RESISTING MY SUBMISSION

RESISTING MY SUBMISSION

The Doms of Genesis, Book 7

Jenna Jacob

Resisting My Submission
The Doms of Genesis, Book 7
Jenna Jacob

Published by Jenna Jacob

Copyright © 2017 Dream Words, LLC
Print Edition
Edited by: Blue Otter Editing, LLC
ISBN 978-0-9982284-4-0

This is a work of fiction. Names, places, characters and incidents are the product of the author's imagination and are fictitious. Any resemblance to actual persons, living or dead, events or establishments is solely coincidental.

Dedicated
To
Lady M. & Master G.

CHAPTER ONE

"OH, FOR THE love of…leather! If I wanted to hang upside down, I'd be a sub who liked suspension," I grumbled, teetering on tiptoes as I stretched my five-foot nothing frame inside the frosty chest cooler. My face and arms were nearly numb, and my boobs threatened to spill out the top of my corset as I quickly counted bottles of pineapple juice. Just when I thought I'd managed to keep the girls free of freezer burn, my left breast plopped out. The sudden blast of cold air caused my nipple to pucker like a trucker's ass on icy roads. I gnashed my teeth, hissed out a curse, and wiggled from the arctic metal bastard.

"Sixty-seven. Sixty-seven." Repeating the number out loud, I branded it to my brain. I had no desire to shove my body back inside the contraption and recount the bottles.

If not for André Perugia—the misogynistic prick who'd invented stilettos—taking the weekly beverage inventory at Club Genesis would truly suck. Truth be told, André wasn't a prick, but my hero. His designs fed my raging shoe addiction and aided me with much-needed height. To give off a larger-than-life appearance for a Domme was pretty important shit.

I tucked my wayward boob back inside my corset and quickly jotted down the number of juice bottles on the requisite spreadsheet as the phone began to ring.

"Club Genesis. Sammie speaking. Can I help you?"

"Hey, it's Dylan," the blond, blue-eyed Dom with endearing dimples announced.

"Hey, doll. What's up?"

"Everything, and all of it bad."

"Uh-oh. What's wrong?"

"We were on our way to the club"—by we, I assumed he meant himself, fellow Dominant Nick, and their shared submissive, Savannah, a.k.a. Sanna—"when a pimple-faced kid, texting while driving, rear-ended us."

"Oh, my god. Is everyone all right?"

"Nick and I are fine, but Sanna might have slight whiplash. We're going to run her by the ER and have her checked out."

"No, we're not. I told you. I'm fine," Savannah insisted in the background.

I couldn't help but smirk. The poor girl could argue until she was blue in the face; it wouldn't change the minds of her Masters. I, too, would want professional assurance for my own peace of mind.

"Keep me posted on what you find out at the hospital. Is there anything I can do to help?"

"Actually, there is. My former captain from the corps is supposed to meet me at the club in ten minutes. Do you mind keeping my man Max out of trouble till we get there?"

"Can I cuff him to a cross?" I teased.

"Good luck trying. He's on our team. The man eats, breathes, and shits Dominance, but he's a good guy. Just introduce him around to the other Doms if you don't mind. You won't have to worry about the subs, they'll come to him…in hordes."

"So you're saying he's a looker, huh?"

"He doesn't do shit for me, but the ladies sure like him," Dylan chuckled. "Fuck. Gotta go. The cops are pulling up. We'll be there as soon as we can. Thanks."

I hung up the phone, sent out a thank you to the universe that none of the three were seriously hurt. A chill slid through me thinking of trekking to the hospital yet again. There'd been a string of bad luck lately where my friends had survived one disaster or another. It was time for the dark cloud of doom to hang over someone else's head for a while.

Counting my blessings, I wiped down the bar and glanced at the clock. An hour from now, Club Genesis—Chicago's premier BDSM dungeon—would be teeming with my lifestyle family busy getting their kink on. My job was to serve drinks and keep the bar running smoothly, but on slow nights, I often had the chance to scene with some of the subs. It was a dream job, at least for me.

From the front of the club, I heard someone pounding on the door. I knew it had to be Dylan's friend. The usual club members knew to wait until I unlocked the place. After pushing past the thick velvet curtains, I released the lock. When I opened the door, a wall of a man stood staring at me. Head shaved, he was dressed in tight leather pants and a white wife-beater. Colorful tattoos covered copious muscles bulging from beneath taut bronze skin. His twinkling emerald-colored eyes slid over me like a caress. I could all but feel his fingers stroking my blonde curls, crimson-colored corset, and black leather pencil skirt with the slit up the side, all the way to my glossy red stilettos. Slowly, a sexy, flirtatious smile speared his lips and sent my heart skipping inside my chest.

"My, my. What a lovely sight you are. Tell me, little one…are you owned?"

His honey-velvet voice had probably lured more women to wrap their lips around him than free coffee from Starbucks. Hell, I'd gladly stand in line for a chance to dance the horizontal mambo with this hunk. There were a couple major flaws with my fantasy. First, he was a fellow Dominant. Even a one-night stand would be pointless. Secondly, his assumption that *I* was a submissive scraped my pride like fingernails down a chalkboard. I wanted to drive the tip of my Louis Vuittons between his legs and send *him* to his knees like a good little sub…another useless fantasy.

Flashing him a plastic smile, I stared straight into his hypnotic green eyes and extended my hand. "Sammie…*Mistress* Sammie. You must be Dylan's friend…"

"Mistress?" He gaped and paused, then flashed me a mischievous smile. "Now…isn't that a pity?"

My girl parts tingled.

He's a Dominant, the little voice in the back of my head reminded. I simply sent him a tight smile.

His voice was gentle, but his eyes pierced through me. With just a blink, I felt him delving into the deepest recesses of my soul as if wanting to discover all my hidden secrets. The fact that I couldn't control my hormones from pinging off each other in some wild sexual dance or the carnal heat spontaneously combusting between my legs pissed me off and sent my inner bitch to rise to the surface.

No man was allowed to control me. *I* controlled them!

"It's a pleasure to meet you, *Mistress*. I'm Maximus Gunn, but all my friends call me Max."

"Maximus Gunn, huh?" I scoffed. "Is that your stripper or porn name?"

Seriously? You had to go there, didn't you? Could you be any more insulting to Dylan's friend?

Yes, I could, but needed to shut the fuck up. It would be much safer and kinder.

Max's eyes widened briefly at my insult before a lazy smile stretched across his inviting lips. He started to laugh, a deep, rich tenor that slid over me like warm honey. Goose bumps erupted over my flesh. Why was I so viscerally attracted to this guy?

Because that man candy standing before you could put Hershey's out of business. And you've got a sweet tooth the size of Texas when it comes to strapping, hot studs like him!

I did, but that was beside the point. Max was a *Dom*. He commanded women to their knees—with very little encouragement, I suspected. He could dazzle me all day and I still wouldn't fall to his feet. I was a Domme, dammit! It was high time I started acting like one, too.

"I've never been a stripper and gave up my porn star days long ago." He smirked with a wink. My knees started to wobble and I steadied myself against the doorframe. Max then suddenly turned serious.

"That's good to know." I forced a chuckle. "It's also good to know you have a sense of humor."

"I do. Is there anything else you'd like to know about me?"

How many inches is your cock and can you lick your eyebrows?

I bit my tongue as a blush warmed my face. "Nope. I'm good, thanks. Come on in."

When I pulled the door open, Max brushed past me. His wide shoulder inadvertently scraped my breasts. My nipples tingled and stood straight to attention. I bit back a curse and locked the door behind him before leading Max into the dungeon.

Glancing over my shoulder, I saw him smiled as he took in the club. "Nice place."

"Thank you. Mika, the owner, puts a lot of blood, sweat, and tears into Genesis."

I rounded the bar as Max took a seat on a barstool. I found the intense and unwavering stare he'd locked on me unnerving. If he'd been a sub, I would have ordered him to drop his gaze until I gave him permission to look at me, but he wasn't.

No, his command was thick, palpable and intimidating. As Dylan had so succinctly stated—which was a glaring understatement—Max really did eat, breathe, and shit Dominance.

I could deal with an alpha-Dom. What I couldn't deal with was his dissecting stare. The man studied me as if he were peeling back my layers, searching for a hint of...

Oh, hell no!

A rush of panic slammed me, sending adrenaline to thunder through my veins. I had to tear his focus off me and fast.

"Dylan is going to be a bit late and asked that I introduce you to the members. He, Nick, and Savannah were in a little fender bender on the way to the club. They're not hurt," I hastily added as a look of horror climbed Max's face, "but Dylan's worried Sanna might have slight whiplash."

"Thank god they're okay. And he of all people would know if Savannah needed medical care. Dylan was one hell of a sniper, but he should have been a medic. He's dressed more field wounds than I can count."

When Max suddenly raised his T-shirt and pointed to a pink scar beneath his ribs, I nearly moaned. Though I glanced at the wound for a nanosecond, my gaze was stalled on his stony six-pack. My mouth went dry. The horny, lonely woman within wanted to tie him down beneath some soft, silk rope and lick every inch of his marbled flesh before riding him like a wild stallion. Of course, I knew it would take the National Guard and a couple dozen tanks to even attempt to restrain the man, but that didn't stop me from dreaming. I forced my eyes back to the scar.

"See? He even patched me up."

"That doesn't look like a war wound, more like a battle scar from taking the wrong hellcat to bed," I scoffed.

Okay, so I was being a bitch, an unwelcoming bitch at that. I was deflecting—in all the wrong ways—the terror and anxiety he provoked that raged inside me. There was no way I'd ever allow him to see how flustered and panicked he made me.

Max scowled. His dark brows slashed at my inept veil of humor. Long, silent minutes passed while the muscles in his jaw twitched and his emerald eyes took on a haunted dullness.

Inwardly cursing myself for being so rude and flippant, I wanted to take my stupid comment back, but it was too late.

"Dylan hooked up with my unit in Ramadi after his captain and most of his team were wiped out in Anbar. One afternoon we were pinned down under heavy fire, next to a shelled-out building. Insurgents were crawling all around us. We'd accidently walked into a fucking Allah ambush. We were definitely SITFU...stuck in the fuck up."

Max's voice was brittle, matching the hard expression on his face. Though he was sitting in front of me, I knew his mind was miles away reliving a hell I couldn't...didn't want to imagine. Guilt for sending him back there made me feel two inches tall.

"Dylan was at my six as we tried to take out as many as we could. My battery-operated grunt was calling in coordinates for an air strike when a bullet sailed through the side of my body armor. I kept firing though it stung like a motherfucker. When Dylan saw the blood, he broke open a butt pack and fixed me up. The cavalry soon landed a few mortars and we got the fuck out of there." Slowly, Max began to focus and a weak smile curled the edges of his lips. "I would have had a hell of a lot more fun getting this scar from a hellcat in bed though."

I had the decency to send him an apologetic smile. I had no idea what to say...sorry for stirring up the horrific memories? Sorry I got my nose out of joint when you thought I was a sub? Sorry for being such a malevolent bitch because you scare the fuck out of me and make me feel like you can see what's buried inside me?

Max wasn't the enemy. My stupid insecurities were. I needed to lower my defenses and stop treating the man like a surgeon bent on slicing open my secrets and start acting human!

"Would you like something to drink?"

"What do you have?"

"Sodas, juices, water...flavored waters, and tea. What can I get for you?"

Once again, he leveled me with a penetrating gaze that left me feeling open and exposed. A foreboding chill slid down my spine.

"You sure you're a Domme? 'Cause the way you word things sounds an awful lot like a submissive."

A tremor of fear solidly shook my body. In an instant, I began slapping bricks and mortar around me. I swallowed tightly and lifted my chin. "I run the bar. It's my job to *ask* the question. Either I can get you something to drink or you can strip off your clothes and step up to one of the crosses. I'll be more than happy to show you exactly how unsubmissive—"

"Whoa, easy." Max held up his hands in surrender. "I was only teasing."

Get a grip. The man isn't a psychic, palm reader, or seer of visions in a crystal ball. Max doesn't know shit about you. He's simply pulling your chain...and you're letting him! Stop!

"Hey, Sammie." Breaching the archway from the hall that housed the members' private rooms, Mika headed toward the bar. As he eyed Max, the club owner's expression grew suspicious. "Everything okay?"

"Fine as frog hair," I replied with a lightheartedness I didn't feel. After introducing him to Max, I peeked around Mika's shoulder. "Is Julianna with you tonight?"

"No. Just me. She's home watching Tristan and Hope. But Drake and Trevor just pulled into the lot as I came in."

Julianna, known as Emerald at the club, was not only Mika's slave but the mother of their child, Tristan. She was also the surrogate birth mother of Hope, Drake and Trevor's six-month-old daughter.

"Tomorrow night, the guys are taking babysitting duty. I plan to bring my mouthy slave to the club and give her a much-needed attitude adjustment." Mika's eyes danced in delight. "I'm going to paddle the sass out of her."

I grinned. "Are you sure you have enough hands to get that job done?"

"I only need one and a big paddle." Mika beamed as he sat down next to Max. "Can we get you something to drink, man?"

I flashed Dylan's friend a derisive smirk, all but daring him to make the same submissive comment to Mika.

Max refused to take the bait and simply chuckled. "Do you have any pineapple juice by chance?"

Of course he wanted the one drink I had to nearly crawl inside the damn cooler to reach.

"We sure do." I smiled and gritted my teeth.

Sliding the metal lid open, I clutched the front of my corset before diving headfirst into the frigid unit. Grasping the can, I wiggled back.

Max had lifted off the barstool, wearing a sly grin as he ogled my ass.

Prick!

I slammed the can on the bar and turned my focus on Mika, dismissing Max altogether. "What can I get you to drink, boss?"

Clearly sensing the undercurrent crackling in the air, Mika simply grinned and shook his head. Seconds later, Daddy Drake—who, until Max arrived, had been the biggest, baddest tattooed Dom in the club—strolled through the archway, leash in hand and wearing a grin. At his side, naked—except for a thick, leather collar attached to the leash his Master held—was Drake's submissive, life partner, and co-parent of Hope, Trevor. The willowy blond sub's boyish features looked none too happy.

"Uh-oh. Is someone spending time with me, chained to the bar tonight?" I asked.

Trevor stuck out his bottom lip and sent a pleading look Drake's way.

"Indeed he is, Sammie," Drake drawled as he sent a stern glare to his sub. "Kneel and bow your head, boy."

As Trevor complied, Max leaned back. He smiled warmly as he watched the couple.

"What did he do?" Mika asked.

"Raise your head and tell them what you're being punished for *this* time, my sweet slut."

"I was… Hope was hungry. I was trying to change her diaper, but she was wiggling all over the place and screaming so hard she was turning red. I hate it when she does that. It makes me feel like a heartless mommy," Trevor moaned. "I tried to hurry with the diaper, but I still needed to fix her bottle. I knew she'd only cry harder and it was tearing me up. Then the phone began to ring, and I-I asked Daddy to answer the call is all."

"Asked?" Drake thundered, clearly stunned by his boy's claim. Trevor quickly cast a guilty gaze to the floor. "I certainly don't recall you *asking* me a fucking thing, boy. But I *do* remember the tone of your voice. You yelled at me at the top of your lungs, and I quote, 'Dammit…the phone! Can you deal with that, for fuck's sakes?'"

Mika, Max, and I couldn't keep from laughing while Drake scowled at his sub.

"Had you looked up, instead of barking out orders to your *Master*, you'd have seen I was reaching for the fucking phone, my luscious, *dictating* slut."

"Yes, Master," Trevor mumbled.

"Yes, indeed. So now you can sit leashed to the bar naked like the naughty boy you are. When *I'm* good and ready, I'll bind you to the bondage bed. I'll wrap your balls off nice and tight, then I'm going to fist your sweet cock until you're nice and hard. Then I'm going to wrap my lips around your aching dick and suck you like a popsicle. Your come is going to be churning so hot it'll blister your goddamn balls. And then maybe…if you wail and beg long and loud enough, I *might* let you come. Of course, I might simply tell *you* to"—Drake changed the pitch of his voice, mimicking Trevor—"deal with that, for fuck's sakes."

Trevor moaned out an apology as his cock grew thick, twitching in aroused anticipation.

"Nice," Max murmured. "That's going to be an exceptionally fun scene to watch."

Drake fastened Trevor's leash to the cleats attached to the underside of the bar, then fisted the boy's long hair in a meaty grip. Jerking his head back, Drake claimed his sub's mouth in a harsh and brutal kiss. "Just be grateful I'm not locking your pretty dick in a cock cage."

Trevor paled. "Thank you, Master."

The cock cage was a molded metal chastity device, shaped like a flaccid penis. Once attached to a male's genital, arousal was impossible to achieve without excruciating pain. It was one of my favorite methods to torture insubordinate subs who wanted to test my Dominance. The delightfully wicked thought of locking Max's cock inside one flittered through my brain. I swallowed back a sinister giggle.

I sent Trevor a sad smile, then flashed him a wink. With a sigh, the sub lowered his head, silently accepting his punishment.

As more members began filing in, Mika introduced Max to the masses. Master Quinn and his submissive, Ava—who'd recently married in Las Vegas and returned to the club after a long hiatus—volunteered to check in the members. I tossed Quinn the keys to the front door.

Soon I watched my kinky family parade into the room. In no time at all, the dungeon was abuzz and nearly every station was in use. I smiled as the scent of leather and sexual musk danced in the air. The soothing, centering sounds of cries and moans from the subs' flesh being whacked and whipped filled my ears.

"What's a Dom have to do to get a drink around here?"

The familiar harsh, patronizing voice of Master Kerr invaded my serenity and turned my blood to ice. The man who'd earned the lackluster title of Biggest Wannabe of Genesis stood at the bar. I'd prayed that after being shot outside the club—for pissing off the wrong loan shark and literally dying on the dungeon floor before the EMTs revived him—that we'd seen the last of the asshat after he'd been hauled to the hospital. My prayers had gone unanswered. As soon as he was back on his feet, Kerr had returned to the club.

It was no secret that I, and other members, loathed the man for his careless treatment of subs. He held little regard for me…well, for women in general. I didn't bother masking my anger. Lifting my chin, I pinned Kerr with an icy stare. Curiosity drew several to the bar wearing expressions of disdain, wariness, and flat-out hatred.

"Ever thought of asking *nicely*?" Max growled, tossing a sideways glance at Kerr.

Great!

On top of the stellar night I was having, the last thing I wanted was to referee a testosterone-induced throwdown. An hour ago, the subbie barback, Joe, called in sick. I'd been schlepping heavy buckets of ice, cases of soda, and juice by myself. Yes, I could have asked for help, but I didn't want Mr. Bowflex sitting at my bar thinking me weak and incapable. I'd be paying for my insufferable pride in the morning. Already my arms ached and my shoes were killing my feet. They made my legs look killer hot, so I simply suffered in silence.

A humorless laugh peeled from Kerr's lips. He sized Max up with a contemptuous sneer. I watched the exchange from the corner of my eye as I hoisted up a bucket of ice. As I was about to replenish the reservoir, Kerr snorted loudly.

"Who are you? Sammie's Master?" the prick asked in a hateful growl.

"Mistress?" Trevor's trembling voice sliced through my flare of panic.

The confrontation brewing between the two Doms was frightening Drake's sub.

Trevor had survived not one but two homophobic attacks. He'd come back from the depths of hell, but conflict still sent his anxiety soaring. I needed to get to the boy and reassure him that all was fine. With my focus on Trevor, the heavy bucket in my arms slipped and tilted to the side. Ice rained across the floor.

"Son of a—" I spat.

Kerr burst out laughing. The mocking sound flayed my flesh like razor blades.

From the very depth of my being I wanted to bitch-slap the son of a bitch. Or egg him on enough that he'd finally cross the line and do something...*anything* to break his contract so Mika could kick Kerr's miserable ass to the curb.

Ignoring the mess on the floor, I snapped my head toward Trevor. Two fellow submissives, Peanut and Tawny, who'd been standing near the bar, were now kneeling beside the scared boy offering reassurance.

"Peanut, unleash Trevor and take him to Drake. Now!" I ordered.

"Yes, Ma'am." The middle-aged redheaded man nervously nodded.

"Take a breather, Sammie. I've got this." From behind me, Master Justice clasped his hands to my shoulders and sent me a tight smile.

The tall, soft-spoken Dom possessed a unique and quiet command. He'd been a longtime friend of Mika's. When Justice moved to Chicago, the two men reconnected. The forty-something, handsome charcoal-haired Dom was now a regular at the club.

Justice gripped my hand to steady the bucket I hadn't realized was still in my arms. He nodded to Destiny. The pretty blonde masochist/bottom who craved pain had been sitting at the bar, watching others scene, and pouting for over an hour. "Would you help me for a little while, girl?"

"I'd love to, Sir." Destiny leapt up and hurried to his side.

"We've got things here under control," Justice assured me in his usual calm and gentle timbre. "Go relax. Sit back and kick up your feet, or find a needy subbie and beat some ass."

His wicked grin was so charming neither the Domme nor the woman in me could refuse.

"Thanks. I owe you one."

As I rounded the front of the bar, Kerr was inching closer into Max's personal space. The fury rolling between the two was tangible and dangerously combustible. A part of me hoped that Max's blasé expression would goad Kerr into throwing the first punch. I knew Max could render the other man unconscious with one blow, but at least Mika could then void Kerr's contract and ban him from the club. The only flaw in my rationale was that Max, too, would be banned. I couldn't allow that to happen.

Dylan had specifically asked me to keep Max out of trouble. I was failing that task miserably. In my peripheral vision, I saw two black-T-shirt clad DMs, Master Ink and Sir Bent-Lee, as well as Drake, striding toward the bar with purpose. I had to defuse this situation, and fast.

Sidling up alongside Max, I looped my arm through his. He jolted and snapped his head toward me. I met his bloodthirsty gaze with a placid smile and swallowed tightly. His whole body felt like reinforced steel. He was as solid as a slab of concrete. But his flesh was warm and soft, like velvet. I suspected his cock would feel the very same.

His cock? Why the hell are you—Stop thinking about his dick!

The man made my estrogen spike like a bad EKG. I needed to unleash a sweet subbie mouth on my girl, and soon.

Max's anger suddenly vanished and he flashed me a knee-knocking grin.

"I'm taking a break from the bar. Let me introduce you to some friends I'm sure Dylan would want you to meet."

"Sounds good." Max replied, seemingly calm, cool, and relaxed.

"Oh, so you're not her Master. You're Sammie's little subbie boy," Kerr chortled. "I get it now. Run along, boy. You don't want to keep your *Mistress* waiting. She might spank you."

I was unsure how it was even possible, but Max's stony muscles flexed even firmer. A tremor of anger billowed through his body. I knew the only thing keeping him from ripping Kerr's heart out and shoving it down the prick's throat was sheer will. Unfortunately, Max understood that no matter how inviting or gratifying, killing Kerr was still a crime.

"Max, allow me to introduce you…this Wannabe Master is Kerr. Better known as the gutless troll of Genesis," I stated, staring the obnoxious asshole straight in the eye.

"Christ, you're a hateful slutbag!" Kerr spat at me before turning and storming off.

"Kiss, kiss. Buh-bye," I drawled sarcastically.

"What the fuck is a clown like that doing in classy club like this?" Max ground out his question between clenched teeth.

"Taking up space and sucking down perfectly good oxygen," I quipped with a saucy grin.

As I started to lift my arm from his, Max clasped his elbow against his side. Trapped to the man, the Domme in me wanted to take issue with his control. Instead, I tempered my knee-jerk reaction and gave into him…this *once*.

"I like you, Sammie. You've got a quirky sense of humor, a beautiful smile, and a softness I find intriguing."

"Don't make me regret being nice to you," I teased. "You won't find my softness intriguing when I cuff your ass to a cross and stretch your ball sac—"

"Okay. Enough. I get it. I'm good." He cringed. "Who are the people you think Dylan wants me to meet?"

"What's the matter? Are you afraid of a little pain?" I giggled.

"No. I like pain…giving it to needy *subs*."

His rumbling seductive tone and the way his eyes caressed the contours of my face nearly made me whimper. He drank me in like a wayward soul, lost in the desert. My skin tingled.

All he did was look at you!

Fuck! The man was far too sexually potent for his own good…and mine.

"This way." I jerked my head toward the numerous tables and chairs situated in the center of the dungeon.

Playing the perfect hostess in Dylan's stead, I introduced Max to the more intimate circle of friends that Dylan, Nick, and Savannah were close to. Starting with Tony Delvaggio—the club's former resident sadist, psychologist, and husband of the beautiful submissive, Leagh; Dominant and world-renowned sculptor Joshua Lars and his gorgeous sub, Mellie Carson—who also happened to be Savannah's older sister; Ian Stone and James Bartlett, supporting Dominants of their stunning sub and ER nurse, Liz Johansson; and last but not least, Master and ob-gyn surgeon Samuel Brooks and his feisty, alluring sub, and Liz' nursing supervisor, Cindy Noland.

As we made our rounds, I introduced Max to other longtime members. I wanted to laugh at the subs who were all but drooling over the new buff Dom. Of course, Max not only encouraged their interest in him, but invited it, as well. The man was an outrageous flirt. He turned a lot of heads…including mine.

"Mistress?" Eli, a raven-haired submissive with soulful dark eyes—who I frequently scened with—approached. He lowered his dark lashes and paused.

"How are you doing tonight, Eli?"

He raised his head at my acknowledgement and flashed me a buoyant smile. "I'm doing well, Mistress, thank you. And yourself?"

I smiled and cupped his chin, holding his gaze. Arousal and a deep-seeded need to please reflected in his eyes. "I'm well."

He glanced at Max before growing suddenly nervous. "I-I…if it would please you, Mistress, I offer myself for your use."

The boy craved a long, hard session. Soaring him into subspace, then cradling him in my arms, swaddling him in aftercare as he tumbled back to earth fed my Dominant needs, as well. But at the moment, with the rigorous heat of Max's body enveloping me, nurturing my own Dominant headspace wasn't even a blip on my radar.

I wanted sex. Hot, sweaty, deliriously mind-bending sex.

Eli would willingly dive face first between my legs. He'd lick, lave, and suckle me to a dozen orgasms, but I refused to steal him away in my private room. I'd never *used* a treasured sub for my own selfish needs; I wasn't about to do so now.

Besides, I needed more than a submissive could give.

I needed someone unencumbered by the dynamics binding Dom to sub.

Someone who'd freely touch me without needing permission.

Someone who wasn't waiting for a command to suck my clit.

Someone who needed to scratch his itch as desperately as I did mine.

Someone to fuck me long and hard until we were both limp and boneless.

My want list eliminated every male in the club.

It had been six months since I'd had a sweaty sex marathon with my occasional fuck buddy, Scotty. The man owned a quaint Italian restaurant not far from Genesis, where members met to eat and visit before heading to the club. Though Scotty knew I was in the lifestyle, he wasn't put off. Of course, I never tried to dominate him in bed, either. Our hook-ups were nothing more than a stress-relieving card-punch kind of thing.

While Scotty was bitchin' hot—built like a linebacker with a fine cock and tongue skills—and always took the edge off my sexual frustrations, nothing flipped my inner Domme switch like fucking a submissive's mind. That was the ultimate rush for me.

Pity I couldn't find a man who was willing to submit a bit before turning into a sexual beast in the sack. One thing was certain; I wasn't going to find him tonight. Eli needed the endorphin rush I could provide. Though it was a catch-22, we were both hungry. Unfortunately we craved vastly different things.

My desires could wait. I needed to feed his.

"I'll see if I can steal some time away from the bar."

His eyes sparkled. A smile lit up his face like a kid on Christmas morning. "Thank you, Mistress. I hope you'll be able to use this boy later."

I couldn't help but grin as Eli happily hurried away. I made a mental note to find a volunteer to handle the bar and give the eager boy what he deserved. Tomorrow, I'd pay a visit to Scotty and see if he'd be interested in giving me the relief I needed.

"And that's why we do what we do," Max mused. "He's a cute kid and quite taken with you."

"He's hardly a kid. He's..." Eli was twenty-four to my thirty-eight. "Okay, he *is* a kid. But he's an exceptional sub. I wish I was able to give him *everything* he needed."

"Why can't you?" Max asked.

"We both know a full-time sub needs a Dom who can devote time to help them grow. I barely have the availability to scene once or twice a week, let alone take a sub under my collar to care for and protect."

"Yes." Max smiled a bit wistfully. "It takes commitment on both parts."

"Do you currently have a sub?"

"No. Not for a long time. But I Top as often as I can." A hint of disappointment laced his voice.

"But it's not the same as—"

"Having one of your own?" he asked, stealing the words off my tongue. "No. Not by a long shot."

Pausing, I watched Lady Ivory secure the cuffs to my former slave's body. Dark Desire was hers now. A pang of longing splintered through me, and I found myself wishing for a simpler time. A time before the economic crash that caused me to close the doors on my successful upscale clothing boutique on the Magnificent Mile in Water Tower Place. A time when my nights were my own and I didn't have to depend on a salary from Genesis to feed, house, and clothe me. A time when I could devote my attention to and fulfill the needs of a collared sub of my own.

Had it not been for Mika's generosity, I'd still be standing in the unemployment line.

"Excuse me, Master Max?" A brave sub with big hazel eyes and strawberry-blonde hair timidly stared up at the massive man. "My name is Honey. I'd be honored to serve you while you're a guest of Genesis, Sir. I'll happily bring you a drink or…"

Or let you spank my ass and fuck me, too, I thought, biting back a snarl.

Max peered down at the girl with the gentle understanding of a Master. An almost humble gratitude seemed to radiated off his skin.

"I am the one honored by your offer, little one." Her cheeks turned rosy and a brilliant smile curled her lips. "I won't hesitate to call upon you if I feel the need. Thank you, pet."

Max placed a tender kiss on Honey's forehead. Out of the blue, jealousy clawed and began shredding my soul. I wanted to lash the girl with my tongue…sink my teeth into her with a scathing lecture, but for what? She'd done nothing wrong. Panic zipped up my spine. Her benign offer was an extension of her need to serve and please. A sub's attraction to a Dom wasn't a crime…

But a Domme being attracted to a Dom might potentially be worse than a crime.

I had no idea where the green-eyed monster had come from or why I'd felt the slightest flutter of jealousy. Still, I'd been blindsided and I was mad as hell about it.

"Thank you, Sir," Honey whispered as if in a daze.

I forced a pleasant smile. "If you'll excuse me, I need to stop by the ladies' room before going back to work. If you need anything before Dylan arrives, I'll be happy to help as well."

One side of Max's mouth kicked up in a crooked smile.

Oh, god. That time I actually had spoken to him like a sub. The only fucking thing I omitted was the honorific *Sir*.

Shit. Shit. Shit. I had to fix my fucking faux pas.

"And if you're a really good boy, I won't make you beg," I added dryly with a brittle smile.

Turning on my heel, I walked away. Once safely in the hall and out of Max's sight, I stomped to my private room. After yanking the key from my skirt pocket, I unlocked the door. Shoving it open, I rushed inside and started pacing the twelve-foot-by-twelve-foot space while bubbling with anger and embarrassment.

Why was I allowing the beefy bastard to unhinge me so?

Because he might be your worst nightmare.

No. Max was the one confusing helpfulness with obedience.

Are you sure?

No one else at the club thought less of me for serving drinks.

You're not worried he thinks less of you…you're terrified he suspects more.

"Oh, god. I am so fucked!"

CHAPTER TWO

AFTER RESTRAINING MY anger and whipping it into submission, I returned to the bar. Max had claimed the same barstool and was nursing a fresh pineapple juice. Though childish and stupid, the fact that I hadn't given him the chance to ogle my backside again filled me with triumph.

"Thank you for holding down the fort."

"You're welcome." Justice nodded. "FYI, Drake and the DMs escorted Kerr out of the club. He won't be giving you any more trouble tonight."

Kerr wouldn't, but there was nothing to stop Max from digging deeper into my psyche. I could feel his eyes boring into me again watching every fucking move I made.

Dylan, for the love of god...where are you?

"Meet me over at that spanking bench, girl." Justice pointed out a particular station to Destiny. "We'll finish our negotiations there and start the scene."

"Thank you, Master Justice." She beamed with joy.

A trace of foreboding fluttered through me. Destiny was a nice girl, for the most part, but she had a bad habit of latching on too tightly to the Doms who worked her. After a not-so-friendly parting of ways between her and Master Sam, Mika—who protected all the unowned subs but didn't scened with them—had to lay down the law. He'd allow Doms who had the necessary experience to safely administer the level of pain Destiny required to work her, but only if she behaved like a free sub. If she started to behave as if they were her Owner, he'd relegate Dommes to fulfill her craving for pain.

I knew from experience the girl found subspace faster and deeper with men than women. Though I didn't think her lesbian-phobic, I suspected the scent of testosterone and the feel of big, masculine hands flipped her trigger far faster and more thoroughly. Since Mika had handed down his new rule, Destiny had kept her end of the bargain. So far she hadn't dug her emotional claws into any of the Doms who Topped her. I hoped the same would hold true for Justice.

"Mad Max!" Dylan bellowed as he, Nick, and Savannah—now sporting a padded neck brace—hurried toward the bar.

"Ghost Man!" Max yelled as he launched to his feet and grabbed Dylan in a brutal man-hug. The two held tight to one another sharing hearty back slaps.

Watching their reunion, I couldn't keep from smiling. They pressed their foreheads together, grinning like loons, and simultaneously yelled, "Oorah!"

I didn't miss the tears filling both men's eyes. I, too, had to blink back the sudden sting of my own.

Dylan introduced Nick, and Max tugged him into a masculine hug. When Sanna was presented, Max lifted her fingers to his lips and placed a tender kiss on the back of her hand. He stroked one thick finger over her medical collar and sent her a sad smile.

When the four finally made their way to the bar, he flashed me a wink. "The son of a bitch finally made it!"

I chuckled and nodded before dragging my gaze from his joyous grin and sent Sanna a frown. "Does it hurt much, sugar?"

"No," she answered, clearly perturbed. "I shouldn't even be wearing this ridiculous thing. It makes me look like a robot, but—"

"But you *will* for the next twenty-four hours, like the doctor instructed, or you'll be dealing with two very unhappy Masters, pet," Nick warned.

"That's right. You'll leave that on, kitten…or else," Dylan chimed in.

Sanna pursed her lips and remained silent. I could tell by the tone of Nick's voice and his serious expression, Sanna's slight injury had shaken him to the core. It was times like these I wished I had more to offer than soda or juice. A shot of whiskey would do the man nicely. But Mika ran a safe, sane, and consensual club. The members and employees respected his no-alcohol rule.

Slamming me with a toe-curling smile, Max plucked his drink off the bar and followed the trio to a table. I couldn't peel my eyes off his sexy marble ass under those tight leather pants. My palm itched to fire up his orbs while my mouth watered. I wanted to glide my tongue all over his rippling muscles.

"Sammie?"

Jerking from my trance at the sound of my name, I spun around to find Mika standing behind me.

"You all right?" His brows were arched high.

"Yeah. Sorry, I didn't see you come down from your office."

Always observant, Mika smirked as he glanced in Max's direction. "You do know he's—"

"A Dom. Yeah, yeah. I do. But sometimes my X chromosome can't help but drool over a fine Y one like his," I drawled. "What can I do for you, boss?"

"Not a thing. I came down to give you a break." Mika nodded toward Eli. "Go get your Domme on with him if you'd like."

The boy was sitting alone at a table wistfully watching the various scenes.

"When have I ever *not* felt like it?" I teased.

As I headed toward the sub, my Dominance awakened within, stretching like a cat after a long nap in the sun. The minute Eli saw me approaching, hope glittered in his dark eyes. His flat brown nipples grew taut. I wanted to pinch those ripe, juicy berries until he moaned my name. When I paused at the table, he sank to his knees in a perfect submissive pose. Eli was willingly handing over his trust, mind, body, and soul to my care. Pride warmed and expanded in my veins.

I gently caressed a hand over the top of his head. His silky hair slid through my fingers. "Rise and follow if you wish to be used, sweet boy."

Eli sprang to his feet. Though he kept his gaze cast to the floor, his smile was bright and wide. God, how I loved playing with passionate subs like him.

Like a shadow, he followed me across the room. My mind became more focused. I was aware of the heat of Eli's body behind me. I could hear his excited breath as it left his lungs. Anticipation prickled my flesh. My nipples hardened. His faith in me, so absolute and pure, sent a thrilling rush of power to fill me, and I hadn't even yet bound him to a piece of equipment.

In the corner station to my right, Trevor lay naked and immobilized beneath a crisscross of rope. His scrotal sac was tied, as well, and his protruding balls were red and swollen. Drake dragged his mouth up and down Trevor's cock, devouring his sub's brittle erection. At the mercy of his Master's loving torture, Trevor helplessly writhed and whimpered. A smile spread across my lips as I drank in the beauty of the magnificent sight.

When I pausing, Eli stilled behind me. I inched in beside him and cupped his chin. While forcing his attention on the enthralling scene, I leaned in close to his ear. "Look at Master Drake and Trevor. You've been watching them tonight, haven't you, boy?"

"Yes, Ma'am." Eli's breath was shallow. His pupils were beginning to dilate, and I could feel the palpable surge of lust heating his skin as well as witness the swell of arousal beneath his thong.

"What do you see?"

"Sweet suffering, Mistress."

"Do you want to suffer sweetly for me, slut?"

"With all my heart, Mistress Sammie." His voice quivered. So did his body.

"Pain or pleasure?"

A shy smile tugged the corners of his mouth. "Both, Mistress."

I chuckled softly. "Greedy little minx. Strip off your thong and wait for me at that cross, boy." I pointed to the empty station. "I'll collect what I need to give you the precious agony and sweetness you crave."

"Thank you, Mistress."

Eli all but ran to the assigned spot, stripped off his black thong, and knelt on a pillow beside the cross. His eagerness warmed me as I gathered an array of floggers, paddles, a nice pliant whip, and a cotton blanket for aftercare. When I returned, his head was lowered and spine straight. With his legs slightly parted, his open palms rested on his thighs. He was the perfect picture of submission.

I couldn't wait to taste his precious power flowing through me.

Spreading out the toys upon an empty table near the cross, I aligned them in order. Innocuous ones to warm him up, followed by slightly harsher ones that would supply the foundation for me to build him to the toys that burned and bit his succulent flesh.

The back of my neck tingled. Pausing my assembly, I glanced over my shoulder. Max's penetrating stare seized me as a slow, incendiary smile spread across his sensual mouth. My pulse began to race. My body temperature spiked, hovering near the brain damage marker, as my traitorous clit throbbed with need. No man had provoked such uncontrollable arousal in me before. Not even Desmond.

No. I couldn't allow my brain to slide down that path. Not now. Not here.

Eli needed a Domme, and nothing—especially Max's provocative stare—was going to distract me from fulfilling those needs. Turning my back on Max, I blocked him from my mind and focused on Eli. The sub's energy, a sizzling current of anticipation, ratcheted higher with each passing second.

"Rise and look at me, sub."

He instantly complied. As he lifted his eyelids, a thrilling shiver slid down my spine.

Confidence.

Devotion.

Honor.

Pride.

Trust.

Those and a whole host of emotions rippled, like a swift-flowing stream, through his dark eyes. Want, need, and a potent willingness to please rolled off his naked flesh, a stark and empty canvas I intended to color and mark with my Dominance. Like a sponge, I absorbed his precious energy until the demand to control him tingled and burst like tiny fireworks beneath my skin.

"Give me your safe word, boy."

"Pasta, Mistress."

I arched my brows. "Did you eat your pasta today?"

Eli coyly smiled and nodded. "Yes, Ma'am. Two plates of spaghetti at dinner."

"Good boy." I reached between his legs and cradled his balls. His quick intake of air and the jerk of his cock on my wrist made me shiver. "We don't want your blood sugar to drop tonight, do we?"

"No, Mistress."

Releasing his sac, I scraped my nails up his flesh. All the tension of anticipation melted from Eli's body. He briefly closed his eyes and moaned as he savored the sensation. I intended to drown him in even more.

"Face the cross." My tone was harsh and impatient.

Without hesitation, he complied. I fastened the sheep-lined cuffs to his wrists and ankles, then stood behind him and raked my nails up and down his back.

Leaning in, I pressed myself against his heated flesh and inched my mouth close to his ear. "Close your eyes, precious. Let go of your will, and lose yourself to me...to my touch, my caress. Everything I use on you tonight is an extension of me...my hands, my lips...my heart."

A soft tremor shook his body. I smiled and stepped back. Lifting the heavy cowhide flogger, I began systematically working my way from his shoulders to his pert little ass. Landing the falls in a slow, sublime tempo, I slid into my own Dominant headspace. The sounds of the dungeon faded into white noise while the movement of the nearby members blurred.

All my attention was focused on one...the benevolent sub before me.

Long minutes later, I was swinging the thuddy flogger with both hands. Driving the leather across Eli's pink, glowing flesh. The slightly brutal massage had him moaning in bliss. His bones liquefied, and he slumped against the cross.

It was time to draw him back to me.

Selecting a leather-covered paddle, I slapped it across his reddened cheeks. He jerked upright before the sassy tart thrust his buttocks outward...silently begging for more. I grinned and landed several furious blows over his proffered cheeks. He grunted in pain and squeezed his hands around the edges of the wooden frame as he worked to process the sting. I lowered the paddle and dragged my nails over his mottled, crimson orbs. He sucked in a long hiss.

Feeding off his sounds and the feel of his fiery flesh, my blood sang.

Determined to give back every ounce of power he so bravely offered, I slid the paddle between his legs. Gently at first, I tapped his balls, hanging heavy between his legs. Slowly, I increased the tempo and force until Eli's muscles tightened, and a cry of distress tore from his throat.

Pausing, I allowed him to process the smoldering burn that engulfed his testicles.

Gripping his hair, I tugged his head back and whispered for only him to hear, "Please me...ride the fire for me, sweet slut."

Having worked Eli numerous times, I used one of the phrases he best responded to as I eased him off the craggy peak of pain.

Turning the paddle sideways, I slapped the insides of his thighs, presenting a new focal point of nerve endings to capture his attention. Eli widened his legs and attempted to dance away from the biting blows but couldn't retreat with his ankles bound to the frame.

His flesh glowed red like embers, and he sucked in a gasp before suddenly stiffening.

"Shit!" he spat.

I inwardly chuckled and landed two more slaps to his angry thighs before pressing myself against his trembling body. Gently caressing the hot flesh with my fingertips, I smiled and bent my lips to his ears. "*Shit* is not your safe word, boy."

"I know, Mistress," he hissed.

"Breathe through it for me, little one."

Eli nodded. He inhaled several deep breaths through his nose and expelled them out his mouth in a noisy rush.

"Good boy," I whispered.

Time and space merged into an ebb and flow as I bestowed him beneath an avalanche of pleasure and pain…drove him to the oblivion he craved. Together we drank in our rewards, gorged on command and submission, as we separately swirled in our own kaleidoscope of serenity.

Eli had escaped reality and was off flying in his own cosmos of peace. The once pristine canvas of flesh he'd offered was now stained with the colors of my command and marked with the welts of his surrender. It was a stunning sight to behold.

As I shook open the soft cotton blanket, Max appeared at my side.

"May I help take your boy off the cross?" he whispered softly.

Stunned by his offer, I nodded. "Thank you."

As Max worked on releasing the cuffs, I wrapped the blanket around my mindless submissive, holding him tight in my arms. Max's eyes didn't leave mine as his fingers deftly worked the leather. As I talked to Eli in low tones, I was taken aback by the respect shimmering in Max's green pools.

"That was a beautiful scene," he murmured before he strode away.

"Can you walk yet, sweet boy?" I breathed softly in Eli's ear.

"Mmm," he murmured.

His nonverbal response was answer enough.

"Let go of the cross and let me hold you."

As his fingers slowly released the wood, I pulled him to my chest before easing us both to the carpet. Tucking the blanket around his boneless body, I strummed my fingers through his sweat-soaked hair and whispered soft praises in his ear. The corners of his mouth lay curled in a sated smile.

Peanut quietly approached and set a bottle of water next to my knee.

"Thank you." I smiled. The sub nodded and walked away.

After coaxing Eli to take a few sips of water, he slowly began to resurface. Reaching up, he pressed his fingers to my face and smiled softly. "Thank you, Mistress."

I sent him a warm one of my own and nodded. "Thank you, sweet sub. I enjoyed myself. How about you?"

A lazy grin split his lips. "Oh, yes. I had a wonderful time, Mistress."

Eli closed his eyes and released a contented sigh. I, too, savored the Dominant satisfaction warming me from within. Lifting my head, I noticed Max, Dylan, Nick, and Savannah had left their table. After skimming a cursory glance over the dungeon, I didn't see any sign of the group. A puzzling sense of disappointment spread through me. I closed my eyes and pushed the absurd sensation away, focusing instead on the warm subbie spread out across my lap.

ROLLING OUT OF bed, a little past noon, I was in a foul mood. I hadn't slept for shit. Max had stormed his way into my dreams and filled them with such explicit sexual fantasies I climaxed a couple times in my sleep. When I woke, the ache between my legs throbbed so hard it felt like fucking menstrual cramps.

I'd never experienced such raw and unsatisfied need before. Pissed, not because I was still incredibly horny, but irked that a man I barely knew, a Dominant man, had my hormones running a marathon with no finish line!

"Argh!" I growled. Flipping on the shower, I slammed the glass door behind me.

Adjusting the temperature to a semi-tolerable scald, I prayed the heat would melt away the gritty residue of my hopeless infatuation with Max that adhered to my skin. It was tragic to be pining and obsessing over a man—to the point of orgasming during sleep. It was beyond pitiful. It was pathetic.

I needed to set a sex date with Scotty. He'd put this ridiculous fire out, and I could return to my confident, sane self again.

After downing a pot of coffee, I headed out to the dry cleaners, grocery store, and post office. By the time I arrived back home, it was late afternoon. Gathering up my clothes for work, I jumped in the car to grab an early dinner at Maurizio's. Hopefully, later tonight, Scotty would be banging this perplexing sexual frustration out of me. But when I arrived, the restaurant was more crowded than I'd expected. While none of the gang from Genesis had shown up yet, I'd be pressed to do much more than proposition the man like a hooker.

"Hey, Sammie," Scotty called out to me with a smile.

"How's it going?"

"Great. Good to see you. It's been a while. Grab a seat. I'll send Carly out to get your order in a sec."

"Good to see you, too. No rush. I've got plenty of time." I brushed away his concern with a wave of my hand.

Taking a seat at a twelve-top table in the middle of the room, I knew a few club members would eventually wander in and join me. As I faced the bar, I watched Scotty. He moved fluidly and seemed at home whipping up drinks, much like I did at the club. His forearms flexed and bunched as he filled a pitcher of beer from the tap. My mind skipped to a different man with larger and more defined muscles...Max.

Dammit. I couldn't purge him. It was maddening that he both enticed and infuriated me with his sexy grin and probing stare. I was a Domme...a woman in control of my emotions and desires! Or I had been until Max came to town.

Carly, the cute waitress who'd worked for Scotty the past several years, pushed through the metal swinging doors of the kitchen. The owner glanced over his shoulder and flashed her a loving smile before nodding toward me. Carly lifted onto her toes, kissed Scotty on the cheek, and scurried my way.

Well, shit! Evidently, while I'd been eating dinner at home, Scotty and Carly had been cooking up a hot and steamy new relationship. My dreams of him annihilating my sexual frustrations lay at my feet in a heap of unfulfilled orgasms.

Maybe it was kismet that I snagged a fresh pack of batteries earlier at the grocery store. I'd need to buy a whole lot more before Max left town. Who was I kidding? He could move to Siberia tomorrow and I'll still be fantasizing about him...buzzing out orgasm after orgasm.

Carly glowed as she cheerfully took my order. I noticed that Scotty couldn't keep his eyes off the girl. Though bummed for purely selfish reasons, I *was* happy for them. Everyone deserved to find their One, in or out of the lifestyle.

An image of Desmond floated to the surface of my mind. The knee-jerk reaction to mentally slam the steel door shut on his face zipped through me. Instead, I closed my eyes and studied the rugged contours of his features. Desmond had been my One, but he'd been ripped from my life sixteen years ago.

There's no going back, Samantha.

The little voice inside my head was right. My ship of happiness had sailed, or rather crashed, a long time ago. I missed the man, still. Thankfully, the bitterness that Desmond left me behind had dissipated. Now, like a patchwork quilt, I filled the missing pieces of my soul spanking submissives and enjoying an occasional friends-with-benefits tumble in bed. Though I now needed to find a new friend, my life was complete...or rather had been until Max slid in under my radar and knocked me on my ass.

Picking at my salad, I analyzed my foolish fascination with the man. I knew my attraction to him was purely physical. Still, he'd surprised me with a few endearing qualities. Like his benevolent kindness to Honey, his brother-like friendship with Dylan, and his chivalrous help with Eli last night. Max definitely possessed a big heart, but the man seemed to take great joy in pushing my damn buttons.

Why did he refuse to get it through his thick skull...I was the pusher, not the pushee?

Setting my fork down, I shoved my half-eaten salad aside. I started to mentally slide barriers around my heart and mind. If I could erect a set of steel walls high enough, I'd be able to deflect Max's cutting submissive innuendos and hide from his intense stares.

Of course, the walls wouldn't keep his scorching hotness from turning me on. That was a different puzzle to solve. I'd find a way. I had to. My sanity and orgasm-free sleeping pattern depended on it.

By the time Carly arrived with a steaming plate of ravioli, I was beginning to feel stronger...more empowered and secure. At least until the door opened and in strolled Nick, Dylan, Savannah, and of course, Max. As was the custom, they joined me at the big table.

I kept my anxiety and fear on a short leash as we ate, laughed, and talked. Outside the club, Max seemed less threatening and intimidating. In fact, he was almost likeable. Maybe it was me...maybe I'd doffed my Domme cloak and had subconsciously combed my hackles down. Inside the club, I always felt as if I had to prove my ability. I abided by a code of conduct, as the other members did, with the exception of Kerr, of course. That asshat played by his own set of rules, none of which lent him an ounce of respect. He was a predator. Bagging subs and slapping collars on the unsuspecting newbies was a game to the prick. He didn't respect women, especially Dominant women like Ivory, Monique, and myself. They, too, ate a barrage of shit from Kerr. Unfortunately, there wasn't a clause in his contract forbidding Doms from insulting or verbally sparring with other Doms. Kerr didn't dare treat the subs the way he did us Dommes, he'd be out the door.

Stuffed to the gills, I sat back and tossed my napkin on my plate. I wanted to groan when Nick ordered Scotty's homemade spumoni for the table. I knew trying squeezing into my corset in another couple of hours was going to be hell, but I couldn't turn down those chunks of cherries, almonds, and pistachios layered in sweet frozen cream.

When Max took a bite of the sinful confection, his eyes rolled to the back of his head, and he let out a long, low moan. If I hadn't known better, I'd have sworn he'd just busted a nut in his sexy, snug jeans.

Okay, so I noticed when he'd walked into the restaurant. I never claimed to be a nun.

Hell, no one possessing a vagina kept from zeroing in on his Hulkish body and handsome face. Even I couldn't peel my eyes off his hypnotic smile, rippling thighs, or the way those faded blue jeans hugged his sinfully tight ass. Still, I didn't need his guttural groan of delight reverberating in my ears and sending sparks of need zooming to my crotch. I bet he'd make those same erotic sounds when I swirled my tongue around his glorious erection.

So much for your super-steel barriers! Obviously they were constructed out of aluminum foil and papier-mâché—meager and useless.

For years I'd thought coffee was my Kryptonite; turned out my weakness for Max was a million times greater.

The man needed to visit his friends and leave.

"So, how long do you plan to stay in Chicago?"

Before I could stop it, the rude question fell out of my mouth. Honestly, I should have chosen a more tactful way. But I needed an end date to know how long I had to batten down the hatches on my hormones.

Max laid his napkin on the table while I drank my iced tea. "Funny you should ask. With Dylan and Nick's help, I found the house I've always wanted. I put a bid on it an hour ago."

If your mother failed to warn you…don't ever gasp with a mouth full of liquid.

Tea spewed all over my luscious spumoni and down my shirt. I choked and coughed like a firefighter in a burning house without a respirator. Gulping for air, my lungs protested as tears streamed down my cheeks. Everyone at the table was up and out of their chairs faster than Maserati's time trials at the Bonneville Salt Flats.

"Jesus, Sammie. If I'd known the news was going to kill you, I'd have kept my mouth shut." Max offered a warped apology as he slapped me on the back.

"Put your arms above your head," Sanna called out. Without waiting for me to follow her instructions, she grabbed my wrists and hauled them into the air.

I was still coughing and sputtering when Nick shoved a glass of water toward my mouth. I shot him a glare and nearly snarled. I was already drowning on iced tea. The last thing I needed was to suck more liquid into my lungs.

Finally able to draw in a semi-deep breath, I grabbed my napkin and covered my mouth. Noises no woman should ever make came croaking from deep in my lungs.

"I'm good," I rasped in the voice of an eighty-year-old phone sex operator.

"Should I call the EMTs, Samantha?" Scotty anxiously yelled from behind the bar, telephone receiver in hand.

"God, no." Waving his offer away, I coughed some more.

"Samantha? That's got a much prettier ring to it than Sammie." Max grinned.

"You call me by that name again, and I'll superglue your junk into the gates of hell." Another favorite cock and ball confinement device comprised of leather and rings.

Max chuckled and leaned in close, dropping his voice to but a whisper. "If that's the only way I'll ever get to feel your slender fingers around my cock, I might let you."

I followed his gaze as he glanced down at his crotch. Instead of tea, I nearly choked on my tongue. Packed sideways and straining beneath his denim jeans laid a massive slab of man-muscle. Saliva pooled in my mouth. My girl parts caught fire. I had to curl my hands into fists to keep from caressing the tempting tube of steel.

Several long seconds passed before understanding pierced my hungry hormonal fog. The cocky bastard was toying with me yet again. No doubt the sequoia strangling in his pants was due to the pretty young redhead sitting across from us. She was wearing a gray Loyola University T-shirt that cupped her pert full breasts. She had a creamy flawless complexion, plump, full lips, and looked like the sorority poster child for Kappa Kappa Dick Lickers. Yet Max had the gall to try and insinuate that *I* was the one responsible for raising his flagpole. Right!

I'd had my fill of his infantile games. I was sick of him poking, prodding, and finding ways to piss me off just to watch me boil. If he wanted to play games...I could, too. I'd give him a taste of his own medicine guaranteed to bring an end to his stupid games.

I sent him a seductive smile and leaned in close until my lips brushed the shell of his ear. God, he smelled good...clean soap and summer sun.

Focus.

I traced my tongue over the outer rim before sucking the lobe between my lips. Thrusting my breasts out, I purposely brushed my nipple against his bicep and watched his eyes grow dark. "I really hate to tell you this, Conan, but I've thrown better-looking meat than yours down the garbage disposal."

Max jerked back with eyes wide in surprise. Then he tossed back his head and laughed...hard.

"Oh, I doubt that, Sammie."

His challenging stare made me want to squirm in my chair, but I stayed in complete control. I wasn't about to let Captain Colossal Cock know how badly I ached to slide my hands, lips, and pussy all over his impressive gun.

"What are you two whispering about over there?" Dylan asked from across the table.

I arched a brow, daring Max to answer.

"Nothing. I was just telling Saman...err, Sammie how much I enjoyed watching her scene last night."

"It's always a joy watching Sammie play," Nick complimented as all three men pulled out their wallets. "I've got the check."

"No. I do," Dylan said, shoving Nick's hands away.

"Put your money up. I'm buying tonight," Max ordered.

Sanna looked at me and shook her head. While the three argued over who was paying the bill, I slapped a twenty on the table and stood. "Try to keep from drawing blood, boys. I'm heading to the club. See you later."

Slinging my purse over my shoulder, I waved good-bye to Scotty as I headed toward the door. I'd barely made it to my car when Max came jogging up beside me.

"Look, I know you have a reputation and image to uphold."

"*Image?* Listen, mister. I don't pretend to be anything but what I am. Got it?"

"No. Wait. I didn't... Christ! Are you always so damn—"

"I'd choose my next words *very* carefully if I were you."

"Testy?" Max bit out in his own testy tone.

"No. I'm actually a nice, loving person to people who aren't constantly challenging my Dominance or trying to piss me off on purpose. Good-bye."

"Piss you off? What the fuck are you talking—"

I turned my back to him and opened the car door. Faster than lightning. Max grabbed my shoulders and spun me around. Heat and lust blazed in his eyes as he pressed his body in close to mine. When I opened my mouth to ask what the hell he thought he was doing, he slammed his warm, soft lips over mine. The kiss was feral, possessive. Alarm bells clanged in my head, but Max silenced them when he plunged his slick tongue in my mouth.

Hot.

Sweet.

Erotic.

As he explored every valley and crevice, I closed my eyes and kissed him back. Lost in the taste and texture of his velvet tongue, I moaned. Max stroked my cheeks with the pads of his thumbs. The kiss grew raw, desperate, and ravenous.

I wanted to shove him back and slap his face for taking his stupid game to such an aggressive level, but I couldn't find the willpower to drag my mouth from his. The luxurious heat of his body slid around me...under me...through me, and I grew dizzy. Every powerful inch of this hungry male called to me on a primitive and animalistic level.

Like sparks from a bonfire, desire sputtered, popped, and sizzled.

The fever of passion soared.

My pulse hammered.

My knees grew weak and I fell deeper under his intoxicating spell.

I knew I had to stop the madness, but his ruthless and sensual kisses stole my mind, my spine, until I was nothing but jelly in his arms.

As fiercely as he'd claimed me, Max tore from my mouth. My heart fluttered wildly as I drank in the sight of his wet, swollen lips...lips that were as soft as silk yet fierce and firm.

Fire blazed in his green eyes.

He looked dangerous, sexy, and more gorgeous than any man had the right to.

"Now you can go," he bit out in a brittle tone. He lifted his hands from my face and took a step backward.

Anger replaced lust so fast it nearly gave me whiplash. "I don't remember asking your permission, *Sir*."

"You didn't. You tried to dismiss me and the chemistry boiling between us. I'm not going to *allow* you to do that."

"Allow me? I don't even know what chemistry you're talking about." Instead of being drawn into confessing something I knew I'd regret later, I feigned ignorance.

"You know exactly what I'm talking about. You can't deny it, Sammie."

"Yes, I can." I lifted my chin. "I can deny Bigfoot, the Loch Ness Monster, and aliens, too."

"None of those are real. We... this... whatever you want to call it, *is* real. Fucking real." A devilish grin replaced his scowl. "Maybe I need to give you more proof."

I wasn't going to stand there and give him a chance to prove anything. The one kiss we'd shared was one too many. If he claimed another, I'd lose what little sanity and control I'd still managed to cling to. The thought of bending to his will, or anyone else's for that matter, filled me with panic and single-minded resolve.

"You try, and I'll stretch your scrotal sac over an embroidery hoop, fix it in place with clothespins, and drink in your screams."

Max cringed and swallowed tightly. "You do shit like that?"

"Of course. How else do you think I maintain my Dominant *image?*"

"I like you Sammie, but you need to pull that stick out of your ass and lighten up. If you weren't so damn sensitive about your capabilities as a Domme, you'd see—"

I did see. I saw red. White-hot rage exploded through me. I drew my arm back, balled my hand into a fist, and punched Max right in the gut. Pain shot up my arm as if I'd slammed my knuckles into a brick wall. For a split second, I thought I'd broken my wrist. The man didn't even flinch. Didn't move. He just stood there gaping at me as if I'd lost my mind.

"You're an asshole!" I barked.

Max stood watching me with an angry scowl as I jumped into my car. I nearly flooded the engine. Finally the damn thing finally started and I lurched of the parking space.

"You're one infuriating piece of work, you know that, woman?"

CHAPTER THREE

IN A HAZE of smoking, squealing tires, I shoved my arm out the window, flipped him the middle finger, then sped out onto the street. I was livid. Curse words rolled off my tongue like a string of pearls. After pulling to a stop at a red light, I jerked my seat belt on and silenced the annoying buzzer.

If there was ever a time I wanted to call in sick, it was tonight. I didn't want to lay eyes on the son of a bitch, let alone have to act civilly when he showed up at the club—and he would show up at Genesis, just to spite me—made me want to punch him all over again.

I could always lace his pineapple juice with arsenic and end my torment. The thought was almost too damn inviting to dismiss at that moment.

After zipping into the parking lot behind the club, I grabbed my clothes and slammed the car door. I stomped up the stairs, punched in the code, and shoved past the portal before storming to my room.

Blazing like a forest fire, both inside and out, I stripped off my clothes and paced the room in my bra and panties. Max's words spooled through my head on an endless loop.

"I'll be more than happy to pull the stick out of my ass, mister...and shove it up yours. Argh! Why does he have to be such a cocky, condescending asshole?"

The knock on my door had me spinning around on my heel and staring at it in disbelief. "You've got to be shitting me!"

The prick had followed me to the club to what? Continue World War Three? The battle would be short lived. I had all the necessary equipment within reach to yank his fucking balls. I might be ready to castrate him but I wasn't ready to face him. Not yet. Not until I could stop acting like a petulant child.

"Go away. Leave me the fuck alone, asshole!"

I heard a snick of metal. Shock raced through me as I watched the knob slowly start to turn. Before I could move to block Max out, the door opened. Mika stepped in wearing a look of confusion and worry. The blazing rage within me lessened. I exhaled a deep breath of relief.

"Asshole, huh? And all this time I thought we were friends."

Embarrassment warmed my cheeks. "I'm sorry. I thought you were someone else."

"Evidently. I was checking out the cameras in my office when I saw you come storming in like a thundercloud. I came down to make sure you were all right. I can clearly see you're not. What's going on?"

"Nothing," I lied. "I'm fine. Just a little argument with—"

"With an asshole, yeah, I got that part, too. But if you thought said asshole had followed you into the club, then it's someone I know. Who?"

"It's not important. I'll deal with it."

"Let me rephrase the question. This is *my* club. You're not only an employee but also a good friend. If someone is fucking with you, I demand to know who the hell it is!"

Mika rarely ever raised his voice, but he was doing so now. I knew I wasn't going to be able to candy-coat this clusterfuck in sugar and rainbows. Dragging my shirt back on, I flopped down on the bed and scooted back against the headboard. Mika sat on the mattress and stared at me with probing amber eyes.

"Max," I stated with a sour expression.

"Dylan's friend Max? How the fuck has he managed to piss you off like this? He's only been in town a whopping five seconds."

"It doesn't matt... Who did you think I was angry with?" I deflected his question with one of my own.

"Kerr. You're always pissed off at that fuck-nut, but then aren't we all?" Mika's lips curled in disgust. "What's Max done? Do I need to call Dylan and tell him that his friend is no longer welcome?"

"No. He hasn't *done* anything."

If you weren't so damn sensitive about your qualities as a Domme... The asshat's words echoed in my ears. I clenched my jaw.

"Sam. I'm not going to sit here and drag answers out of you. Spill it. Now!"

"God, you're impatient."

"Yes. I know. Julianna reminds me of that all the time. You're stalling, and I'm losing the little patience she hasn't already stolen from me."

"Okay. Okay. Damn." I scowled. "He hasn't *done* anything. He's a bastard who thinks it's funny to tease me about…being a sub."

"Max, huh?"

I nodded. "He thinks just because I *ask* the members what I can get them to drink…which, I reminded him, is my *job*, he says I sound like a submissive."

Mika's lips twitched as he bit back a grin.

"Don't you dare," I warned with a glare.

He stayed silent for several seconds as if struggling not to laugh. A whole new level of anger and hurt sliced through me.

"Obviously, you think I'm weak," I bit out. "How many other members think I'm a sub in Domme clothing?"

"None," he replied with a growl as if understanding the fragility of my emotions. I hated anyone to see me this way, even Mika. "Do you think Max senses something deeper inside you? Maybe he can see the—"

"Don't say it. Don't you dare let that word roll off your tongue."

Mika scowled and sucked in a deep breath. "You can lie to me all you want, Sam. But don't lie to yourself. Take a good hard look at why he infuriates you so. His playful teasing pulls deeply at you for a reason. I see the way he looks at you, but more importantly, I see the way *you* look at him. Max stirs something more inside you than anger."

"I can't. I can't open that shit back up, Mika."

"I don't think you have a choice, sweetheart. You and I…we talked about this years ago. Remember?"

"Yes. I remember." I closed my eyes as dread rippled through me.

"What I told you then still holds true today…tomorrow…forever. I support you a hundred percent."

"Thank you. I love you for that."

"I love you, too. That's why seeing you like this rips me up…makes me worry."

"Don't. He'll leave town soon and… Oh, god. No, he won't," I groaned. "He's buying a house here in Chicago. But look on the bright side…you'll soon have a new member of the club."

"I don't want you focusing on him becoming a member right now, Sam. I want you to go home. Soak in a bubble bath and figure out what you want. According to Julianna, relaxing in the tub rates right up there with ice cream and sex."

"I don't want time alone to strip back the layers of my head or my heart."

"That's exactly what you need, baby." He sent me a sad smile. "Sort it out, and then meet me in my office tomorrow afternoon at four. If you haven't come to a conclusion, we'll figure where we need to go from there. All right?"

My stomach twisted. I couldn't do what he was asking. Fear of what I might discover all but paralyzed me.

"There's nothing to figure out. I know who I am. I know what I want."

You did, but then Max walked through the door, and...

"Like I said, honey...lie to me all you want." Mika stood. Effortlessly, he lifted me to my feet and hugged me tightly.

I wasn't fooling Mika, and I certainly wasn't fooling myself, especially when I felt my soul start to shift. Like tectonic plates, shimmying ever so slightly and rippling outward. Fissures split open, releasing an upsurge of dread, and threatened to spew a life long lost into the air for all to see.

I clutched Mika tighter as fear quaked through me.

As if sensing the ground cracking open beneath my feet, Mika issued a sympathetic sigh and rested his chin on the top of my head. "What can I do for you, Sam?"

I squeezed him hard and backed out of his hug. "Nothing. It's something I have to do alone. In fact, I'm going home to sort this shit out once and for all. Don't be surprised if I show up for work tomorrow with a whip slung over my shoulder." I smiled with false confidence worthy of an Academy Award.

"If not, that's fine as well. You know that, right?"

"I do." I nodded resolutely.

Mika pressed a kiss to my forehead and left the room.

I suspected he'd dash back up to his office and park his ass in front of the security monitors and watch me like a hawk. Each of the private rooms was fitted with hidden cameras and microphones. Not for voyeuristic pleasure but for the members' safety. The images fed upstairs, where he and the security staff could keep a watchful eye on private play.

Since big brother…err, rather, Mika was probably watching, I played to the camera and pretended all was fine as I dressed. When I headed down the hall to leave, I blew a kiss to the camera above the back door and strolled to my car.

Once I was inside my vehicle, tension and anxiety started to spike. I felt like a pressure cooker atop a high-flickering flame and struggled to tamp down the need to start dissecting my emotions then and there. As Dylan, Nick, and Sanna could confirm, texting while driving was dangerous. It would be suicide for me to peek under the lid of my churning past while behind the wheel.

Luckily I made it home before the lid blew off my inner shit pot. I'd managed to change into my robe, pour a glass of Hennessy, and drag down the dusty box from the shelf in my closet before the first tear fell.

Sitting on the couch, I placed the box containing my happiest and most horrific memories on my knees. I took a fortifying sip of brandy and then slowly lifted the lid.

On top were the newspaper articles I'd saved. I'd barely glanced at the image of smoke billowing from the twin towers when brittle fingers of pain clenched my heart and froze the blood in my veins. Time had done nothing to heal my wounds, only mask them behind layers of gauze and tape.

I made myself study the image. Questions that had plagued me for years, quickly resurfaced. Had Desmond been alive after his plane slammed into the North Tower? Had he suffered and called out my name, or had he been granted a merciful and instant death? Closing my eyes, I sent my mind wandering back to that dark September morning. Not because I was a masochist but because I was on a mission.

"I'll be back in a week. You'll barely notice I'm gone," Desmond reassured.

He'd been so wrong.

As he sat on the edge of the bed beside me, he bent and tied his shoes. I rubbed his back before he straightened and caressed my naked body with a loving dark-eyed gaze. Goose bumps peppered my flesh as I drank in the sharp lines of his nose and the defined angle of his rugged jaw. The man was beautiful, both inside and out, and I loved him more than life itself.

"When I get home, I want to find you just like this…waiting for me.

Naked, wet, and ready." *The lurid promise in his eyes made my heart skip.*

"If you didn't have to be gone a whole week, I'd stay right here...of course, I'd starve to death before you got home."

His rich, deep laughter warmed me like summer sun, the way it always did. Rising, I kissed my way up the back of his cotton shirt until I reached the patch of exposed skin above his collar. I breathed in his clean scent of soap and woodsy cologne before I pressed my lips to his neck.

Gripping the glass of brandy in my hand, I licked my lips. I could still taste his warm, familiar flavor. The air stilled in my lungs. Letting my tears flow, I rode the wave of anguish as it bore down hard upon me. These would be but the first of many I would shed before I was finished flaying myself open with the wicked knife of memories.

Lifting the newspapers, I placed them beside me. Steeling myself to look inside the box, I sucked in a ragged breath. Staring back at me was the beautiful man who'd owned my heart, the love of my life, Desmond. This single photo of him was the only one that remained. In a fit of rage and desertion, I'd burned all the others two weeks after he'd died. Looking at the gutting reminders of the joyful times we'd shared was like a slow suicide. I'd had to destroy them...all except this one print.

As I peered into the box, he smiled up at me. He looked so carefree, content, and happy. God, we were so fucking happy. The photo showed him leaning up against a tree in Central Park. It was summer, and the canopy of leaves overhead had danced shadows on his face. Still, I could see the unconditional love twinkling in his dark eyes. It had been a spectacular day. After a picnic lunch, we'd lain laid on a blanket, laughing and making grand plans for our future...a future of kids and a house in the suburbs.

But that wonderful future never came.

I took another sip of brandy and traced the tip of my finger over his dark hair. The wind had blown a shock of his black strands to carelessly fall across his forehead. Seconds after I'd taken the photo, Desmond had brushed it back and made a goofy face just to make me laugh.

Drawing my finger down the photo, I traced the outline of his sculpted cheeks, pausing at his lips. Every fiber in my being wanted to feel his warm, silky mouth against mine...just one more time.

Lifting the picture, I closed my eyes and pressed my lips to his as a strangled sob tore from my throat. Clutching the edge of the photo, I doubled over and tried to hold in the gutting grief, but it was too vast…too raw…too overpowering.

The unmitigated agony I'd resurrected burned hot. It was as scalding and violent now as it had been sixteen years ago. I sat there for a long time, rocking and sobbing as the desolate void consumed me. Through blinding tears, I compelled myself to set his photo aside.

Shoving the blade of the knife all the way to the hilt, I reached back inside the box.

The leather was still soft but cold…meaningless to my life now, but not my memories.

I clutched the collar that once adorned my neck and bound me to my One…my Master, my husband, my world. A bleak and abandoned wail rolled from the depths of my soul. The walls began to close in, trapping me in a prison of self-exhumed pain.

Leaning to his side, Desmond dragged his tongue up my stomach. I giggled and squirmed but remained open, giving myself freely to him as his mouth left a trail of fire on my flesh. The muscles of my stomach rippled and bunched beneath his tongue, and I felt him smile before he latched onto my right breast. His low, silky moan of approval vibrated over my nipple, and I softly exhaled, lost in the freedom of pleasing my Master.

Even after he'd kissed me good-bye and left our brownstone to catch a cab for the Newark Airport, my body and lips still tingled. I hugged his pillow, breathing in his soothing, comforting scent, and fell back to sleep. The phone woke me sometime later. A friend of ours who lived on Long Island was frantic and crying and told me to turn on the television.

Within seconds, my whole world crumbled like the mighty towers.

Lost in memories of heartbreak and pain, I sipped the brandy. Tasteless now, its warming burn had grown absent. I was numb and hollow, except for the lesions I'd sliced open again. They blistered and seared as the hemorrhage within flowed in a river of misery.

It didn't matter that I no longer lived in New Jersey—unable to stay in a city surrounded by Desmond's ghost, day and night—the raw ache for him to walk through my door and command me to my knees blazed deep in my soul. I longed to feel the foundation beneath me...that submissive security that encapsulated the world he'd provided with his powerful Dominance. But like the air heaving from my lungs, Desmond was gone, and he was never coming back.

Tears hot and free-flowing coursed down my face while sobs for life's cruelest betrayal burned my throat. I'd never found a way to purge the anguish that scorched my soul. Even slicing my wrists—which I'd shamefully given thought to in the days following Desmond's death— wouldn't have rid the raw, corroded emotions within.

Brushing a hand across my cheeks, I absently smoothed away my tears and sucked in a quivering breath.

"Kiss the leather, princess."

The centering command Desmond had uttered before the start of our sessions, whispered through my brain. Lifting his collar to my trembling lips, I kissed the soft leather. Its scent was still sweet and pungent. The craving to succumb to his will and savor his glorious direction enveloped me in a fiery blanket of desperation.

"Mark it with the same promise I gave you when I first placed that lovely leather band around your throat. That's it, princess. I'll always keep you safe, treasured, and loved. Hand yourself over to me, sweet slave. Let me mesh your power with mine and set you free."

Shoving the box to the floor, I sank to my knees. A howl of forbidden surrender clawed up the back of my throat. Lowering my head, I raised the collar upward, offering the symbol of submission on open palms to the ghost of my Master.

Tears rained down my cheeks and splattered my thighs. The collar would never again be secured around my throat. Lost forever was the security and peace that once bloomed through my soul, so sweet and heady.

Desmond had left me...left me all alone to pick up the pieces of my shattered life.

Abandonment, like millions of blades, ripped me open.

I knelt before an apparition as anger, anguish, and anxiety consumed me. Ripped and tore at my heart and soul with their jagged teeth until the bloody carnage slowed and thrummed hollow within.

My arms trembled. My body shook.

Sobs of regret and fear echoed in my ears as I tore the cloak of Mistress Sammie from my bones and summoned Samantha— Desmond's slave—into my heart, once more.

The submissive I'd buried deep inside spread her wings. Like a phoenix rising from the ashes, she blazed to the surface, fiery, hot, and screaming.

My power.

My control.

My Dominance lay smoldering at Samantha's feet.

Stripped of my Dominant protection, I felt naked…scared…alone. I closed my eyes and searched the dark recesses of my soul. I opened my heart and embraced the somewhat awkward submissive from long ago and let the feelings rise up from deep inside me. Though standing on the cusp of a slippery and dangerous precipice, I had to determine—once and for all—what level remained of my former slave self.

She was still there, though fragmented and frightened. Curious and cautious, wondering why, after all this time, I chose to awaken her now. But then I felt it…that ancient warmth…a yearning to please smoldering beneath a black and charred veil of denial.

I hadn't vanquished the yielding woman within, merely abandoned her. A scream of sorrow tore from my lips as I dropped my collar and crumpled into a ball.

Suddenly, my front door exploded inward with a deafening shriek. Shards of sawdust and splintered wood littered the air and tumbled to the ground as Max charged into the room. Snapping his head from left to right, as if looking for an enemy, he finally locked his stare on me…sobbing in the middle of the room.

Confusion, shock, and embarrassment surged within, while hot on their trail was a blast of rage and resentment. He'd not only violated my privacy but invaded my submissive inquisition as well. But Max ignored the daggers I tossed his way and thundered toward me, like an animal, with long, measured strides.

Crouching beside me on the floor, he desperately searched my eyes. "What's going on? I heard you scream. I thought someone was trying to…"

He reached out to brush the hair from my face, but I slapped at his hand.

"Get away from me." I leapt to my feet.

Guilt pumped through my veins as I darted a nervous glance at the condemning evidence scattered on the couch and floor. Spying the collar, Max reached out to pick it up.

"Don't!" I yelled. "Don't you dare touch that. It doesn't belong to you."

He drew his hand back as if I'd burned him with a blowtorch. Studying me with an even sharper gaze, he slowly dragged his eyes off me and stared at the collar lying on the ground. Lifting his head, he glanced around the room. Without a word, Max stood and walked to the couch. He stared at Desmond's photo before locking on to the newspaper clippings.

"Oh, jesus…no. Fuck no." Mournful understanding slid from his lips.

"Go," I murmured.

He jerked his head in my direction. I expected to see a look of victory…hear him shout out a triumphant, *I told you so!* Instead, I saw a million questions swirling in his eyes. Max strode toward me. Without a word, he wrapped me in his arms.

He was warm.

Alive.

Offering salvation to the scattered fragments still circling inside me.

I longed to drown in the human comfort of his touch.

Cocoon myself in his hot breath that caressed my neck and savor the much-needed sliver of peace his compassionate embrace offered.

But too much was at stake.

My Dominance—that *image* Max had teased me about—wasn't simply a mask or costume I'd chosen to hide behind. The reinvention of myself was real…a living, breathing entity of survival. When Desmond died, I had no choice but to lay my submission to rest alongside him. Still, I was unwilling to give up the lifestyle I'd come to love. So I did the only logical thing…I studied and learned to become a Domme. Changing my mindset from surrendering to controlling was hard, but over the years I found a certain satisfaction and was able to satiate the emptiness left by Desmond's death. I knew I'd never connect with another on such a pure and absolute level or hand my power over to anyone but him.

Yet here I stood, surrounded in Max's arms, fearing that not only could he salvage my submission but also pulverize my Dominance into unrecognizable dust.

I tensed. My skin crawled with fear and dread. He knew my secret. Struggling, I tried to break free of his grip, but the man simply held on tighter.

"Shh," Max whispered. "Don't fight. Just let me hold you. Forget code or status, Sam. Just let me hold you as a man."

I felt his hard length lying hot against my stomach. Trembling, like a virgin, I ached to feel his lips graze up the sway of my shoulder, past my neck, and nibble that sensitive hot spot beneath my earlobe.

His offer of mercy slid over me in a gentle glide of satin while allowing him to comfort me scalded like lava. I didn't know if I could trust him. I'd exposed my vulnerable underbelly. Would he choose to use these fragile emotions against me and slaughter my reputation as a Domme? I'd allowed him to see too much.

"Thank you," I mumbled. "I'm fine. You can go now."

"You're not listening to me, Sam."

Oh, I was. I'd heard him loud and clear. He no longer called me Sammie. No, he'd already cast her aside and was attempting to strip away the rest of my skin to inspect the submissive that lay within. But on the other hand, he wasn't calling me Samantha, either, which was a damn good thing. I didn't trust myself to keep from sliding to my knees before him.

Samantha was still alive and breathing. A fact I couldn't deny. I'd willingly shoved myself into this emotional blender. My confidence and the ability to control myself was now nothing but puréed liquid. I had to put myself whole again. But being nestled in Max's strong arms was making that nearly impossible.

As if sensing my conflict, he lifted me into his arms and cradled me against his massive chest. He started to carry me down the hall.

"Wait. My front door..."

"Shh. Relax. I'll take care of it in a minute."

I began to protest further, but he simply placed a warm, thick finger over my lips. Peering first into the guest room, then the bathroom, Max grunted when he discovered my bedroom.

Sex? He wanted sex now?

I didn't know how many more emotions I could cram inside my psyche before needing a padded room. Panicked, I wanted to twist in his arms and cling to him like a crab and, at the same time, push him away and bar him from ever touching me again.

Max gently laid me in the middle of the bed and sent me a tight smile. "Take some deep breaths and relax. I'll be right back."

The Domme within wanted to rise up and challenge his directive, while the submissive nodded and longed to make him proud and follow his instructions to the letter.

Fuck! I'd already battled this rebellious uprising. I'd spent years warring the two opposing entities vying to win the title. The thought of having to relive the war between submission and Dominance again was bleak and depressing. Sucking in a ragged breath, I closed my eyes and listened to Max's steady footfalls as he walked down the hall.

Of all the foolish notions! What had possessed me to rip the scabs off my mortal wounds and think I'd find some cryptic meaning to my chaos? Even more irrational was the notion that I could simply suture the gaping chasm back together and magically find that missing peace of mind.

Maybe I could have. Unfortunately, Max had burst into the room, riding atop a fucking white horse, before I'd had time to begin processing my epiphany or come to terms with Samantha's existence. The only thing I'd accomplished was to resurrect a ghost I now lacked privacy to send toward the light.

Maybe I didn't need Dominance or submission…or even sex after all! Maybe what I truly needed was a couple million psych sessions with Tony Delvaggio.

A thunderous crash from the living room shook the house. I launched out of bed and raced toward the door. Turning the corner, I ran chest-first into Max's unmovable body.

"Whoa." He clutched my waist and lifted me off the ground before carrying me back to my room.

"What was that noise? What did you do?" I demanded as I squirmed against his hold.

Setting me on my feet, Max lifted his shoulder in an absent shrug. "I pulled the rest of your door off its hinges."

"You what?" I screeched.

"Don't worry, I texted Dylan. He and Nick are sending out a guy to install a new one. I locked the exterior glass door. No one can walk in."

"You *ripped* the whole thing off?"

"Yeah. There wasn't enough left of it to close, so…" I scowled. He volleyed with arched brows. "Don't start getting pissy. I heard you scream and thought someone was raping or murdering you. I was trying to save your life."

"Your chivalry is endearing, but you *destroyed* my door."

"Nick and Dylan—"

"I know. I know." I held up my hands. "They're getting me a new one. Stop bitching, right?"

"Now you're learning." He grinned and winked.

"Don't press your luck, pal. How did you even find me…and what the hell are you doing here?"

Max looked at me as if I'd lost my mind.

"Seriously? You punch me in the gut, flip me off, and then tear out of the parking lot like Danica Patrick…and you ask *why* I'm here?" His expression softened. "When I found out you weren't working tonight, I asked Dylan to give me your address. We need to talk. So I borrowed his car and came over." His voice dropped to barely a whisper. "I'm glad I did."

I wasn't glad. I was embarrassed. He'd stormed my castle to find me losing my shit and sobbing like a baby. But fear that Max now knew my secret superseded any wounded pride. I'd gone to great lengths to make sure that no one but Mika was privy to my former life. I wanted to keep it that way. No good could come from giving credence to the stigma that I wasn't a capable Dominant. There were already a few Dominant counterparts who thought that. Their remarks were nothing but bullshit. Any strong woman threatened their fragile male egos and three-inch penises.

Still, I needed to do damage control to ensure Max wouldn't spill my secret to anyone.

"We could have talked later. You didn't need to check on me. As you can see, I'm fine now."

Liar.

Okay, so I was a solar system out of orbit and light-years from fine, but I wasn't going to admit that to Max.

"I'd appreciate it if you wouldn't say anything to anyone about the collar and…my deceased husband/Master."

"Aw, Sam. He was also your husband?" The pain in Max's eyes nearly had me sobbing all over again. I clenched my jaw and nodded. "How long had you two been married before…nine-eleven?"

He'd seen all the evidence. I felt the need to tell him the whole story to ensure he at least had all the facts straight. I exhaled a heavy sigh, expelling the fear-mixed anxiety within. "Four years. We got married when we were both eighteen. We'd been grade school sweethearts. Desmond lived two doors down from me. He asked me to marry him when we were in third grade. I said yes," I said in weak and humorless chuckle. "He was my destiny…my soul mate. There'll never be another like him."

I felt my chin begin to quiver. I bit my lips and swallowed tightly. Turning away from Max, I sat down on the edge of my bed. He followed and eased in beside me.

"So you turned to the Dominant side to keep from kneeling to another Master. I get it now."

"I need you to keep this between the two of us, please."

"I still don't know why you feel you need to keep your former submission quiet, but trust me. Your secret is safe with me. I respect anonymity. Trust and honor as well. I was a fucking Marine. I know all about rules and regulations."

The tiny smile that curled his lips told me he was trying to insert a bit of levity, but it didn't quite reach his eyes. Max was worried about me. Aside from Mika, no one ever worried about me, except, of course, my mother. But since I'd moved to Chicago, I strived to make sure no one ever had a reason to.

"I'm not trying to be nosey," Max began a bit cautiously, "but do you revisit the past often? I mean…shit. This is going to come out wrong, and I apologize, but do you torture yourself like this a lot?"

A bitter chuckle rolled off my tongue. "Never. Today was the first time."

"Why today?"

"I'd rather not talk about it. You can go now. I'm fine."

"Sam," he whispered. Moving in closer, he brushed the hair from my face. His finger grazed my cheek and tiny pulses of desire warmed me. "Don't shut me out. Please. It's my fault we got off on the wrong foot. I'm sorry I teased you. Truly I am. I'd like us to be friends."

"We can be friends, Max. I have no problem with that."

No, the issue was the decadent heat rolling off his massive body and his masculine smell assaulting my senses. Maximus Gunn was a powerful aphrodisiac. I could easily turn into a Max junkie, but I had enough on my plate at the moment.

He inched in close and lifted my chin with his finger. With his dazzling eyes locked on mine, his voice dipped low and seductive. "I'd like us to be *good* friends, Sam."

Please don't kiss me…please don't kiss me.

But he did. The feather-soft nudge of his lips sent my pulse fluttering. I didn't pull away. I couldn't. The attraction was too strong, too potent. When he kissed me again, harder…more insistent, I selfishly took the tenderness and compassion he offered. The jagged edges scraping raw inside began to soften and smooth.

"Damn. You taste sweet like honey, Sam."

The way he kept saying Sam made me feel as if there was yet another identity trying to take shape inside me. Not Domme or submissive, but a woman in desperate need of the salvation he offered.

Locking my wrists around his neck, I kissed him back. Hungry tongues mated, sliding over slick, wet heat. My mind screamed not to let him inside. He was the villain, the rogue who forced me to question my decision to become a Domme. But my brain refused to listen, and my body delved further into his sweltering kiss. I was lost in the luxury of Max, and it wasn't until he moved over me that I realized he'd pressed me onto the mattress.

The sheer size of the man overwhelmed. Enveloped in his solid steel and liquid heat, I wanted to wrap myself around him and stay safe and protected. But that was the lost sub inside screaming for security. Mentally and emotionally exhausted, I yielded to the restless sexual desire smoldering inside me. Demand ignited like a spark to kindling. The flames danced up my spine and licked at my core.

Max pressed his stunning erection between my legs and I gasped in need. Heat against heat, throbbing and pulsing, I couldn't keep from spreading my legs and inviting him deeper against me. He hissed like a nest of rattlesnakes and lifted. Supporting his weight on muscular arms, he gazed down at me with such blinding openness I wanted to weep. He showed me what words couldn't say, that he, too, was lonely and desperate and searching for those missing pieces of his soul. Deep down I knew I couldn't fill his empty places any more than my own, but I wanted to try and give back a sliver of the comfort he offered me.

Scraping my nails down his arms, I felt the flesh ripple as muscles bunched and flexed beneath my fingers. The man was sculpted marble covered in warm silk. Max repositioned himself, leaning his weight onto one arm. Lifting his hand from the bed, he cupped my breast.

Warmth seeped through the fabric onto my skin as he slid his thumb across my nipple. My pussy clenched and my hips arched involuntarily, longing to be next in line for his magical caress. Nerve endings danced in hot sparks, and my hormones tripped over themselves. I melded into his palm with a low moan.

CHAPTER FOUR

"I WANT YOU, Sam." Max's voice had grown thick and husky. His eyes turned as dark as fir trees in winter.

The attraction between us was raw and real like he'd claimed outside the restaurant. I couldn't deny that fact. Yet I was still very much Mistress Sammie and wondered if prying open Pandora's box was such a wise idea. I might be able to sate my cravings for the man, fuck him out of my system, so to speak, but at what cost?

"You don't want me as Domme. And I can't give myself to you as a sub." The stark reality of that crossroad made my voice quiver.

"I don't want to make you feel like a Dominant or a sub. I want to make you feel like a woman…a woman who's starving for the touch of a man again. Let me help heal some of your scars. How long's it been since anyone made you feel…alive?"

Years. Too many years.

Max somehow sensed my answer as if I'd broadcast it over a radio frequency only he could hear. He responded by kissing me again. Slowly and sensually, latching his teeth onto my bottom lip, he gave a little tug. Sucking the swollen flesh into his mouth, Max caressed it with his hot tongue.

I could tame the controlling and the malleable segments of myself, but I couldn't temper the anxious butterflies dipping and swooping low in my belly. Unconsciously rocking my hips, I was hungry for more than his kiss. I needed his attention focused on the pounding ache between my legs. Of course, grabbing him by the ears and shoving his head down there would only incite a riot between us. Okay, so maybe I couldn't lock away all my Dominant tendencies. I doubted Max could, either. Only time would tell if we managed to find a mutually suitable rhythm within this crazy dance we'd invoked.

Using his lips and tongue, he trailed fiery kisses along my jaw and down my neck while slowly inching the robe off my shoulders. Leaning back, he balanced his knees on the edge of the bed and released the sash of my robe. Peeling the fabric open, he stared at my naked breasts, totally entranced. I grinned but he didn't see me. His glazed look stayed glued to my boobs.

"I take it you're a breast man?"

He didn't respond. Oblivious to me, and everything around him, Max licked his lips. I nearly laughed.

"Would you like me to sink to my knees and suck your cock now?" I teased.

"Uh-huh."

If he'd been a sub, I would have secured him to a bondage bed, tightly wrapped his sac, and tit-fucked him until the pain grew so intense he cried like a baby.

When my question finally registered in his brain, Max's eyes pinned me with shock and confusion. "Wait. What?"

I couldn't help it. I laughed. "Nothing. I was just testing to see if you were with me or off at the booby carnival, eating cotton candy and trying to win a stuffed teddy bear."

"It's not cotton candy that I'm dying to taste. It's your pretty breasts. I know they're going to be much sweeter."

"You'll never know unless you..." My voice had taken on a sultry tone.

"So pretty," he murmured. As he skimmed the tips of his fingers from one swell to the next, a look of hunger and awe lined his face. "So silky soft, too."

Dipping low, Max traced his tongue over my crinkling flesh. The moist heat of his mouth made my nipples draw tighter. The delicious ache throbbing in time with my heart was pure bliss. Opening wider, he sucked the pebbled tip into his mouth. When he scraped his tongue back and forth over the sensitive peak, I sighed and cupped my hand to his bald head. Pings of pleasure ricocheted through me. Zapping reality, he tossed me into a euphoric world of sensations. My pussy wept. My clit pulsed. The temperature in the room soared with every nip, lave, and suckle.

"Oh, my god. You have a sinful tongue," I moaned.

He released my nipple with an audible pop and grinned. "I'm just getting started. They don't call me Mad Max for nothin'."

A crooked smile tugged my lips and I purred. That's exactly what I wanted to hear. His non-commanding approach hadn't flipped any of my control buttons...not yet.

"You plan to drive me mad?"

"Insane," he growled against my flesh. Lifting his head, he claimed my mouth in another breath-stealing kiss. Our silky tongues tangled as I dragged my palms over the expanse of his broad chest to his narrow hips. I groaned as he rocked his erection up and down against my sweltering mound. I raised my legs, placed my feet on the mattress, and bent my knees, opening myself up for the taking.

My body blazed in a primitive feminine fire while all sanity evaporated from my brain. Willingly surging ahead with Max was madness. Absurdity. Total insanity. Making love to this man would only complicate my life. Make any kind of friendship messy and awkward. Yet I couldn't shut off my demanding desires. For a woman who'd kept her emotions on a short leash for years, Max had effortlessly busted mine clean off the chain.

But allowing him to do so only reinforced the fact that I was certifiably insane. But then again, a normal woman, I'm not.

As I tugged at his tee, Max drew back briefly so I could yank it over his head. I gaped at the slab of man above me, and the fabric fluttered off my fingertips.

Holy shit!

And I'd thought his shoulders and arms were stunning. The man was beyond beautiful. Mika was buff and built. Drake was massive and intimidating. But Max...Max was his own species of muscleman candy.

Take him. Take all of him.

The need to feel his hot flesh against mine annihilated all my inhibitions. Reaching for the button on his jeans, I deftly worked to get him naked. As my fingers skimmed his abs, I felt his muscles flutter and tighten. He was no more immune to my touch than I was to his. Empowerment, heady and demanding, sang through me.

You're not a Domme right now. You're simply a woman. He's neither Dom nor sub, just a man, a man hungry for the same thing you are...release. Heeding the inner voice within, I exhaled the drive to command and control.

As if sensing my inner conflict, Max lifted off me and stood. His breath was shallow, and his massive pecs rose and fell with each rapid draw of oxygen. He toed off his shoes and drew down the zipper of his jeans. With a moan of relief, he bent and slid the denim off his ass and down his thighs. I only caught of a glimpse of the massive shaft between his legs. But when he straightened once more and kicked the fabric free, I bit back a gasp. My mouth had gone dry, but I forced an arid swallow and stared at him in all his naked glory. Every inch was sculpted and defined…*every inch* including the seven or eight of the long, thick erection pointed toward the sky. My mouth was no longer dry…it watered.

"Your turn."

With a sultry smile, I started to inch the red lacy thong off my hips.

"Wait. I want to do that."

He bent and strummed a thumb up the center of the fabric. I could feel my wetness that saturated the silk. With a low growl Max leaned in farther and pinched the material between his teeth before slowly peeling the thong off my hips, down my legs, and off my feet.

His nostrils flared.

The mixture of our heady hormones clung in the air. Soaring the unrelenting urge of man to claim woman and woman to claim man past desperation.

Max cupped my nape and pressed his lips to mine, kissing me with a mindless passion. I floated off the ground as his tongue sought to devour every ridge and crevice. Inching his fingers up the back of my scalp, he sank a fist into my hair and angled my head back to delve deeper. I couldn't miss his assertive need to control.

Reaching down between his legs, I feathered my fingertips over his shaft. His body tightened and I swallowed his groan. Sinking farther down, I clasped his balls and squeezed until he tore from my lips with a curse.

"Play nice, and I'll do the same." I arched my brows in warning.

Max dragged his hand down my back and over the flair of my hips. Pulling me flush against his rugged body, he aligned his heated sex to mine.

"I lost my head."

A soft chuckle rolled off my tongue. "Not the one between your legs. I can feel that one just fine."

Max grinned. "No. That one's definitely not lost. He knows exactly where he belongs."

"I like his GPS tracking skills."

"You're going to like what he does next a whole lot more."

I had no doubt whatsoever that he'd thoroughly and completely sate my savage needs.

Then what? What are you going to do after he puts out the fire? Strap on your corset and stilettos and pretend Samantha was just a mirage? Smile and wave to him in the club as if none of this ever happened?

I didn't want to think past this moment, but the niggling voice in the back of my head asked valid questions. Was I simply using sex with Max to avoid negotiating a peace between the two opposing forces within me? Did it matter? Why couldn't I simply enjoy a raw and dirty fuck with the man? There wasn't a happily ever after in my future, only the here and now. Closing my eyes, I willed my analytical brain to silence, at least long enough to achieve a mind-bending orgasm or two…or five.

"Hey." Max tucked his fingers beneath my chin and lifted my head. I opened my eyes but wanted to slam them shut again when I saw his dissecting stare. He pressed a cotton-soft kiss to my lips. "We don't have to do this if you're having second thoughts."

I both loved and hated how easily he read my emotions. No one since Desmond had been able to home in on my feelings. Max's innate talent wasn't normal, but it was comforting.

"We can stop right here…right now," he assured.

"You even think about stopping and I'll get my whip."

He palmed my breasts and lightly pinched my nipples. I sucked in a hiss. "I thought you said play nice?"

"I did. So how politely do you want to fuck me?"

"In every raw and nasty way we can," he growled.

"Bring it, big man," I taunted in a sultry tone.

Turning from his arms, I crawled onto the middle of the bed. I rolled my hips and teased him with a tantalizing show.

"Oh, yeah," his gravelly voice rumbled. "This is going to get dirty…fast."

Without asking, Max yanked open the drawer of my nightstand. A wicked grin tugged his lips as he pulled out a string of condoms, bottle of lube, my long, slender vibe, and thick rubber dildo. "Real. Fucking. Dirty."

My body trembled but I boldly lifted my chin. "I can make it ten times dirtier if you pull out the strap-on that's in there."

"Not tonight, sugar," he said with a chuckle.

As he inched toward the bed, I reached between his legs and cradled his heavy erection. Hot and throbbing, he pulsed in my palm. Slowly, I stroked up and down with a featherlight touch. Max moaned, pressed his mouth to mine, and cupped my mound. He dipped one finger between my folds and toyed with my clit. Gripping him tighter, I glided up and down his cock from root to tip. He was thick, so thick I couldn't get my hand all the way around him.

Swallowing my soft moans, he slid from my mouth. He dragged his tongue down my neck and over the swell of my shoulder, then dipped lower and latched his lips onto my nipple. Every thrust of his fingers and stroke of his thumb, along with every suckle, nibble, and lave of his tongue sent me floating higher and higher. I closed my eyes, lost in the tropical heat of his mouth and the wicked rasp of his fingers exploring my core. I squeezed tighter as I pumped my fist along his velvet-shrouded cock.

He awakened a dormant primal woman within, and she roared to life, hungry and ready to feed.

"More," I demanded.

His tiny chuckle vibrated my nipple and I growled. Max sank his teeth into the pebbled tip. "Play nice, or I'll put you on your knees."

Inwardly turning to stone, I jerked back and pulled free of his mouth and fingers. I dropped his steely cock and inched backward on the bed. Narrowing my eyes, I clenched my jaw. "I won't ever kneel to you or any other man again."

Max blinked, surprised by my intense reaction. "Easy, tiger. I was only kidding. Like you did with me about the strap-on."

If you're big enough to dish it out, you'd better damn well be willing to take it.

"We're doing this as man and woman. Remember?" he continued. "I've not only restrained my inner Dom but I've also locked away any expectation of you submitting to me, Sam."

"But you'd like for me to, wouldn't you?"

"Hell yes. I'm not ever going to lie to you. It would be phenomenal. But the cost to your mental well-being is too high. I might have chained up my control, but I can't cordon off the need to protect you. I'll walk out the damn door before I cause you any emotional or physical pain."

His pledge took the wind out of my sails and neutralized my fear-based anger.

"Relax, baby. All we're doing here is having some consensual fun. Clear everything from your mind and let me make you feel good, all right?"

I nodded though I was still a mental hot mess. Why was he even staying? Was he as pent up as me? Was he dealing with my cluster-fucked emotions just to get laid? Evidently. He hadn't gathered up his clothes and rushed out the door, at least not yet.

Let me make you feel good... His words turned over and over in my head.

Maybe Max was right. Maybe all I really needed was to stop psychoanalyzing the nipples off every word he said and simply let go. Fuck the man's brains out, send him on his way, then deal with my inner selves and make a final decision about my Dominance.

One thing was certain—trying to fuck Max and internally sort it all out at the same time was *never* going to work.

"You'll let me make you feel good, too, right?"

"Baby, I'll let you do anything you want to me…within reason."

"What do deem as unreasonable?" I asked.

"Your strap-on, for one. No lifestyle stuff. No whips, floggers, paddles, needles, electricity, or fire. And absolutely no embroidery hoops or clothspins anywhere near my junk. Got it?"

The corners of my mouth twitched, fighting back a grin. "How long's it been since you've had strictly non-lifetstyle sex?"

His brows wrinkled as he pondered my question. "Let's see…I was seventeen when I started experimenting with bondage and learning about Dominance. That makes it about…twenty-three years."

"Wow. That's a long time."

"What about you?"

"Six months ago, give or take."

"So you have a regular—"

"Fuck friend?" I interjected for him. Max nodded. "No." *Not for over six months, and not anymore, thanks to Carly.*

"You have sex with your subs, though, right?" he asked.

"Not intercourse."

It wasn't unheard of for men to join the lifestyle assuming they could get laid every night at the club. Once those types discovered BDSM had nothing to do with sex and everything to do with the power exchange, they usually didn't return. While I allowed my subs to masturbate—as a reward—I didn't permit any of them to fuck me. The only exception was Dark Desire, when he was mine. The man was too perfect a slave—which made it doubly hard when it had come time to un-collar him—and had a cock too beautiful to deny myself the pleasure he provided.

Max raked me with a hungry stare. Wrapping a wide fist around his cock, he slowly stroked himself up and down. "Would you lay out on your back for me again, Sam?"

"Yes," I softly whispered.

Centering myself on the middle of the mattress, I watched as Max prowled over me. Hovering above for several silent moments, he gazed into my eyes, then bent his elbows and slowly lowered his lips to mine. I wasn't sure if the gentle kiss was his way of testing the waters or if he meant to imprint his vow and shield me from having to claim myself as anything but a woman. Either way, it soon didn't matter. I was lost in the feel of his lips, the texture of his warm, slippery tongue and calloused hands as they raked over my naked body.

As he worked his mouth down my flesh, pausing to tease and torment my nipples, his fingers delved between my folds, adding to the fitful pleasure restlessly writhing inside me. My own gasps and moans echoed in my ears as Max's mouth grew closer and closer to my throbbing mound.

"Such pretty blonde curls," he whispered, threading his fingers through the wet ringlets. "I love the scent of your pussy. It's sweet…rich…earthy. I'm going to love smearing your thick juice all over my face, too."

"Max," I hissed.

"What?" He chuckled. "You don't want my mouth on you, Sam?"

"No. I do. Just stop talking about it and do it."

"Is that an order, or are you begging me?" He grinned as he arched his brows.

"Neither. It's a request."

"Well, in that case…I'm gonna have to grant your wish, fair maiden."

I watched him settle in between my legs, and the air stilled in my lungs as he dropped his mouth to my cunt. His moist breath teased my swollen and sweltering core. I fisted my hands to keep from gripping his head and forcing his mouth to my pussy. Extending his tongue, Max streaked it quickly over my engorged clit. My muscles twitched and my body jolted as a sliver of fire raced through my veins. Flattening his tongue, he drew it up between my folds in a long, slow, deliberate swipe.

"God, yes," I hissed.

Rocking and rolling my hips, I met each lap and plunge he bathed me with. Pressing my shoulders into the mattress, I arched as he hungrily fucked me with his talented, curling tongue.

"Your cunt's so soft and silky. Your cream is sweet and tart. My cock's as hard as steel and jealous as hell of my tongue."

He burrowed in even deeper while his nose and thumb batted and burnished my clit. Max worshiped my body not like a sub but a man, rendering me powerless. All I could do was lie back and savor the silky feel of his tongue and fingers dragging in and out of me. Trapped in the sublime boundary of verve and *le petite mort*—the little death—Max kept me suspended and writhing on the cusp of euphoric bliss.

My moans and whimpers grew to mewling cries of self-inflicted, passion-mixed pain. He would command me neither to hold back or to release. I was free to sail away all on my own. While I desperately wanted to free-fall into the exploding light, I couldn't let go of the spine-melting sensations he bestowed.

And just when I was ready to pirouette over the edge and crash into a million shards of ecstasy, Max sat up in an urgent rush.

"I have to feel this. Fuck. You're burning me up. I'm on fucking fire."

Hastily he ripped open a condom. Hissing, he sheathed his swollen and weeping cock. Max aligned the engorged crest to my pussy. Gripping my hips, he slowly impaled me. My swollen tissues stretched as he packed inch after glorious inch into my gripping core. I was stretched and filled to the hilt. When his pubic bone brushed my clit, pulses of pleasure ignited and spread outward…consuming every cell in its path. I threw back my head and screamed as the orgasm engulfed me in a blistering wave of fiery heat.

"Jesus," Max barked. Digging his fingers and thumb into my hips, he dragged in and out of my clutching core, hammering into me with such force another orgasm layered over the first, and I exploded again into a million quaking particles.

Max cursed again, his face contorting as he fought to hold back, making sure I rode the crest up and over yet again. Sweat dripped from his face as I continued to cry out and moan while uncontrollably gripping at his driving cock.

"So goddamn hot. So fucking tight. You're strangling me," he bit out between clenched teeth.

As I slowly floated downward, his expression slightly softened. Then without warning, he pulled from inside me. Without a word, he lifted me up with his strong arms, and flipped me onto my stomach. I opened my heavy eyelids to discover the room had finally stopped spinning, but everything appeared hazy and surreal. Wedging an arm beneath me, he pulled me up to my knees and dragged his fingertips down my spine.

Before I could remind him that I wasn't going to kneel for him, Max gripped one hand to my hip and plunged his thick cock back into my fluttering cunt. He issued an animalistic grunt as I sucked in a gasp. As he dragged his bulbous crest over my G-spot, I began climbing that familiar summit once more. Suddenly a drop of cold gel plopped onto my puckered rim. *Lube.* Oh, god, surely he wasn't going to try and shove his massive cock up my…

"Max," I cried. "I-I can't take you there."

"Shhh, baby. I'm not going to try and squeeze into your ass. Your pussy's too tight as it is. I'm not going to last long enough to work my way into this tiny hole."

He pressed a lube-covered finger through my gathered ring. Lights exploded behind my eyes, and slivers of delight detonated outward as my tiny opening sucked at his digit. Swirling his finger around the ridged rim, Max opened me wider as my eyes rolled to the back of my head. Lost in the sweet burn engulfing me, my clit throbbed incessantly. Dragging a hand between my legs, I strummed the aching nub and melted as Max wedged another finger inside my rosebud.

My keening cries echoed off the walls, nearly drowning out the sound of the vibe as I soared to the peak again. Cold plastic replaced his fingers. As he thrust in and out of my cunt, Max pressed the pulsating toy into my ass. The sensation was indescribable. My nerve endings felt as if they'd burst open and pinged off one another in an oscillating cyclone. The frantic driving rhythm of his cock was the only anchor keeping me from levitating off the bed. My limbs tingled out the warning as fire, light, and convulsions melded in an earth-shattering conflagration that splintered me apart.

Screaming until my throat turned raw, I clamped down around Max like a vice. He cursed and yanked the vibe free only to shove his fingers deep inside my clutching ass. Shouting my name, he slammed his cock in deep and stilled. I felt his seed jettison along his pulsating shaft as he followed me over. I whimpered as I clasped around his emptying cock and buried fingers.

Tremors and aftershocks rippled through us both, prompting jolts and quivers to consume our throbbing flesh. My arms trembled and my elbows gave out. Just as I was about to crash to the mattress, Max wrapped a steely arm around my waist and hauled me upright. With my back pressed against his slick chest, I purred. He bent and left a trail of kisses across my shoulder and up the side of my neck. Shivering, I clutched around his still-erect cock.

"Such a sweet, spent little kitten," he whispered in my ear. "I've never felt anyone quite as spectacular as you."

I'd never had my world rocked the way Max had just done, either. But my mind was too lethargic to try and decide if that was a good thing or a bad one. Hell, I couldn't even form words yet. I could only moan my reply.

His low chuckle tickled my ear. Lifting my heavy arms, I slung them behind his neck and sighed. Max cupped my breasts and nibbled my neck. His cock lurched inside me and I grinned.

"You're a sex machine."

"Not normally…not like this. I don't know what you've done to me, Sam, but I could stay inside your snug tunnel all night long and still not get my fill of you."

The idea sounded too tempting for words. But eventually we'd have to get out of bed. Whether or not we'd be able to walk was a different story.

Taking me with him, Max tumbled us onto the mattress. Spooning on our sides, we lay silent for a long time cocooned in one another's body heat. Blessedly, my mind hadn't yet engaged, and I turned to look over my shoulder at him. Max smiled, then lifted his head and pressed his mouth to mine in a soft, soulful kiss. My feminine musk clung to his lips and stained his tongue. Thumbing my nipples, he caressed my body while I softly purred and trailed my fingernails over his rugged arms. His erection declined slightly, but I could feel he was still rigid wedged within me.

Lifting from my lips, Max nipped the lobe of my ear and whispered, "Wait here, Sam, I'll get you cleaned up."

While it wasn't an order per se, his words pierced my skin in a pinprick of defiance. Shoving the sensation away, I wasn't going to ruin the most incredible sex of my life by turning into a confused, insecure shrew.

The loss of his body heat sent a shiver of abandonment through me. I brushed the ridiculous emotion away as I lay boneless, liquid, and body humming. Listening to the water running in the bathroom, I partially lifted my heavy eyelids. I smiled as Max swaggered toward me—cock bobbing at half-mast, washcloth in one hand and clean vibe in the other. He was a sight to behold. As he sat down on the edge of the bed, I reached out for the cloth. The idea of him cleaning me up felt too much like aftercare.

"Roll over, I've got this."

I shook my head. "I'll do it."

He handed me the warm, folded cotton with a troubled expression, then stood and stepped into his jeans. I quickly cleaned myself and sat up. I could feel his eyes on me as I paraded into the bathroom and tossed the washcloth into the dirty-clothes hamper. Turning, I found Max, in just his jeans, hands on his hips, staring at me. His expression was a cross between anger and lust.

"What's wrong?"

"Why wouldn't you let me do something as innocuous as clean the lube off your backside?"

A whole host of excuses swirled in my head, but after the starkly intimate act we'd just shared, I wasn't going to sully it by lying to him. "I didn't want you giving me aftercare."

He scoffed and shook his head. "The only aftercare I gave was holding you in my arms a few minutes ago. But the thought hadn't even crossed my mind, then or when I went to get the cloth to clean you up. Sometimes a man simply wants to do things for the woman who just blew his mind. Did you ever stop to consider that? No. Because you're so afraid—"

"I know what I'm afraid of," I snapped.

"I do, too." Max issued a heavy sigh and scrubbed a hand over his head. "I'm walking on eggshells here, Sam. I don't like it, but I'm doing it for you. Look, I get that you're caught between two worlds."

"No. I'm really not." My words were clipped. My anger began to churn.

"Then why did revisiting your submission rip you apart? I saw the state you were in when I got here."

"Because of you!"

Max blinked. "Me? What the hell did I do?"

Suddenly, I was too naked and exposed. I stormed to my dresser and dragged on a pair of yoga pants, then slapped on a bra and grabbed a shirt. The clothing left me feeling only slightly less vulnerable, but aside from crawling into the closet and slamming the door, it was the best I could do. I had a sneaking suspicion this conversation was about to take an ugly, unwanted turn, but I couldn't back down now.

"Why did you constantly tease me about being submissive?"

Max opened his mouth, then closed it. He stared at me for several long seconds, then flattened his lips. "You want the truth?"

"Always."

"Okay. First of all, you are an impressive Domme. You handled that boy last night with an expertise most Dominants, male or female, don't possess."

"Thank you. But?"

"The minute you opened the door to the club, a feeling punched me in the gut so hard it about knocked the wind out of me."

"What feeling was that?"

"You don't want to know, Sam. Trust me."

"I do, or I wouldn't have asked." I slapped my hands on my hips.

"It's not important." Max's mouth curled in a look of grim resignation. He bent and picked up his T-shirt, then pulled it over his head.

"Obviously it is, or you wouldn't have brought it up." He'd opened a door to something uncomfortable or too revealing. But just as quickly, Max had slammed the damn thing shut again as if I weren't capable of handling its contents. "Tell me. I'm a big girl."

"You're a beautiful girl," he softly murmured. Moving in close, he cupped my shoulders and sent me a weak smile. "But you've been through the emotional wringer enough for one day. We'll save this conversation for another one. All right?"

"No. It's not all right," I bit out. "I need to know why you kept needling me about being a Domme."

"Why?"

I closed my eyes. I had to look away from his penetrating gaze.

Suddenly the doorbell rang.

"Fuck!" Max spat. "It's probably Dylan and Nick's guy. I'll—"

"I'll get the damn door."

Turning on my heel, I stomped out of the room. I didn't even know why I was mad, but my blood pressure was spiking like a porcupine. Plastering on a manufactured smile to the workman standing on the porch, I unlocked the etched-glass outer door and pushed it open.

"Samantha Radcliff?" the older man with gray hair asked.

"Yes."

"I'm Fred Sidewell. Nick Masters sent me over."

"Thank you for coming on such short notice."

"No problem, ma'am."

Though Fred hadn't used the honorific, *ma'am* in the context of the lifestyle, a sudden calmness came over me. I felt a shift within and a familiar control lock in place.

"If you'd like to follow me out to the truck, Mr. Masters suggested I bring a few styles with me for you to choose from."

I could feel Max standing behind me. Not just the heat of his body but the tension rolling off him, as well. While our conversation was far from over, I felt more equipped to handle whatever it was that he was hiding from me.

"That was thoughtful of him. Yes. I'd be happy to."

I followed Fred to his truck. He showed me several doors, some stained in light oak and couple more a deep mahogany, but I really wasn't paying much attention. I could feel Max's stare boring into my back. Sweat broke out over my face. I dotted it away with the back of my hand as Fred tugged out a couple more, painted white, from his truck. I lifted my finger, pointing to the last door he offered when I spotted Max walking toward me.

"I'm going to take off. I know you're going to be busy for a while, but we're not done talking, Sam. There's still a whole lot we need discuss. I'll see you tomorrow, all right?"

"Okay," I replied, darting a glance at Fred who was busy dragging power tools out of the cargo hold in the bed of the truck.

Max brushed a soft kiss against my cheek, flashed me a gentle smile, then turned and walked away.

I watched his sexy retreating form as a mixture of emotions clamored through me. I was disappointed that he'd decided to leave, and it left a hollow feeling inside. Yet a sense of relief I couldn't deny swirled through me, too.

"I should have you put back together in about an hour," Fred announced.

"Sounds good," I murmured, watching Max drive away.

When I wandered back inside, I noticed that my collar, Desmond's photo, and the newspaper clippings had been tucked back inside the box now sitting on my couch.

CHAPTER FIVE

TRUE TO HIS word, Fred had installed the new door and replaced the splintered frame in a little over an hour. Alone again, I paced the living room, staring at the box still poised on the couch. As darkness settled outside, I plopped down beside the container of broken promises and dreams. Unanswerable questions about Max still raced through my head. But since figuratively stepping into my Domme shoes once again, I felt competent to deal with whatever lay ahead.

Without an ounce of timidity, I lifted the lid on the box. Desmond's smiling face stared up at me. While the familiar empty sadness wormed its way into my heart, I simply smiled back at him.

"I miss you. I always will." My voice softly trembled.

I clutched my old collar. I needed to find out if the pieces of Samantha were content in her isolated cell or if she indeed yearned to rise from the ashes. I didn't want to spend another minute riding this roller coaster of doubt. It wasn't me. Lashing out at Max for my own shortcomings wasn't the answer.

It had taken years for me to become this cast-iron bitch, and I couldn't shake that side of me off in a matter of days or hours. But Max hadn't signed up to be my whipping boy, either. I wasn't being fair to him or me.

Once I sorted this clusterfuck out, I'd tuck the past away where it belonged and offer my apologies then. That or venture down a new road and fucking kneel at his feet.

Not hardly, my subconscious scoffed.

Closing my eyes, I drew the leather to my nose and inhaled its scent. Longing and sadness rushed in. A few tears of mourning slid down my cheeks, but the pain was bearable now. Maybe forcing myself to relive the past had numbed me. Or maybe I'd already purged the majority of debilitating pain. Of course, the cloak of Dominance protecting me might simply be deflecting more self-induced agony.

Sweeping my jumbled emotions aside. I held the collar and focused on the feelings it induced. I slowly plucked each sentiment from my mind and studied it.

Security. The memory of the constant shelter Desmond had provided lent an unequaled level of safety. But I had provided my own safety and protection for years.

Trust. Holding the feeling was like balancing the blade of a knife in my palm. I'd trusted him to always be there for me, but that trust had been broken. Not by the man himself but by forces that neither of us could have ever imagined. Still, there were people in my life who had earned my trust. Mika, Julianna, Drake, Trevor…the list could go on and on. But over time I had learned how to trust again.

Peace. Submitting to Desmond had completed me. The amount of serenity I'd found in serving him was greater than the universe. My heart had overflowed each time he praised me. But I'd resigned myself to the fact—learned to live with it even—that I'd never find such all-encompassing solace with another. In switching from sub to Domme, I'd found a pseudo-replacement of fulfillment in accepting a submissive's control. It might not be as perfect as what I'd once had, but it was rewarding, and I could remain among my kink-minded family.

Love. A lump lodged in my throat. I worked to swallow it down. Desmond had been the love of my life, and always would be. I couldn't wrap my head around the idea of sharing the depth and breadth of devotion with anyone else. My husband…my Master had known me inside out, backward and forward and all the hidden cracks and crevices in between. He'd unconditionally accepted all the parts of me, the good, bad, and ugly. While I still maintained the capacity to love…my mother, my friends, no man would or could ever love me as much as Desmond had.

Placing the collar back in the box, I exhaled a heavy sigh. Wiping my eyes, I tucked the lid in place and silently carried the container back to my room.

I hadn't had any life-altering epiphanies; I'd simply come to the sad conclusion that I pined for a life lost…a ghost of happiness that I once had. I could no more recreate those glorious days than I could conjure Desmond from the dead.

"This is as good as it gets. This is all you'll ever have." The words of reckoning spilled off my tongue. It was as if I needed to hear them out loud before I could take the first step on the only path available for me…the road I was already on.

Placing the box on the shelf in my closet, I pressed my palm to its side.

"Until we meet again in the afterlife…good-bye, Desmond."

I closed the door. It snicked in place with a chilling finality.

Another tear leaked down my cheek, and I let it fall to the floor in tribute to the man who still owned my submissive soul.

AT FOUR O'CLOCK on the dot, I stood outside Mika's office. Whip in one hand, I raised my other and rapped on the ornately carved wooden door. He opened it from the other side and drank me in. From my black shiny stilettos to my short black leather skirt and black leather corset to the whip clutched in my fist. He grinned.

"I see you've found your answer, *Mistress*. Please come in," Mika chuckled.

"I told—"

"Don't say it." He held up his hand. "I assumed you knew what was in your heart, but sometimes it doesn't hurt to take a step back and make sure."

"I know what's in my heart. And I know exactly where I'd be if Desmond were still alive. But he's not. Therefore, I'm not, either. If it were a perfect world, we'd all be idyllically happy, shitting rainbows and unicorns, but it's not and we don't."

"True." Mika nodded toward the couch. I sat down and he took a seat beside me. "But are you settling for second best or charting a new life course?"

"Honestly, both. I can navigate Dominant waters, but as a sub, I can't."

"I understand. So this friction you feel with Max, are you able to rise above it now?"

"There's a hell of a lot more than just friction. I won't lie."

"I'm glad. About the not lying part, I mean. I heard about the grand entrance he made over at your place last night."

My brows shot up in surprise. "Who told… Dylan, right?"

Mika nodded. "I ripped him a new asshole for compromising your privacy, but he assured me that Max was as trustworthy as Nick and Sanna."

"I think he might be, too."

The corners of Mika's mouth curled slightly. "Did you find out why he was giving you such a hard time?"

"No, and it doesn't matter. Either Max and I will come to an understanding as friends or we'll co-exist in the club. I've learned to tolerate the few narrow-minded Dominants who are here. I can do the same with Max if I have to."

"He's still a guest of the club. If his behavior is annoying and he persists taunting you, I want to know."

"Sure."

"That wasn't a question, let alone a rhetorical one." Mika narrowed his eyes.

I rolled mine. "Yes, boss."

He stared at me for several long seconds. "You look more relaxed than you have in a long time."

Yeah, well…you would, too, if you'd had the world fucked out from beneath your feet.

As the heat of guilt rolled up my chest, I jumped from the couch before it could reach my cheeks. "Time to get the bar set up for tonight. I'll see you downstairs later."

"Sammie," Mika called out to me as I reached the door. I peeked back at him from over my shoulder. "Try not to get hurt, sweetheart."

Fuck! He knew. I obviously wasn't hiding the satisfied woman very well. Mika knew Max and I had done the sweet, dirty deed. *Dammit!*

"I won't," I croaked, then dashed from his office.

The sounds of whips, paddles, whimpers, and moans blended with the sizzle of violet wands unleashing ozone to mix with the scent of leather and sex. The familiar cacophony was soothing.

Nick, Dylan, Sanna, and Max breached the foyer through the wide velvet curtain. A ripple of arousal I didn't want to feel slid through me. As Max locked his gaze on mine, a sad smile lifted the corners of his mouth. I wanted to sprint across the dungeon and kiss those magical lips until I was senseless. Instead, I jerked him a nod and then focused on wiping down the bar. I couldn't control the zaps of lightning setting my traitorous body on fire, but I could keep a grip on my outward reaction to the man. My heart thrummed and my blood pumped like lava. My clit tingled as if anticipating an invitation to another orgasm party.

I inwardly scolded my hormones as a massive shadow moved over the bar, darkening the spot I polished. I didn't have to look up to know it was Max. I could feel the heat of his body...smell him, like an animal senses its mate.

Stop being ridiculous. You fucked him. That hardly qualifies as being marked as his mate. Get real!

I wanted to believe the chastising voice in my head, but in my heart, I knew we'd more than fucked. We'd carelessly intensified the weird and highly combustible connection between us.

"Good evening, *Mistress* Sammie," he murmured, a hint of disdain in his voice.

"Max," I replied, not raising my head. Okay, so call me a coward. I wasn't ready to look him in the eye—not until I calmed my wrecked nerves. "What can I get you to drink?"

"Diet cola, please."

Head down, I prepared his order and placed it on the bar atop a napkin.

"Sam," he whispered softly. "Look at me."

I slowly raised my head and was nearly taken out at the knees. He was once again opening his soul to me. In those sparkling green eyes, I saw apology, reassurance, trust, honesty, and a wealth of sadness, swirling in a storm of want and desire.

"Are you okay?"

I swallowed tightly and nodded.

"Did your door get replaced?"

Again, I nodded, unable to trust my voice to keep from quivering.

Dammit. Just one look and he was crashing through my heart like he'd done to my damn door. Like a riptide, there was no way to keep from being dragged out to sea.

"After the club closes, can we go somewhere to talk?" he quietly asked.

I shook my head, denying his request. With one slow blink, Max slammed the door of emotions shut and barred me. His lips flattened to a thin line.

"I have errands to run in the morning," I lied. "I'll need to get to sleep as soon as I can."

"I promise I won't keep you up too late."

"I-I'll see what I can do."

"Master Max. I would have gladly served your drink, as well," Savannah announced, moving in beside him.

"It's all right, girl. You only have two hands. Save them for your Masters. But to keep you from having to make another trip to the bar, I'll help you carry our drinks back to the table."

"Thank you, Sir. I appreciate that." She grinned.

I couldn't help but smile. Sanna's bubbly personality was contagious. "What would you and your Masters like, sweetheart?"

"Two cran-apple juices and a cola, please."

"Coming right up."

Before he turned to escort Sanna back to her Masters, Max sent me a dangerous smile and winked. "I'll be back soon."

A nervous hum droned inside me, but as another member stepped up to the bar, I focused on work and shoved the looming discomfort of our pending discussion down deep.

"Red! Red!" Lil'tigger, the fairly new submissive, screamed her safe word from across the room.

I jerked my head up in time to see Kerr land one more brutal blow to her ass.

"I said *red*, you asshole," she shrieked.

Kerr grip her purple-dyed hair and brutally yank her head back. Cuffed to a cross and immobile, she fought against the bindings as Kerr whispered something in her ear. Lil'tigger furiously shook her head as tears streamed down her cheeks. Blood dripped from a cut on her butt cheek.

Master Ink and Sir Bent-Lee, the head DMs, converged on the scene as conversation in the club fell silent. The Doms working their subs stopped and shielded them with their bodies while quietly reassuring them.

From the archway, Mika stormed into the dungeon. His jaw was clenched, lips pressed tight, and fire blazed in his amber eyes.

Please let this be the last straw.

As Mika made his way toward Kerr, Bent-Lee pressed a cloth to Lil'tigger's injured flesh before working to release the sobbing sub from the cross. Master Ink stood glaring at Kerr, who seemed to be losing his patience at having to explain his actions. Several Doms, who'd been sitting at their tables, converged at the periphery of the station. Tony, Joshua, James, Ian, Justice, Sam, Nick, Dylan, and Max stood like menacing citadels, ready and waiting for Kerr to do something stupid.

"Keep an eye on things," I murmured to Joe before rounding the bar to join the others.

Leagh, Liz, Cindy, and Savannah along with her sister, Mellie—who looked pale and shaken—stood at the ready with a blanket and bottle of water to help settle Lil'tigger once she was free. Several years ago, in another city, Mellie had worn Kerr's collar. The irony that the two would once again meet as members of Club Genesis was a sick twist of fate.

Wearing an angry glare that conveyed the depth of his fury, Mika quietly spoke to Kerr. Suddenly the prick reared back. His face contorted with rage.

"You can't do that. I didn't do anything wrong!" Kerr bellowed. Crimson stained his cheeks. With nostrils flaring, he heaved the paddle in his hand across the room. A group of subs quickly dove for cover as the wooden toy splintered across the floor.

Mika grabbed Kerr by the shirt and effortlessly lifted him off the ground as I reached the cluster of Doms, and moved in beside Max. He glanced at me and did a split-second double take, then frowned. Ignoring him, I watched Savannah grab her sister's arm. Mellie lifted her chin as she looked at Kerr with loathing. Joshua, her new Master—a highly respected member of the club and well versed at the dynamics of the lifestyle—took one look at his girl and ate up the distance between them in three long strides.

Bent-Lee finished with the last cuff, and Leagh rushed to Lil'tigger's side. Wrapping the trembling sub in the blanket, Leagh led the crying girl away from the confrontation while the rest of the submissives followed.

Like an angry mob, we Doms gathered in closer now that Lil'tigger was safely out of harm's way.

"Kerr. Your membership is officially terminated," Mika bellowed for everyone to hear.

A resounding cheer went up among the crowd and I started to laugh.

"I'll notify every club owner in a five-state radius of your abusive behavior." Mika released the man's shirt. Kerr crumpled to the floor on his ass.

"You can't do this," he roared, launching to his feet once again. "You can't interrupt a scene. I was handing down a punishment, you stupid prick!"

"*I* can do whatever the fuck *I* want." Mika sneered. "Lil'tigger is not your sub. She's unowned and is protected by *me*. Any behavior that warrants a punishment comes through me…by me, and you damn well know it!"

"Your punishments are worthless. All you ever do is talk to the subs; you never beat their asses the way they deserve."

A collective gasp rippled through the club. I wanted to grab Kerr by the balls and show him exactly what he deserved…castration.

"You come anywhere near this club again, you won't need an ambulance; you'll need the fucking coroner." Mika's threat was arctic and low. He turned to the DMs. "Get him the fuck out of here!"

I wanted to jump up and down and scream out like a cheerleader. When Ink and Bent-Lee grabbed Kerr by the arms, he started to struggle. Kicking and cursing, he fought for freedom. Mika rolled his eyes and shook his head, unimpressed with the asshat's tantrum.

Turning to the group of us watching with glee, Mika chuckled. "Anyone who wants to help the DMs, please. Be my guest."

Like a piñata being busted open at a kid's birthday party, the Doms rushed forward and gripped their hands onto Kerr. They lifted him off the ground. I was anxious to join in, as well, but aside from his junk, there wasn't a place on his body for me to put my hands. I definitely wasn't going near the toxic shit between his legs, so instead, I led the way toward the front of the club.

"I'll get the door for you gentlemen," I volunteered with a wide grin.

As I held the portal open, Kerr passed me with a snarl. I blew him a kiss and flipped him off. They tossed the man to the sidewalk with a thud. He let out a scream, but the Doms simply turned and walked back inside. I couldn't resist high-fiving each and every one of them.

"Thanks for taking out the trash, boys," I laughed, then slammed and locked the door.

When I turned around, Max was the only one left in the spacious entry area. Butterflies dipped and swooped in my stomach, and the giddiness within turned to something solid and hungry.

"I'm glad that shitiot is banned. I didn't like the way he treated you, or any other woman for that matter."

I nodded. "I am, too. Finally he crossed that line I'd been praying for. But now I'm worried Kerr will try to get back at Mika in some way. It's happened before."

"I heard about that from Dylan a few years ago. That crazy son of a bitch shooting him was bad shit."

"Yeah. I know he'll take precautions, both coming and going from the club."

"He'll be fine," Max assured. "How are you doing?"

I could lie and tell him I was fine, or I could rush to his arms and lock my lips to his, or I could just tell him the truth.

"So far, so good. I can live with that."

"But are you happy?"

"I'm as happy as I'll ever be. I came to terms with that a long time ago."

A thoughtful expression lined his face and he gave a single nod. "You know, yesterday at your place when I came out of the bathroom to clean you—"

"We've already discussed that. I overreacted. I'm sorry."

The memory of his hot body against my back, his calloused hands gliding up and down my body exploded in my head. I could feel his labored breaths, rushing like a furnace over my neck, still smell the tart scent of sex that hung in the air. Need, want, and desire coiled in my belly. My nipples grew taut, aching for his touch again. While my pussy clutched the emptiness within, my clit throbbed for the lash of his talented tongue. The attention he lavished on me was spellbinding and more.

I knew better than to start dissecting his logic or motives for having sex with me. I'd have to put my own rationale under the microscope, and that chafed. Max had made me feel helpless and small...like a sub.

"Why did you show up tonight in all your Domme glory?"

"Excuse me?" I blinked.

"I thought you were struggling to decide which side of the fence you belonged?"

"So now that you see I'm still a Domme, all your bluster about us simply being man and woman was just bullshit? Did you only seduce me to try and gauge how much submission was left inside me?"

"What? No," he barked. "Christ, Sam. I'm attracted to you. Why are you so damn suspicious of me? You thinking I've got some hidden agenda to squash your Dominance with my own is what's bullshit."

He moved in closer until our noses nearly touched, until his enticing hot breath spilled over my lips. "I know why you demanded to wipe the lube away. You needed to reestablish a sense of control."

I lifted my chin. "So what if I did?"

"Exactly. So what?" He shrugged. "Be honest with yourself, Sam, and with me. You don't have to shut me out or set your sexy ass on your Domme throne. If you feel the need to slide into your badass spiked shoes…just tell me."

I stared at him with my mouth hanging half open and my eyes wide.

Max started to softly chuckle. "I'm not intimidated by your Dominant side, Sam. A lot of men might be, but I'm not like a lot of men."

Boy, that's the truth.

"I don't want you to be intimidated by mine, either," Max stated.

Yeah, good luck. That was going to take a serious amount of work.

"Last night was something new for both of us, but I"—he sent me a wicked smile—"I liked it. I know you did, too."

I felt my cheeks catch fire. "Yes, I did."

His eyes smoldered and he pulled back a fraction of an inch. "I'm glad that's settled. Tomorrow is Sunday. The club is closed. I'd like to take you to dinner."

"You're asking me out on a date?"

"Yeah, I am. So what?"

I couldn't remember the last time I'd been on a date. I suddenly felt as if I were eighteen again. "So okay. Dinner it is."

"Great. I'll pick you up at seven." He brushed a soft kiss to my lips, flashed me a devilish smile, then turned and swaggered past the velvet curtain.

Excitement tingled from my toes to the top of my head. Good grief. I was acting like a silly schoolgirl. Rolling my eyes, I shook off the ridiculous sensation and headed back to the bar.

Mika and Bent-Lee were sitting beside Lil'tigger, who'd stopped crying. Sam, Cindy, and Liz—who worked in the medical profession—

were nearby packing up the first-aid kit. With Kerr banished, the rest of the members had resumed play and conversation. There was an overwhelming sense of relief…a palpable lightness in the air.

Dragging my gaze toward Max's table, I saw Honey sat kneeling at his feet, staring up at him in visible awe. The same irrational wave of jealousy plowed me once more, stopping me dead in my tracks. Unable to peel my eyes from the couple, I watched as Max cupped her chin and smiled. There was no tangible reason for the pang of envy that pierced through me, but it was there all the same.

Tamping down my ugly emotions, I turned on my heel and hurried behind the bar. Replacing the hurt and anger that was bubbling up inside me, I forced a cheerful smile. There was no excuse for the feelings pinging within. Max was a Dominant, like me. We had a job and a right to help submissives in the club achieve growth. There was no room for the petty woman's jealousies rising inside me. If Honey had come to me, I'd be commanding her to a station and guiding her fulfillment, too.

The masochistic urge to glance Max's way was like a dark force that no lightsaber could vanquish. With each glass I filled, the same question as to why I let his actions with a submissive bother me spooled through my brain. We fucked. We planned to do dinner. Neither meant we were in a relationship. Hell, we weren't even going steady.

"Oh, wow. That's intense," Liz murmured to Cindy as they waited for their sodas.

"Way intense," Cindy agreed.

Raising my head, I turned to see what scene had the two subs so enraptured. Across the room, Max stood next to one of the bondage tables. Honey lay splayed out, naked and writhing beneath the crackling violet wand. Metal clamps adorned her nipples, connected to a chain that trailed down her flat stomach and attached to a stainless steel closure cinched around her clit. Her legs were spread wide, and cotton rope held her ankles to the corners of the table. Even from the distance of the bar, I could see copious juices pouring from her pussy. Honey gripped the handle of a contact cable from the violet wand in her fist. The reverse technique passed electricity from the wand, directly through her, keeping Max free of the current. Each touch of his fingers, or various metallic toys, bypassed the man's nerve endings and sent electricity to dance and sing over the sub's flesh. Honey's moans and the rock of her hips told me that Max had set the wand low. He wasn't trying to fire her up, simply torture her nipples and clit with tingling heat.

Focused relentlessly on the sub, Max controlled each sensation igniting inside her. His fluid and graceful elegance exemplified both his knowledge as well as his experience as a Dom. His commanding style was simply breathtaking. Out of the dark depths within me, a longing to trade places with Honey seeped into my blood and settled like a heavy weight beneath my bones.

Unable to turn away from Max's scene, I watched as he glided a Mylar flogger over the chains against her flesh. I could almost feel the pulses of electricity stimulate her nipples and clit. A chill raced up my spine as Honey wailed and begged for permission to come in a desperate keening cry. Yanking the probe from her hand, he gripped a thick pink dildo and shoved it deep inside Honey's tunnel. Bending, Max whispered in her ear. As she screamed out her release, I knew that he'd granted her the command to come.

My pussy clutched, gripping nothing but emptiness. Throbbing in tandem, my nipples and clit pitifully pulsated in need. Swallowing tightly, I watched as Max released the clamp on her clit. He strummed the rubber cock in and out of her cunt while his mouth moved with words that only she could hear, as he slowly eased the sub back to earth.

"Good god," Liz groaned. Grabbing a bar nap, she fanned her face. "I think I'm going to find my Masters, kneel at their feet, and beg them to take me home…pronto."

Cindy moaned. "You and me both, girl. Dayum! That was hot."

I couldn't even force a smile, let alone drag words past my tongue before the pair grabbed their drinks and hurried away. Peering at Max once more, I saw he'd freed Honey from the ropes and now stood behind her. He wrapped a blanket around her naked body and simply held her, back flush against his chest the way he'd melded me to him the night before. Tears stung the backs of my eyes. My body trembled. A void I hadn't felt in sixteen years began eating its way within. Turning my back to him, I squatted to the row of cabinets behind the bar while jealousy gouged my heart. Pretending to reach for a stack of plastic cups, I closed my eyes and dragged in several long, ragged breaths.

Yes, he was a Dominant, but did he have to engage the sub in such a blatantly sexual scene?

That was obviously what Honey needed…what they'd negotiated.

I squeezed my eyes shut tighter. I didn't want the little voice inside my head making excuses for her, or Max or attempting to sooth the pain of insult away. I wanted to rush to my private room, crawl inside the shower, and scrub the sickly film of betrayal away. Sucking in a deep breath, I stood.

"I'll be back in a minute."

Joe absently nodded as he shoved cans of soda into the metal cooler. Casting my eyes to the archway, I hurried out of the dungeon. Inside the safety of my private room, I sat on the edge of the bed and tried to sort out my erratic emotions.

Yes, I was jealous. Honey had felt Max's touch, his attention. She'd been granted the pleasures I greedily wanted to experience again. *They were mine, dammit!* Angry with myself for letting the little green-eyed monster consume me, I tried to rationalize why I felt so slighted and raw.

The man hadn't promised me a damn thing besides a good time in bed and a date for dinner. He'd worked a sub. Big deal. Every Dom in the club did the same damn thing on a nightly basis…including me. Max taking care of Honey's needs was no different than me doing the same for Eli. While I didn't jack the boy off, I'd done so plenty of times in the past.

"You're losing your damn mind," I murmured in disgust.

The light tap on my door had me rolling my eyes. No doubt Mika had been watching me coming unglued on the security monitor in his office. I truly loved the man, but sometimes he acted like an overprotective father. Gripping the handle, I pulled the door toward me.

Before I'd even looked up at Mika, I stepped aside so he could enter. "I'm fine. I'm fine."

"Good," Max replied with a soft chuckle.

Yelping in surprise, I jumped and slapped my hand to my chest. "What are you doing here?"

"That's what I came back to ask you."

"No. I mean what are you doing in my room?"

"I just told you. I came to see if you were all right."

"Why wouldn't I be?"

Max didn't answer. He simply arched his brows and studied me with a cocky stare that screamed: *You're wasting your time. Blowing smoke up my ass won't work.*

"The mirrors in the club are quite revealing. I could give Honey aftercare and still see every teeny tiny emotion that rolled across your face. At least until you ducked down behind the bar and out of sight."

My stomach began to swirl. He'd been watching me? *Impossible.* Max had been transfixed on the sub…hadn't he? Obviously not.

"When you stood up, I saw the tears in your eyes. And then you took off toward your room. I had to know why me scening with Honey upset you."

"I knew you were full of yourself, but honestly," I scoffed, trying to dig myself out of an endlessly collapsing tunnel. "You think I'm upset about you and a sub?"

"I don't think it, sweetheart. I *know* it." Max took my hand off the doorknob. As the portal closed, giving us total privacy, he pressed his massive body against me until I felt the cool drywall at my back. "You don't need to be jealous of anyone in or out of this club."

"Seriously?" I hissed. "How the hell can you clear a doorway with a head as big as yours?"

"Which head are you talking about?" Max smirked.

With a growl of frustration, I shoved at his pecs. Of course, I didn't move him even a fraction of an inch. Grasping my design, he took an obligatory step back.

"First of all, I'd have to feel something toward you to feel the least bit jealous." I lifted my hand and poked him in the chest.

"So you *do* feel something toward me. That's a plus."

"Shut up," I spat. "Secondly, why on earth would I feel the least bit threatened? Honey's a sub. I'm not!"

"Yes, you are."

"Out!" I yelled. "Get the fuck out of my room!"

"Sam, it's not a bad thing. You're losing your shit over a title…a role. You don't have to choose one side or—"

"You know why I can't go back to being a… Oh, just get out. Leave. I don't want or need you trying to convince me I'm something I'm not."

Shaking with rage, I backed away from him and pointed toward the door as it flew open. Mika, Ink, and Bent-Lee stormed into my room.

The trio looked intimidating and fierce, but not half as fierce as the fury blazing in Max's eyes.

"I believe the lady asked you to leave," Mika reminded in a calm, even tone.

"I'm not here to hurt Sam. I simply want to talk to her."

"She's made it clear that she's done talking."

CHAPTER SIX

THE MAN WAS worse than an overprotective father. Charging into my room in such a way told me he thought me weak and helpless. Instead of extending my thanks—which I knew he wanted to hear—I extended an open palm.

"Stop. I can handle myself, Mika." Slapping my fists on my hips, I turned toward Max. "It's best if you go join your friends in the dungeon. Besides, I need to get back to work, anyway."

"Sammie," Mika began.

I shook my head. "Mika Emile LaBrache," I growled in warning. "I don't want to talk about this or anything else the rest of the night."

"Fine," Mika bit out. "But we will discuss this later, *Samantha Abigail Radcliffe*."

The corner of Max's lips twitched. I narrowed my eyes at him, then shot the other three testosterone-laced Neanderthals in my room a scathing glare.

"So will we," Max assured, undaunted by my visible fury.

"I'd rather talk to a wall, thank you very much." I mocked both Mika and Max.

After storming out of my room, I charged down the hall. Snapping my boss's head off wasn't the smartest decision I'd ever made. But I hoped Mika would take my internal conflict and my caustic attitude with a grain of salt. If not, I could always move in with Mom down in New Orleans. At least I wouldn't have to see Max again.

How the fuck did my life get so damn complicated?

Behind the bar once more, I watched as Ink and Bent-Lee returned to the dungeon. Mika and Max, however, were nowhere to be found. They were probably upstairs in Mika's office, sharing a glass of McClelland he kept stashed in his desk drawer and plotting ways to bring me to my knees…literally. Either that or they were in the back parking lot, slugging out who was the better protector of poor lil' Sammie.

Sammie. Sammie. Sammie. Sometimes it's not always about you, sugar, the self-righteous voice in my head mocked.

"Oh, shut up!" I snarled.

"I'm sorry, Mistress, but I-I didn't say a word." Joe blinked in confusion.

"No. Not you, boy." I dismissed him with a wave of my hand before grabbing a bottle of water. Twisting off the cap, I tilted it back and closed my eyes. As I gulped the liquid down, I prayed this clusterfuck of a night would end soon.

I didn't catch sight of Max or Mika again. By three a.m., the club was nearly empty. Ink and Bent-Lee had enlisted the help of several Doms to escort members to their cars. Per protocol, the extra security was put in place anytime someone's membership was revoked. None of us put it past Kerr to stir up trouble outside the club now.

After cleaning up, I mopped the floor behind the bar. Joe wiped down the tables and stacked chairs. The DMs pulled the heavy velvet curtains to cover the equipment, in preparation of the arrival of the early-morning cleaning crew.

"Can I walk out with you, Mistress?" Joe asked, looking as exhausted as I felt.

"Sure. I'll protect you," I teased with a wink.

"I-I meant I'd..." Joe stammered, then grinned. "Thank you, Mistress."

As my submissive bodyguard and I reached the metal back door, I darted a glance at the camera fixed above my head. I raised my hand in my nightly wave to Mika, and probably Max, as well, then pushed through the portal and headed to my car.

After a long, hot shower with my favorite honey-almond bath gel, I dried off and crawled into bed. The green iridescent light from the clock radio on my nightstand showed four forty-five. I closed my eyes and fell sound asleep.

Max lightly dragged a finger from between my breasts, up my throat, and past my chin. His warm flesh stilled on my lips and I opened my eyes. He stood before me, wearing nothing but a placid smile and a thick, weeping erection poised near my mouth. Licking my lips, I tore my gaze from his cock and sent him a beseeching stare.

"What is it you want, my beautiful slut?" he asked in a low, husky voice.

"To please you, Master," I whispered shyly.

I realized I was naked and on my knees. Thighs spread wide with my palms splayed open atop my thighs. I drew a hand to my throat. It was naked, as well, and a pang of sorrow swelled within.

"Soon, pretty slave. You'll wear my collar soon."

My heart nearly burst with joy at his promise.

"Open your lips for me, Samantha. I need to feel your sinful mouth," Max whispered as he sank his wide fingers into my hair and tilted my head back. "You're so fucking gorgeous…so perfect and pleasing, my precious pet."

Gazing up at him without remorse or guilt, I parted my lips and offered my tongue as a pillow for his shaft. I studied the hard lines of uncompromising muscles along his abs and chest, the masculine outline of his jaw, and the sensual bow of his mouth.

Sliding his thick, throbbing cock between my lips, Max hissed as he slowly fed me each spine-tingling inch. His wide crest prodded the back of my throat as he cupped my chin.

"Worship your Master's cock, beautiful," he whispered beguilingly.

The heat of serenity enveloped me as I made love to his length with my mouth. I met his thrusts with the swirl of my tongue as Max grunted and moaned in delight. His sounds of pleasure fed the starving submissive within. I gorged on him while I drowned my One in all the love and devotion blazing in my soul.

All too soon, he issued a feral growl. Gripping my hair, he jerked his cock from between my lips. Gripping his wet, swollen shaft, Max pumped himself in quick uneven strokes. He cried out my name, and his thick, pungent streams jettisoned onto my chin, over my breasts, and dripped onto my thighs. The slippery heat scalded my flesh and reinforced his claim of me while tears of happiness streamed down my cheeks.

His chest heaved with each labored breath, and as his smoky green eyes slowly began to focus, Max sent me a smile so bright it dimmed the sun. Swiping his fingers across my chin, he gathered his seed. I smiled, proud of the joy I had brought him. Dutifully, I opened my mouth and extended my tongue as I cleaned his offering from his fingers.

"Such a good girl," he praised in a low sigh filled with love.

Suddenly, the door burst open. All the submissives of the club stood peering into my bedroom wearing looks that ranged from shock and sadness to disgust. Tears spilled down Eli's cheeks while Destiny threw her head back and cackled in an evil, sickening tone.

"How could you betray me like this, Mistress?" Eli wailed. "I trusted you! I put my life in your hands!"

"Quiet, boy!" Max roared. "I'm Samantha's One now. You will show her the respect she deserves."

"I did once," Eli screamed defiantly.

A dark shadow pushed through the throng of subs. When the man stepped into the light of the room and raised his head, I screamed.

"Why do you kneel for another, Samantha? I'm your forever One." Desmond's voice was teemed in anguish and heartbreak.

"No!" The scream tore from my throat as I bolted upright in bed.

Sweating.

Shaking.

Tears streamed down my face.

I lunged out of bed, raced to the bathroom, and flipped on the light. As I stumbled to the sink, I blinked, adjusting my eyes to the brightness. Peering into the mirror, I shook my head. The reflection staring back at me was of a woman I didn't recognize. Her eyes were rife with guilt and fear, haunted in a way I hadn't seen since 2001. The dream—"dream nothing," I scoffed, "that thing was a fucking nightmare."—had annihilated me.

Max wanted...no, needed a sub, but I'd never be able to fill that role. The peace and serenity that had enveloped me in my nocturnal fantasy couldn't erase the grizzly consequences if I... No. I couldn't. The risk of being shunned by the submissives or condemned by a few pious Doms was only partly the reason I kept my compliance chained and gagged. I was terrified that kneeling at Max's feet would disgrace and tarnish Desmond's memory. That would lead to a total emotional meltdown, and I knew it. Yet I couldn't erase the familiar serenity that filled me as I knelt at Max's feet in my dream. I was more terrified than ever.

There's no going back, Samantha, the little voice in my head reminded once more.

That sliver of insight didn't stop me from yearning. I ached to feel my submissive splendor again.

You can't always have what you want.

"No shit!" I scoffed at my nagging conscious. I had to find contentment with the things I had...once more.

"Damn you, Max! Damn you for stirring this hopelessness up inside me." The words tore from my mouth as I balled up my hand and slammed it against the sink. Pain shot up my arm. I remembered punching Max. His stomach gave as much as the porcelain...not at all! Remembering his shocked expression made me choke on a watery laugh.

Turning on the faucet, I bent and splashed cool water over my face before returning to the bedroom. The sheets lay in a rumpled heap just as they'd been after Max and I'd made love.

"You didn't make love. You fucked. Big difference," I chided.

No matter how big, bad, and bold I wanted to be, the fallout from my dream left me bruised and tender. Instead of crawling between the sheets to torture myself with Max's scent, I padded to the kitchen.

From the pantry, I plucked out a bottle of tequila. Bypassing the lime and salt, I drew down a glass and poured a healthy swallow. I tossed back the first shot and savored the bitter burn as it smoothed its way down and warmed my belly. The second swig sent a shudder through me. The tequila burned hot. The residual heat of my dream was hotter and more beautiful than the sweeping brush of orange and blue sunrise that painted the morning sky. I twisted the cap back on the liquor, walked back to my room, and crawled into bed. Max's scent was everywhere. Pulling the sheet to my face, I savored his lingering presence meshed within the thread count as it caressed my flesh.

I wrapped the memory of Max around me and fell asleep. Thankfully, I didn't dream, but when I awoke, I felt empty...almost hollow. Determined to keep the blues at bay, I downed my coffee, tucked my phone into the surround-sound speakers, and got to work. I sorted and started the laundry, cleaned the bathrooms, dusted, and vacuumed.

Throughout the day, I wondered if Max would even show up for our date after the hateful way I'd behaved last night. Fear brought out the worst in me. But then I was confident he already knew that. Max was too observant, bold, brazen, and in command to be swayed by my unruly temper. At seven on the dot, he'd be outside ringing my bell. Of course, that wasn't the bell I wanted him to ding.

"God help me, I'm in way over my head."

When the house was spotless, I darted to my bathroom and relaxed beneath a piping-hot shower. After drying my hair, I added a touch of makeup before sliding on a pair of soft, faded blue jeans and a tank top. Glancing at the clock, I was shocked to discover I'd spent more time primping than I'd thought. It was five till seven. I left my heels in the closet and quickly slipped on a pair of sandals—Sunday was my guilty pleasure day of comfort.

Just as I'd expected, at seven o'clock on the nose, the doorbell rang. I answered to find Max in faded jeans, a white cotton tee, and a pair of flip-flops as well. Evidently, he enjoyed comfort, too.

"I'm glad you didn't get dressed up all fancy and shit." He grinned.

"I wasn't sure where we were going, so I went with really relaxed casual. Looks like I made the right choice, huh?" I flashed him a sassy smile. "Come on in."

As he stepped past me, Max dragged his knuckles down my cheek, then bent and brushed a kiss to my lips. He cocked his head and looked down at my feet. "Did you shrink?"

"You're funny," I said with a sarcastic edge.

"I know, but you're not laughing. When they put you together—and they did a fine job, I might add—I think they forgot to put in your funny bone."

I bit my lips together trying not to grin. "They must have given you mine."

"I'll give it back. It's not a funny bone, but it's a bone, all right."

I rolled my eyes and shook my head. "You've been using that line since third grade, haven't you?"

"Fifth, actually. I didn't know what my junk was for prior to that."

"Fifth grade?" I blinked. "You've been boning girls since fifth grade?"

"No. Seventh."

"I don't want to know. Are you going to feed me, or are we going to spend all night discussing your sexual prowess?"

"Only if we can talk about yours, too?"

"No. Your sexcapades are undoubtedly more extensive."

"I'm not sure I want to compare notes, anyway. I'm liable to get jealous."

A low laugh of disbelief rumbled from the back of my throat. "You don't seem like the jealous kind."

"There's still a lot you don't know about me."

I slung the strap of my purse over my shoulder. "I know everything I need to about you, Maximus Gunn."

"Perceptions can be far different from reality."

The double entendre wrapping his words did not go unnoticed. "Trying to push my buttons already? We haven't even left the house."

He flashed me that devilish smile that made my pussy weep. "I can't help it. You're too much fun."

I pressed the tip of my glittery fuchsia-polished fingernail beneath his chin and sent him a cocky smile. "So are you, when your mouth's on my pussy and you can't talk."

The twinkle in his fern-green eyes told me he enjoyed the banter. "Peel off those jeans and I'll shut the fuck up real fast. You'll be the only one making noise. I just love all the sexy sounds you make when you're building up to explode."

"Take me to dinner. We'll discuss dessert later."

Max drew back his hand and slapped me on the ass. My eyes grew wide as I bit back a yelp. The slow burn made my pussy even wetter. It took everything I had not to close my eyes and savor the sting. Instead, I sent him an evil glare. "Don't ever spank my ass again."

"Then don't tell me what to do. I stopped taking orders when I retired from the Marines six months ago." He arched his brows as if daring me to challenge him.

Touché.

"Point taken," I conceded. "Just remember, you're the one who started poking first."

"I like hearing you moan and whimper when I poke you." A crooked smile kicked up one corner of his mouth. He pulled me against him and rolled his hips, pressing his erection between my legs.

"Good lord," I purred. "Is that M-16 you're packing always ready for action?"

"Only when I'm around you, Sam."

Visions of surrendering to him crowded my mind. It would be so easy to kneel at his feet, but the fallout would be brutal. Tensing, I could feel him combing through my psyche, searching for my unease.

When our stomachs growled in tandem, he chuckled. "Are you ready to go?"

"Yes." I was ready for anything, except his discerning stare. "I'll drive."

Max smirked. "No. *I* will."

I rolled my eyes as we walked toward the door. "That wasn't a ploy for control, Conan."

"Oh, really?" he scoffed.

"Really. In know you're new to the city, I was simply trying to be helpful."

"Dylan's car has GPS. I typed in the address to the restaurant already."

After opening the door of Dylan's Lexus, Max extended his hand to me. Though his gesture was purely chivalrous, I was capable of plopping my ass onto the seat. I bit my tongue and accepted his assistance before sliding onto the buttery-soft leather. Fastening my seat belt, I watched Max jog around the car and climb in behind the wheel.

"Where are we going?"

"To a steak place Nick recommended. It's called Sully's." Max darted a glance at me. "You okay with steak?"

"More than okay. I love red meat *and* I'm starving."

We continued bantering, landing little digs here and there, but as soon as Max brought up Honey's name, the playful humor inside me vanished.

"We negotiated and I gave her what she needed, Sam. That's it."

"I know." Well, my brain did, but my heart wasn't listening. "I was surprised that she asked for sexual release from you because—"

"Because she barely knew me?" he finished. I nodded. "It surprised me, as well, until I learned during our negotiation that she has a stranger fetish."

I was stunned. "She does?"

"Yes. Evidently she's been mentally pretending that she doesn't know any of the Doms when they scene with her. Honey's a smart girl; she knows exactly what flips her trigger, but she's not careless enough to pick up guys at bars to live out her fantasy." Max shrugged. "She's been improvising in a safe way."

"That's good to know. And yes, she is a sweet sub. I've worked her a few times myself. Next time, I'll dig a little deeper and see if she'll open up so I can help feed her fantasy a bit."

"I think she'd like that. I'm curious. When you played with her before, did you allow her to come?"

Sneaky bastard. Exposing the parallel rewards we'd each given the sub mitigated my unwarranted jealousy. But the *gotcha* tone of his voice and flicker of triumph dancing in his eyes was a bit over the top. I instantly realized the reason my green-eyed monster had crawled out of the box was because I'd watched his scene as a *woman* and not as a Domme.

"I have, numerous times."

"I hope I'm there to watch you next time. You've a dynamic Domme style."

"Thank you. I think you're damn intense yourself."

He acknowledged my compliment with a smile as we pulled up to the restaurant. We were seated at a cozy table where muted sounds from the bar mingled with the soft music piped in on overhead speakers. Tossing aside our Dominant dynamic, Max and I laughed and talked as we sipped glasses of Pinot Noir and devoured our succulent steak dinner.

He told me about his childhood, how he grew up on a ranch in South Dakota. I had a hard time picturing Max as a cowboy. He seemed more the motorcycle type. He had bad boy written all over him. I told him about growing up in New Orleans. How I'd been an only child raised by two loving parents. I even told him about my dad's passing from a cerebral embolism just six months after nine-eleven. Over a decadent dessert of crème brûlée, I explained how Desmond's job with a financial conglomerate led us to New Jersey. While I skirted the BDSM aspects of our marriage, I revealed how I'd ended up in Chicago and about the success and subsequent failure of my clothing boutique.

"Beauty, brains, and an entrepreneurial spirit. You're an impressive woman, Sam." Max raised his glass in a toast.

I blushed and lifted mine. After clinking our goblets together, we each took a drink. I was more relaxed than I'd been in years, and the hours slid by as we discussed nearly every topic under the sun. It was only when I glanced over my shoulder that I discovered we were the only patrons left in the restaurant.

"I guess we should leave so the employees can close, clean up, and go home," I stated.

"Probably not a bad idea, though I'm certainly not ready for our *date* to end. How about you?"

I wasn't ready to call it a night, either. Mellowed by the wine, I wanted to invite him back to my place and fuck like bunnies. The thought had my clit cheering in a needy throb.

"What did you have in mind?" I asked coyly.

"I have an idea." His mischievous smile told me he was already reading my mind. Or at least I hoped so.

But Max surprised me. Instead of driving us back to my place, he headed toward the North Shore district. I knew the area well. Mika and Julianna lived close. Max pulled onto West North Shore Boulevard and found a place to park. He took my hand, and the warm summer air blew across my skin as we walked toward the sand. With a purely romantic glint, the moon reflected off the water of Lake Michigan.

We walked the shore for what felt like miles, talking and laughing about nothing and everything. Max paused from time to time, brushing his lips to mine with a passionate tenderness that filled me with nervous excitement.

"So, now that you're officially retired, are you going to turn into a club bum and hang out at Genesis every night, or are you going to find a respectable job?" I teased.

Max laughed. His low, rich tenor blanketed my body like warm cotton. "What job is more respectable than a Dominant, unless, of course, it's submission?"

"No. I meant something outside the club, like a stockbroker or a lion tamer."

"A lion tamer?" He barked with a laugh. "If you want me to leave you alone, I will. You don't have to plot my death by vicious animal attack."

I swatted his arm. "I didn't mean it like that. If I wanted you to leave me alone, I'd damn well tell you. You're just twisting and bending my words like you always do."

Max stopped and spun me in front of him. The lake winds whipped my hair across my face. He reached up and tucked the errant strands behind my ear as he leaned in close. "The only thing I want to bend is you over that picnic table. Then I'd twist you up until you were hot and wild and make you shatter all over my cock."

My mouth went dry. I briefly darted my attention to the wooden table a few feet away. Images of Max driving deep and hard inside me crested like a tidal wave in my head. A slash of fire zipped down my spine and licked the nub between my legs. Whether it was a smart move or not, I knew I was going to fuck him again. Any plans of distancing myself from Max vanished like a boat in the Bermuda Triangle. This time I took *his* hand as we all but ran back to Dylan's car. Neither of us said a word. We didn't have to. A sexual chemistry arced and streaked between us like firework trails in a night sky. Once we were inside the car and making our way back to my place, Max reached out and placed his hand on my thigh.

"Will you do me one favor tonight?"

"What?"

"Don't take the cloth from me."

My knee-jerk reaction to seize his need to have the upper hand gripped me hard. Instead of arbitrarily shutting him down, I waited for my impulsive storm to pass. It didn't. I broke out in a cold sweat. Empty seconds ticked by as I wrangled my chaotic fear of handing over my control.

As usual, Max read all he needed to in my silence. Threading his fingers through mine, he gave my hand a squeeze. "It's not what you think. I only want to pamper you. Nothing more…nothing less."

His logic sounded reasonable, but the suspect part of my brain warned this was but the first of many concessions to come. If I allowed him to wheedle a little here and there, before I knew it, Max would hold all the power.

Good god. He doesn't want to chain you to a spanking bench, simply clean your cooch! Lower your damn drawbridge and relax like you have been with him all night.

The little voice within smacked me upside the head with a two-by-four, or so it felt. The night *had* been fabulous. We'd shucked our individual cloaks of Dominance, thrown conformance and protocol to the wind. It had been a relaxing, carefree, and easy breath of fresh air. So what possessed me to try and paint the canvas of our picture-perfect evening in dark and distorted colors?

Your fears.

But fear wasn't a good enough reason to sabotage my night with Max.

"I'll try and keep my angst in check."

"I don't want you keeping any parts of you in check," Max stated matter-of-factly. "I want you untamed and wild, not gauging every touch of mine on some scale of Dominance or submission. I'd rather you be mindless as I wring all the orgasms I can out of you."

A tremor slid south and my pussy clutched. I crossed my legs to quell the ache. Max gave me a sideways glance and grinned.

Yeah, and the big, bad wolf wanted the little pig to let him in. All bacon-boy got out of the deal was a house blown to smithereens.

Still, sitting on the damn fence post was getting me nowhere. If I hadn't flunked the balance beam in high school, I'd sail across that narrow rail and ignore the quicksand below. I needed to stop letting fear rule me…hike up my big-girl thong, and enjoy the time I had with Max until it all came to a screeching halt.

"Thank you." I squeezed his hand back. "I like it when you're honest with me."

"You're welcome. How about sharing some honesty with me then, Sam. You already know we're like a match to gasoline in bed…explosive in all the right ways. I'm not going to ask you to kneel before me until you're—"

"Stop right there! In one breath, you tell me you won't try to control me, but in the next, you assume that *one day* I'm going to just hand it over to you. That's what freaks me out. I'm on pins and needles waiting for you to slip up and try to take me to my knees."

The muscles of his arms bunched as he gripped the steering wheel tightly. There was a long, pregnant pause before Max pulled the car to the curb. He shoved it in park, then turned and pinned me with an angry stare.

"If you won't even try to trust me, what the fuck are we doing, Sam?"

"I have no idea." I tossed my hands in the air in frustration. "Yes, we're combustible in bed, but that's hardly a reason for me to hand over my trust to you like a damn sub."

He gaped at me as if I were from Jupiter. "Usually when two people are in a sexual relationship, they have a basic level of trust between them. You're grasping at straws because you're scared to let that *damn sub* inside you see the light of day."

CHAPTER SEVEN

I STARED AT him, speechless. He'd nailed the hammer on the head so vehemently I didn't know what to say. There wasn't anything I *could* say that wasn't a lie. Yes, I was afraid of Samantha, afraid she was going to leak out from inside me and destroy me.

Without another word, Max pulled from the curb.

"What makes you so certain she even wants to come out?" I asked quietly.

"I doubt you really want me to answer that."

"I wouldn't have asked if I didn't want the truth."

"Fair enough." Max nodded. "The second you opened the door to the club, I saw a sub. Even when you introduced yourself as Mistress Sammie, my gut screamed bullshit. Even when I watched you work Eli—which was stunning, by the way—you still possessed the heart of a sub…a sub yearning to be free."

"You see me as weak?"

Max scoffed. "Show me a unicorn, and I'll show you a weak submissive."

"I meant a weak *Domme*."

His lips flattened in a tight line. "When you decide you're ready to listen to what I'm trying to say, we'll finish this discussion."

Bam! Max had brought his big, bad Dominant hammer down.

Miffed, I turned and stared out the passenger window. The silence was uncomfortable. I'd disappointed him. Guilt slowly sluiced through my veins. Memories of failing Desmond crept through me and woke feelings of remorse and shame from a deep slumber. I wanted to crawl out of my skin.

Suddenly my mind tripped back to my initial interview with Mika when I'd first joined Genesis. I'd told him about my years as Desmond's slave and how I'd lost my husband, Master, security, and submission in one fell swoop.

"I can't give up the lifestyle any more than I can cut off my own arm. I need to be among like-minded people who respect and find contentment in the power exchange. But I can't join your club as a submissive."

"What are you asking for, Samantha?" Mika asked.

"First, please call me Sammie. Samantha was my slave name. I'm not that girl anymore, and I never will be."

"Okay." Mika nodded, a hint of skepticism flickering in his pretty eyes.

"I'd like to ask you to recommend a Dom to mentor me. Someone who wouldn't mind helping a woman find a way to fulfill the needs of the subs."

"How about me?" Mika offered.

"You'd do that for me?"

"Absolutely." He smiled.

Several months later, we'd sat in his office watching the scenes playing out in the dungeon. As part of Mika's mentorship, I'd been working submissives for a couple of weeks. He'd commented on how I seemed comfortable in my new Domme skin. Then out of the blue, he'd turned with a look of worry.

"What happens when a powerful and intuitive Dom crosses your path and discovers the sleeping slave within?"

Slowly, I turned and stared at Max in disbelief.

He *was* that powerful and intuitive Dom who'd discovered my sleeping slave.

But Max had done far more than simply cross my path. He'd shown me a whole new road, one paved in compassion, understanding, and trust.

He'd discovered my Achilles tendon, but instead of slicing the ligament in two—by sabotaging my status at the club—Max had opened his arms, ready and willing to protect both the Domme and submissive parts of me.

As he pulled into the driveway, I softly whispered, "I'm sorry, and thank you."

He turned off the engine and looked my way. The anger melted from his eyes as a gentle smile inched over his lips. "For what?"

"Sorry for being angry and confrontational. Grateful for all you're doing to help me."

I unclasped the seat belt and all but crawled onto his lap. Wrapping my arms around his neck, I pulled him to my mouth and kissed him with apology, promise, and passion. When he kissed me back, I feared my heart might explode. Slowly, Max pulled away and toyed with the hair by my face.

"Relax, Sam. Everything is going to turn out fine."

For once, a sense of surety and peace settled through me. I believed him. But more so, I finally understood he'd go to any lengths to protect all of me…the woman, slave, and Domme.

I knew I could trust him.

As we made our way inside, Max steered us straight toward the bedroom. Anticipation spiked as he whipped off his tee and tossed it to the floor. I peeled mine away, as well, before he palmed his powerful hands around my breasts and strummed my pebbled nipples.

With practiced finesse, Max unfastened my bra with the flick of a finger and thumb. The lacy cups hadn't even hit the floor when he latched his mouth onto my flesh, laving and scraping his teeth before suckling my aching nipple. Paying homage to the other, he burnished his thumb over its stony peak.

With a moan, I palmed his nape and closed my eyes. Pulses of lightning flashed while thunder churned between my legs. In seconds I was wet, willing, and eager. Writhing and rolling my hips, I silently urged Max to hurry. He moved his mouth to my other breast, oblivious…or purposely postponing my escalating need.

Impatience ruled.

The impulse to take control burned like lava.

I clutched his shoulders and rubbed my weeping pussy against his heated erection. Max let out a growl and sank his teeth into my flesh. Blissful pain flowed across my chest, past my belly, and settled in my already throbbing clit. I could feel my pussy swelling, growing plump and ready, while my breasts grew heavy and full. But inside, the battle of control and surrender still raged until I felt like a ripe plum, split down the middle.

Max's claim of walking on eggshells rolled to the front of my brain. I finally understood. I was ankle-deep in the fragile casings, unsure of how or where to step next.

Slowly easing his mouth from my breast, Max stood and pressed his forehead to mine. "Turn off your brain, Sam."

"I can't."

"Then let's stop and figure—"

"No! That's the problem. I need…" I closed my eyes and exhaled a long, heavy sigh.

"What, baby? Tell me what you need."

"I need you to fuck me." My impatient tone and the cold, meaningless sound of the words made Max's eyes widen briefly.

"I want to do more than fuck you." He frowned. "Right now, I'd like to take you over my knee and spank your ass red, then shove my cock into your tight cunt so you'll stop thinking."

A part of me ached for that freedom, too. I didn't want to think, only feel—to let go and put my whole being in the palms of his hands. But the fear of never wanting to crawl back out kept me clinging to my control. I had to let go, for his sake and mine.

"No. Wait. Let's start over. Can we?" I wanted a clean slate.

"Okay." The intensity of his gaze told me that Max was running out of patience. "How do you suggest we proceed?"

"Can we both get naked and take it from there?"

"All right."

He released the zipper of his jeans and quickly kicked them aside. I nearly forgot to remove my own as I gazed at his chiseled body and rigid cock. Seconds later we were both nude and staring at each other. An awkward uncertainty filled me. Instead of trying to seduce me, Max moved to the bed and sat down.

"Sam," he whispered. "Come over here and tell me what's going on with you."

His benevolent understanding caused the dam holding back the flood of emotions inside me to weaken. Tears stung the backs of my eyes, but I quickly blinked them away as I eased to the mattress beside him.

"Eggshells," I whispered as I quickly rubbed my eyes.

"Yeah. Prickly suckers, aren't they?"

"Awful," I grumbled.

He lifted my chin with his fingers, forcing my gaze, but I stalled on his smiling face. *What the hell was he happy about?* I didn't find this predicament the least bit funny.

"When I'm with you, I tuck my control away. It's not easy, but I have to shift into a vanilla mindset in order to keep the Dom in me at bay."

Vanilla mindset.

That was it! Instead of worrying about what I'd have to give up and preparing myself for a pissing match with Max, I should have been working out a vanilla peace treaty in my head. Having sex with him—even though he was a Dom—shouldn't be any different than the sex I'd had with Scotty. Dammit! Why hadn't I realized this sooner?

Maybe because were too busy letting the Dom dynamic paralyze the logical parts of your brain?

The churning clouds within me parted. Not only could I see a ray of sunshine but I could also breathe again.

"Good grief! I get it now. Finally!" I mumbled.

"Get what?"

"The vanilla mindset," I explained. "We just have to get it on like a regular old vanilla couple."

"We're not that old," Max chuckled softly.

"No. You know what I mean."

"Yes, and remember, you did just fine the other night."

"I did, didn't I?"

"Oh, yeah," he murmured in a low, sensual rumble.

Max pulled me into his arms and kissed me senseless. Like an eagle taking flight, freedom filled me, and I soared with renewed hope. Our tongues tangled. Our hands fondled and caressed hot, naked flesh. That urgent and demanding hunger had returned. I couldn't slake it fast enough.

I gripped his cock and gently stroked him from base to tip. Max nibbled and nipped my lips while his talented fingers toyed with my pussy. Peeling my mouth from his, I trailed my kisses along the ridge of his jaw and down his neck. His flesh was hot and salty. Max moved with me. His arms flexed and bunched as his busy fingers drove in and out of my slippery core. Moaning, I paused at his pecs to swirl and flick my tongue over his dark nipple. He sucked in a hiss before exhaling a curse. Triumph filled me and I smiled against his steely flesh.

The rich, masculine scent of the liquid seeping from his crest and dribbling down my fingers made my mouth water. I nipped the tip of his berry-hard nipple, and Max let out a feral growl before sinking a fist into my hair. I felt his fingers twitch as if he wanted to clench my mane and take control, but he quelled the urge. It made me want to stay inside the vanilla lines, as well. It was difficult, but I felt freer than I'd ever thought possible.

As I worked my lips and tongue down his ripped-velvet torso, I stared at his engorged red crest, slick and oozing copiously in need. My breasts were pressed against his forearm, and my progress southward was halted. Frustration pelted me. The need to swirl my tongue over the tip of his cock, to taste his salty nectar as it exploded over my taste buds, was driving me insane.

I thrust my hips backward until Max's fingers slid from my tunnel before easing onto the floor. Eye level with his glorious shaft, I flattened my tongue and stretched my mouth around him.

"Ah, fuck. Fuck. God...Sam. Yes. Your mouth... So fucking hot. Slick. Feels... Oh, god. Yes. Incredible."

I loved that I'd inundated him with so much pleasure that he'd gone mindless and couldn't string a sentence together. With my eyes locked on the blissful expressions rippling over his face, I fisted his throbbing shaft and cupped his balls as I sucked and swirled my tongue around his pulsating veins.

Max massaged my scalp, sending tingles to race down my spine as I bobbed up and down his hot shaft. I could almost feel the burn of him stretching my pussy as he inched through my folds to fill my core. I rocked my hips, anxious to experience that incredible splendor again.

He sucked in a ragged breath as he gazed down at me with a glassy stare. "You're so fucking beautiful, and your mouth...it's way past sinful."

Pride and peace, like glowing embers, warmed the empty places inside me.

Slivers of my submissive dream fluttered through my mind. Like feathers brushing at memories, the abandoned sub within ached to slide into the sublime serenity of long ago. But thoughts of dismantling Sammie wove together like a fence, barring me from stepping closer to the paradise that beckoned me.

Vanilla. Vanilla, I inwardly repeated as I struggled to gain a foothold on the present. Then on a cold gust, the realization that I was sucking Max's cock on bended knees blew through me on a gale-force wind. Panic roared in my ears. Somehow I managed to maintain the rhythm of my undulating mouth as Sammie crumbled within.

A cascade of excuses spilled in my brain as I clawed to retain an uncomplicated balance within.

You couldn't reach his cock any other way.
You're still in control of the pleasure he's receiving.
This is the best position to give head.

Okay, I knew that last one was a lie, but the frenzy within began receding, so I clung to my rationale like a child to the string of a balloon.

Still, the vow to never kneel before another thrashed inside me.

I slowly pulled my mouth off him and stood. When I gave Max's shoulder a slight shove, he willingly fell back against the mattress. With a hungry stare, I climbed on top of him. As I straddled his narrow waist, he gripped my hips and slammed me onto his wicked cock. I let out a yelp as my muscles stretched tightly and burned so sweetly.

With a guttural moan, Max bucked into my hot core. My muscles fluttered around him, welcoming him inside me. He thrust deep and cupped my breasts in his palms before thumbing my nipples, sending me sailing higher than the heavens.

His eyes locked on mine, and I stared in awe as they shimmered like fiery opals.

"You fucking glow, Sam…like alabaster."

Glancing down, I noticed the shock of my pale ivory skin melded around his waist. His sun-kissed flesh gave off a startling contrast.

He made me feel safe…in this strange and different world.

Protected…though vulnerabilities—like wily ghosts—floated beneath my veil of denial.

Desired…as a woman and sub, while my Dominant alter ego stood silent on the sidelines.

Max reached up and tangled a hand in my hair, guiding my lips to his mouth. I melted across his solid chest as friction flamed to an all-consuming inferno of raw and desperate passion.

I clung to his shoulders, feeling his copious muscles flex and roll beneath his velvety flesh. Max sank his strong fingers into the cheeks of my ass. Picking up speed, he grunted as he shuttled me up and down, slamming me into each savage thrust.

I whimpered and wedged a hand between our slapping flesh to stroke my aching clit.

Unable to form words, I pushed off his chest with one hand and purred his name. A flicker of delight danced in his eyes as a tiny smile tugged his mouth. Max didn't have to read my mind...he already knew my weakness was him.

Jolts of pleasure burst through me, igniting a chain reaction that would all too soon decimate me. A part of me waited, expecting him to whisper the command for me to come. Such a blatant submissive notion should have crushed a part of me, but demand—alive and spiking—overruled all rationale of right or wrong.

I whimpered his name in a blatant plea. Max might have ignored the slip of submission I'd dangled in front of him, but his eyes flared with fire. His face contorted. His body tensed. Clutching my hips in a beastly hold, he drove in deep and held me fixed to the base of his shaft. My fingers whirled over my clit. I felt his cock expand. Heat blasted through me like a cannon. White light, bright and blinding, exploded inside me. I threw my head back and screamed his name. With a roar, Max bellowed mine as well as his hot seed showered my quivering walls.

Equal parts bliss and fear shot through me.

We hadn't used a condom!

The outer edges of ecstasy began to grow dark, stained with a foreboding fear. Max thrust deeper as he emptied the last of his seed inside me with a long, satisfied moan. Bliss warred with fragments of logic that desperately tried to swim to the surface. Either he hadn't thought about being bareback or the ominous consequences of our actions hadn't yet registered. They would soon enough. I tensed.

"We're in trouble. We forgot the condom, and I'm not on the pill," I blurted out, stealing the look of sated euphoria clinging to his face.

As if a bucket of ice water had been dumped over his head, Max bolted upright, nearly tipping me off the bed backward. Gripping my hips, he dragged his wide eyes to our joined crotches. Terror morphed over his features. A spike of insult pierced my chest. Looking up at me, he didn't say a word, simply stared for several long seconds before he raised both brows.

"You're not on the pill?"

"No. Have you...uh..."

Shit! I didn't know how to ask him how many women he'd ridden without a saddle before me. Was he a carrier of any STDs? Overwhelmed, I could feel a full-blown panic attack bearing down on me.

Max just looked at me and started to chuckle. "We both got a bit carried away, didn't we?"

"How can you laugh at this?"

"There's not much else to do." He shrugged. "What's done is done. We can't go back and change anything. I've... Wow! I've never once forgotten to glove up. I mean, I get checked regularly and haven't been with anyone but you since my last check-up, so I'm clean."

He arched a brow, silently asking if the same held true with me.

"I'm clean, too, but that still doesn't... Oh, god," I moaned.

Max cupped my cheeks and fixed me with a firm stare. "If we happened to have made a mini-Gunn just now, we'll deal with it together. All right?"

"No! It's not all right. I'm thirty-eight years old. Women my age are becoming *grandmothers,* for shit's sake. I don't want a *baby*. I'm too damn old!"

A troubled look lined his face. "I'm not laying blame on you, Sam, but if you don't want kids, why aren't you on the pill?"

His caveat and the lack of accusation in his tone might have freed me from feeling guilt but did nothing to stop the embarrassment climbing within. Honestly, who wants to admit they haven't a normal sex life in...forever?

"There wasn't a need for me to take the pill," I replied with feigned self-assurance. "I don't do relationships. They only complicate things."

Max's lips twitched. "I'm sorry you feel that way, 'cause your life's about to get a whole lot more complicated, Sam."

I suddenly couldn't speak past the lump in my throat. Oh, my mouth was moving, opening and closing like a trout on dry land, but not one word came out.

"Easy, baby," he whispered. "Don't freak out on me. Got it?"

I swallowed tightly and finally removed the blockage. "I'll freak out any way I want!"

"Yes. I know. You always do, but now's not the time to push me away and take off running."

"I-I-I don't run from anything."

Liar!

Bristling, I tried to wiggle off his cock still speared inside me. "Don't, Sam."

"Don't what? Don't get pissed? Too late!"

"I can see that. Your eyes go dark and turn a pretty shade of sapphire when you're ticked off. I don't want you angry. We have to talk this out."

"No, we don't. If I'm pregnant, I'll deal with it."

Max reared back as if I'd slapped him. "Deal with it how? I won't let you abort my child."

"I'd never do that. I was raised Catholic. I meant I'd raise the baby...*alone*."

He grunted and shook his head. "No, you're not doing that, either. If you're pregnant, we'll raise our child *together*."

I closed my eyes and counted to ten...twice. When I'd calmed to a slightly more rational level, I looked at him. Max stared back at me with a blank expression, as if he was safeguarding his true emotions until I'd had my say.

"I can't raise a child with you. I can barely navigate the fact that we're two Doms. This...thing between us isn't going to last, Max. It will eventually burn out or self-destruct, and we both know it. There's absolutely no way I'm going to compound one mistake with another."

"Babies aren't mistakes and neither is the attraction between us." A secret smile played over his lips. "I've always wanted to be a dad."

Though I was technically old enough to be a grandmother, I'd been young once and dreamed of having Desmond's child. The fact that I'd never conceived was both a blessing and a curse. There wasn't a living breathing part of him left in the world, but I'd barely managed to keep myself together after his death. I'd have been a complete and total failure as a mother.

"Fine. If I'm pregnant, I'll give you the kid to raise. How's that?"

As the lie flew off my lips, the devastation and pain reflecting in Max's eyes filled me with regret. No way could I carry a child in my womb, give birth, and cast a baby off as if it were a pair of unwanted jeans.

"I'm sorry. I didn't mean that."

"You did, or you wouldn't have said it," he replied flatly.

Begrudgingly, Max lifted me off his cock and eased me onto the mattress. He sat up and stood before striding across the room to pluck up his jeans and tee.

"No, I honestly didn't. I was lashing out in anger," I confessed. "I do want children...or I mean I did...once upon a time."

"Just not with me. I get it." The rejection etched over his face singed me to the core.

Rising, I moved toward him and cupped my hand to his face. "I think we'd make beautiful children, Max. You'll make a phenomenal father. I'm sorry. I say things I don't mean when I'm scared. I didn't mean for my words to stab and hurt you."

"I know why you do it. But you still managed to slice open an artery. Don't worry, I heal quickly." Max pressed a tender kiss to my forehead. "I need to go…get some fresh air. I'll see you at the club tomorrow night."

Now who's running?

"I'd appreciate it if you'd let me know when you find out if you're pregnant or not. Okay?"

"Of course. Max…I truly am sorry. It's just…"

I can't stand feeling so out of control. Feel too much for you already. Don't want you to leave me. Want you to hold me and promise everything will be all right.

"I know." With a sad smile, he turned and left the room.

As the front door snicked shut, I wrapped my arms around my waist and sank to the edge of the bed. An empty hollowness ate at my soul until there was nothing left of the brilliant light Max had gifted me with.

Numbly, I rose, grabbed my robe, and padded to the kitchen to fix a cup of tea. While the leaves steeped, I flipped through the pages of the calendar on the wall. I noted the stars on the dates, indicating the start of my menstrual cycle. My periods had been like clockwork since I was a teen, but when they'd started going berserk, I'd gone to see my gynecologist. Last fall she'd confirmed that I was in the beginning stages of menopause.

My cycles were as hit and miss as a blind man tossing darts in a bar. There was no way of knowing if I was ovulating right now or not. The only pot of gold at the end of my bleak rainbow was that Max and I were both clean. His gun might have fired a live round and mortally shot up one of my eggs, but at least I was free and clear of herpes.

"If I hadn't been so damn fixated about being on my fucking knees, I might have remembered to grab a condom," I groused. Pressing a palm to my belly, I closed my eyes and sent out a plea to the universe. "Please don't let me be pregnant. Please."

Like a living, breathing thing, apprehension pulsed through my veins while anger at myself for verbally lashing Sam *again* smoldered. I couldn't control whether or not the rabbit was dead, but I had to accept one truth: Max could see through my Dominant veil. It was pointless to deny that fact or try to run and hide from the visceral attraction I felt toward him.

I cupped the mug of tea, wandered into the living room, and curled up on the couch. I started scrolling through the channels. The first movie I stumbled upon was *Baby Boom*, followed by *Mommy Dearest*, *The Stepmom*, and finally *Little Man Tate*. It was a single-mom marathon. With a growl, I turned off the TV and tossed the remote aside.

It was after midnight, but my internal clock—which had adjusted itself to working until the wee hours of the morning—refused to unwind enough for me to try and go to bed. Since theaters and restaurants were now closed, my entertainment options were limited. I could take a jog or hop in my car and hit the all-night grocery for a tub of ice cream. My mouth began to water. I bolted off the couch and ran back to my room. After changing into a pair of yoga pants and an oversized tee, I grabbed my purse and raced out the door.

Standing in the frozen foods section, I vacillated between chocolate almond fudge and praline pecan. The sound of male laughter grew loud, and I turned my head as Eli and two college-aged boys rounded the aisle, shoving one another and playfully shouting insults. As Eli and I made eye contact, the grin on his face was replaced by a look of shock. He briefly dragged a gaze over my casual clothes before awkwardly lowering his lashes. The wave of embarrassment and fear rolling off him was sturdy and palpable.

I snatched the tub of chocolate almond, and without a word—protecting his anonymity and mine—I brushed past him. After I rounded the corner, I pressed my fingers to my forehead and tried to rub away the headache I'd been ignoring since Max had left.

Max.

I pressed a palm to my stomach as a shudder quaked through me.

"Miss...err, Sammie?" Eli murmured from behind me. As I spun around, my eyes grew wide. "I wanted to apologize for...well, you know. I didn't know if I should say some—"

"Don't apologize. You did exactly what you were supposed to do." Grabbing a bag of potato chips off an endcap display, I shoved them into his hand. "Here. Take these to your friends before they see us talking. You can't explain how you know me without lying or confessing about being a member of the club...and you know that's against the rules."

Eli gave me a weak nod, then clutched the chips and hurried away.

I exhaled a heavy sigh and hurried in the other direction. Standing in the aisle amid feminine products, I stared at the various home pregnancy kits, trying to determine which was the quickest and most reliable. Giving up, I grabbed four different brands and hurried toward the cashier. After placing the items on the belt, I heard the rowdy boys once again.

Please let them keep shopping. The silent mantra spooled through my head as I blankly stared at the cashier while he finished with the customer in front of me. In my peripheral vision, I saw Eli and his friends crowd in behind me. The pregnancy tests lay in the open flashing like neon signs. Turning slightly, I saw Eli's eyes widen as he stared at the kits. He paled and darted a look of sadness and confusion my way.

Shit! Why had I decided to buy the damn things now?

"I need to get some air. I'll meet you guys outside," Eli announced to his friends before turning and racing away.

My head pounded even harder. I briefly closed my eyes and exhaled a heavy sigh. After paying for my purchases, I hurried toward my car.

"Are you?" Eli's angry words stopped me in my tracks as he jogged from behind a stone pillar. "Are you pregnant?"

There were big, fat crocodile tears in his eyes.

"They're not mine, boy. They're for one of the subs at the club," I lied, donning a cold Dominant tone.

"Oh, thank god." A rush of air exploded from his mouth. "Who's pregnant?"

"That's none of your business now is it?"

"Right," he mumbled and lowered his gaze. "I'm sorry, Mistr—"

"Christ, Eli," cried one of his friends now hurrying toward us. "We'll get you laid before the night's through, man. You don't have to hit on old ladies."

Eli cringed.

"Go," I ordered under my breath.

He flashed me a look of apology and turned, then jogged toward his friends. "Fuck off, Henry. She wanted to know what time it is."

Without looking back, I climbed into my car, chafed at being called an old lady. The mouthy little shit could have used the words *mature woman*, but then boys would be boys. With a growl, I peeled out of the parking lot. I knew Eli was mortified by his friend's insult. I'd have to soothe the boy's ruffled feathers tomorrow night at the club.

Once back home, I crawled into bed, container of ice cream on my lap and book in hand. I devoured the tub while I lost myself in a mystery novel until three a.m., when I put the book aside and snuggled in beneath the covers.

Max's virile scent lingered in the sheets, on the bedspread...my pillows—he hadn't even touched my pillow—yet he was there in every breath I took. My brain and body came alive as memories of making love to him assailed me. Images of us at the club, Maurizio's, dinner tonight, our walk along the beach, and of course, the spine-bending sex we'd shared filled my mind. I couldn't shut them out. I wanted to scream, but mostly I just wanted the chance to make up for my ugly, bitchy behavior.

After tossing and turning for hours on end, I threw back the covers and stomped to the guest room. If I was going to get an ounce of sleep, I had to find a bed that held no trace of Max.

I woke with a start to the sound of someone banging on my front door. With a curse, I pulled the pillow over my head, but the drumming continued.

"Somebody better be dead," I grumbled.

Shoving my wild, disheveled hair from my face, I rushed to the living room, and yanked the door open. Max stood on the porch wearing the same clothes he'd had on the night before and a weak smile. In his hand was a tray with two cups of coffee.

"I brought you a cup—"

"Do you know what time it is?" I scolded.

"Yes. Early. Lose the attitude. We need to talk"—his voice suddenly softened—"and I wanted to make sure you were all right."

"I'm...okay. But do we need to talk now? Can't it wait until—"

"What I have to say can't wait, Sam."

I eyed the coffee, then relented and invited him in. I plucked a cup from the tray as Max walked toward the living room. I might have still been half-asleep, but like a bloodhound, one sniff of coffee—already brewed and ready to sip—and I was hot on the scent. I shut the door and turned toward him. Without the blinding sun at his back, I noticed the pale, dark circles under his eyes. He looked like hell.

Because of you!

Guilt swept through me. I stroked his face. "You didn't sleep at all last night, did you?"

"No." Max shook his head before he dropped his gaze to my stomach. He splayed his hand out over my belly and looked up at me. "No matter what happens, Sam, I'm in this for the duration."

CHAPTER EIGHT

EMOTION CLOGGED MY throat. Tears stung the backs of my eyes as he curled an arm around my waist and dragged me to his chest.

"I don't care what we have to do…whether it takes contracts, arrangements, promises or vows, we'll work things out between us. Understood?"

"We don't even know *if* we have a problem. Let's wait and see—"

"I'm not only talking about the possibility of a baby. I'm talking about us…you and me."

Did he mean a future?

I groaned as my shoulders slumped. "I don't know if there'll ever be a you and me. I still haven't figured out if I'm a Domme or a sub. I don't have a clue in hell where I belong."

A gentle smile touched his lips as he brushed the pad of his thumb to catch the tear spilling down my cheek. "You belong with me, Sam. Plain and simple, you belong with *me*."

A tiny sob slid from my throat. Max took the coffee from my fingers and placed both cups on the end table. Then he lifted me into his arms, like he'd done the night he broke down my door, and carried me down the hall. When he noticed the covers strewn across the bed in the guest room, he sent me a startled stare.

"Has someone else been here?"

I shook my head. In a quivering voice, I confessed that I couldn't sleep with his scent surrounding me. A look of relief swept over his face as he pressed his lips to mine, a soft, tender caress filled with understanding and promise.

He laid me on the mattress before gently tugging off the clothes I'd worn to the store and had fallen asleep in. Stepping back, he undressed. There was nothing provocative or sexy in his movements, but I was mesmerized all the same. An easy comfort had formed between us. It was as if we'd known each other a lifetime instead of only a few short days.

Without a word, Max crawled in beside me. He pulled the blankets over us and wrapped me in his arms. Placing a tender kiss to my lips, he rested his head on the pillow and closed his eyes. Nestled in his warm, protective arms, I laid my head on his chest and listened to the steady beat of his heart as I slid into the inky darkness.

When I woke, he was gone. I glanced at the clock. It was nearly one in the afternoon. With a languid stretch, I turned and buried my face in Max's pillow. As I breathed in his familiar scent, tingles ignited beneath my flesh. I couldn't help but smile.

We hadn't come to any conclusions in regard to the litany of issues hanging over our heads—hell, we'd barely said a word at all—but a flicker of hope and security had awakened inside me. For the first time in a long time, I didn't feel completely alone.

After tending to business in the bathroom, I tugged on my robe and opened the bedroom door. The scent of bacon and an undertone of coffee hit my senses before I'd even stepped into the hallway. My tiny smile turned into a full-blown grin as I hurried into the kitchen. There, beside the stove, stood Max, flipping a skillet of hash browns and sipping coffee. The hopeless romantic in me imagined how wonderful it would be to wake every morning and find Max in my life. Shaking off the foolish thought, I kissed him on the cheek and went straight to the coffeemaker.

He smiled as he watched me fill a mug to the brim.

"Did you sleep well?" he asked as I took a sip of the steaming hot liquid.

"Like a rock," I purred.

"Me, too. I hope you don't mind me commandeering your kitchen."

"Commandeer all you want. I haven't had anyone cook me a meal outside restaurants and fast food in forever."

"Then it's high time you did. Sit back and relax. I'll have everything ready in a couple of minutes."

"Thank you."

It was blatantly obvious we were trying to put our best feet forward while ignoring the hulking elephant in the room.

You belong with me. His words echoed in my head, yet I couldn't help but wonder if Max simply might have *his* in the clouds. Aside from whether I was pregnant or not—which was another elephant all its own—the pressure to decide my role in the lifestyle pressed in around me.

I stared out the window contemplating the conundrum while I sipped my coffee. Soon my mind was trapped in a flowing circle, like the infinity symbol. The most practical solution would be to embrace both parts of me and become a switch: Top submissives and surrender to Max. Genesis had several switches who gracefully reveled in having one foot in both worlds, but the option didn't appeal to me. I was an all-or-nothing kind of creature.

"Talk to me, Sam. I need to hear what you're thinking."

Max set plates of scrambled eggs, bacon, and golden-brown potatoes on the table before easing into the chair beside me. I needed to stop trying to chart my path alone. Max had proven, more times than I could count, that he wouldn't use my weaknesses against me. Still, my stomach knotted as I loaded up my plate and began telling him about the disturbing dream I'd had the other night.

"So, are you more afraid of letting the submissives in the club down or being humiliated by the idiots who think because you have a vagina, you can't command?"

"A little of both, but that's not the real—"

"We'll discuss Desmond in a minute. Right now, I want you to examine the biggest concerns regarding the club."

"They're equally damaging to my *image*." I smirked. "I've worked hard to earn the reputation I have."

Max nodded as he bit into a strip of bacon. "But it's that *image* that keeps hanging you up in here." He tapped his finger to my head. "Does it really matter if you're a Domme or a sub? I mean, to anyone but you?"

"Of course it does. The free subs at the club rely on me to work them."

"There are plenty of other Doms who do that. The responsibility doesn't rest solely on your shoulders."

"No, but...I-I don't want to confuse them, either."

"And we're right back to the issue of image again, Sam. Declaring yourself a Dom or a sub only defines what's in here." He reached out and placed his palm on my heart. "I know in order for you to remain in the lifestyle, you wrapped yourself in a protective layer. You've adjusted and adapted, but you've paid a price for it, as well. You abandoned the submissive within who needs to be nurtured, treasured, and fulfilled."

Chewing on his words and my breakfast, I pondered his statement before setting my fork down. "But I'm not sure how abandoned she really is. I mean…I haven't let Samantha out, except in that dream…and you know how awful it ended."

"Yes, but it was only a dream. Question is…are you willing to try?"

"Try to let her out?"

"Yeah."

"No." My response was fast and adamant.

"Why not?"

"Desmond," I softly whispered.

"Ah, yes." Max paused and set his mug down, drawing his thumb around the rim. "You're not going to like my next question."

"Then don't ask it."

He grinned. "Don't start slapping up your walls, Sam. We're finally getting somewhere."

God, it irked me when he busted me like that.

"Desmond was a perfect Master for you in every way, correct?"

"Yes," I whispered, suddenly losing my appetite.

"When you handed him your heart and all the power you possessed, he completed you."

I nodded, blinking back tears.

"But don't you see, little one? You completed him in every way, as well." Max's voice had dropped to barely a whisper. "You met one another's needs, like it's supposed to be. Do you think after all the years he immersed you in such love and devotion that he'd want you to deny yourself that fulfillment simply because he wasn't able to provide it to you anymore?"

I'd asked myself that question a million times as I struggled to fit into my Domme skin, but when Max bid the same question, a sword of betrayal slashed my flesh.

Tears slid down my cheeks as I lowered my head. He shoved back from the table and, in one fluid movement, plucked me out of my chair and settled me onto his lap. He tucked me against his chest and simply held me.

He was right. I'd given up Dark Desire to Lady Ivory when I

realized I could no longer fulfill his needs. I found a sense of peace, happiness even, when he started to thrive under her care.

Desmond would be destroyed if he knew I'd divided myself into pieces...shoved Samantha away and molded myself into Sammie to take her place. Sure, he'd understand that I'd cut myself up like diamonds in order to survive, but he'd still be angry that I'd sacrificed fulfillment—even at the hands of another Dom—because I was too weak to let go of his ghost...let go of *him*.

Still, that realization wasn't enough to force me to draw a definitive line in the sand.

"I'm not mentally ready to kneel again, Max."

"How many years has it been since you did?"

"Sixteen," I mumbled.

"How many?"

"Sixteen," I repeated louder.

"How many more are you going to spend denying yourself?"

"I don't know. As many as it takes." I wiped my eyes and lifted my chin.

"All right. We'll find out together. Baby steps."

"I'm not sure I want—"

Max cut me off with a kiss. "The only way you'll find the answer is through your heart. But first you have to want to move forward. Do you?"

"I think so."

"I get that you're scared for a multitude of reasons, but if the desire is truly there, you only have two things left to do. Give yourself permission to surrender and reach out and take my hand."

Putting that permission into motion was going to be the tricky part. I fully thought I'd said good-bye to Desmond when I shoved the box of sorrow back on the shelf, but that was a cop-out. I'd never let him go. He'd always been in my heart and in my memories. I wasn't sure I possessed the willpower to fully close off the past.

Baby steps, Max had assured. I'd already started taking them. While it certainly hadn't been one giant leap for mankind, I had lowered my walls and let him in. Ironically, doing it felt right. Maybe it was time to keep taking those tiny steps to see where they led.

"I know." I snuggled back against him and closed my eyes.

"When you're ready to start, tell me. I'll help you."

I sat up and shot him a curious stare. "Help? How?"

"By introducing you to Samantha again."

"No way. I'm not going to open up that can of worms at the club in front of God and everyone."

"I'm not talking about doing anything at the club, Sam. I'm talking about doing it here…in the safety and security of your own home."

"I'm not sure about this." A tremor of fear quaked through me.

"Not today, and not until you're ready. When you are, I promise I'll be beside you, ready and waiting to catch you if you fall."

"You mean *when* I fall." I rolled my eyes.

"No. *If.* Don't start psyching yourself out before you've even stepped up to the plate. You're stronger than that, and we both know it."

I was strong and in control, or thought I was, until Max showed up and blew my perceptions into a storm that pelted my Zen. He'd rained down on me, and I was now caught in a landslide called Max. I knew I had to ride this slurry of emotions to the bottom before I could discover what parts lay in ruin at my feet. Surprisingly, that didn't scare me. It was discovering what parts survived that terrified.

I leaned up and kissed him, a wordless thank you for his understanding and patience.

A good Dom is always patient and understanding, pet. Desmond's voice softly echoed from far off inside my head. I closed my eyes and burrowed against Max once more.

We spent the next hour and a half in bed, burning off breakfast, until I had to get ready for work. When I stepped inside the shower, Max followed with a wicked smile, a hard-on from hell, and a condom packet between his fingers.

"I thought men your age had to recoup after sex," I laughed.

"Men my age?" He blinked. "What's that supposed to mean? How old do you think I am?"

I stroked his erection and grinned. "Eighteen by the feel of things."

"You make me feel like I'm eighteen again." His voice was a low rumble as he latched onto my mouth with a hungry kiss.

I knew I'd be late for work, but at that exact moment, I didn't give a shit.

He pressed me up against the cool tile walls, nibbling my neck and telling me all the lewd and erotic things he wanted to do to me. After rolling the condom over his cock, he thrust inside me, plowing deep into my tender core. I gasped and moaned and rocked my hips, working to relax against his delicious invasion. He cupped one breast, pinching and plucking my nipples, while his other hand busily strummed my clit with the perfect amount of pressure and design. Every ruthless drag and thrust set my enflamed tissues ablaze. I was dizzy and panting as Max soared me higher and higher into oblivion.

When my whimpers and moans morphed into keening cries of need, he sank his teeth into the lobe of my ear. His ragged and shallow breaths drowned out the sounds of water cascading down our naked flesh.

"I'm ready to split this condom apart. Come hard with me, Sam. Let me feel your tight cunt suck the come from my balls again."

A scalding wave slammed through me. My muscles strained and gripped his driving cock. Blood roared in my ears. Lights exploded behind my eyes and I screamed his name. With a feral growl, Max briefly stilled before manically pounding into me. He bellowed out "Sam" as he followed me over.

Clinging to one another, we struggling to catch our breath. I closed my eyes and basked in the hum of pulsating pleasure. Several minutes passed as we floated back to earth, then Max lathered me with soap and tenderly washed every inch of my flesh. With thick, skilled fingers, he massaged shampoo through my hair, adding to my already boneless verve. I wanted to crawl back in bed with him and take a power nap, then spend all night lost in lust.

But duty called. I had to leave our carnal paradise and go out to join the real world. Clad in only his jeans, Max watched from the doorway of the bathroom as I readied for work. I dried and curled my hair, then brushed a bit of mascara over my lashes before adding a hint of blush to my cheeks.

"You don't need any of that. You're gorgeous just the way you are," he murmured. Pushing off the doorjamb, he brushed the curls off the back of my neck and pressed a soft kiss there.

"You're just trying to sweet-talk me into going back to bed with you," I said in a sultry laugh.

"Actually, I'm not. I need a few hours to let the skin grow back. But tonight, after the club closes…" He waggled his brows at me and grinned.

"You're an animal," I jokingly replied. "I love that about you."

His stare intensified. "What else do you love about me?"

Love? Oh, hell…I'd picked the wrong word. It was far too soon to make any such declaration. Though I was deeply attracted to the man, love—if ever—was far off on some distant horizon.

"I love what you did to me in the shower, but I'm not loving the fact that I have to leave for work."

Max wrapped his arms around my waist and nipped the lobe of my ear. Sparks of arousal ricocheted through me. "I don't love that fact, either."

He slid on his tee and watched me dress, then walked me to my car.

"I'm going to head over to Dylan's and change. I'll see you at the club in a while."

"Sounds good. See you there."

As usual, Genesis was empty when I arrived. After scurrying to set up the bar, I poured myself a glass of water as Eli rushed through the curtain. Dressed in his street clothes, he clutched a backpack in one hand.

"Mistress, I want to apologize for last night. My friend Henry, he's an ass. The things he said—"

"It's all right, Eli. You're not responsible for what your friend does or says. In his eyes, I *am* an old lady," I chuckled.

"No. You're beautiful," he protested.

"Thank you, boy. I'm flattered." I eyed his backpack. "Go change into your thong. I'll have a cherry cola waiting when you return."

"Yes, Mistress." Eli sent me a grim nod before he darted toward the men's room.

My words hadn't eased his niggling guilt. I'd have to spank the shame from him. Normally the thought would thrill me, but for some reason, the notion held little appeal. I was probably still a bit harried from hustling to ready the bar or drained by my recent sex marathons with Max. I'd make it up to Eli tomorrow night.

But I didn't, nor the next night, or the one after. I hadn't abandoned the boy. He visited the bar often. We talked and even laughed a bit, but as more nights came and went, Eli's hunger for another session grew stronger and stronger. For some reason, I couldn't muster the motivation to play with him.

I tried blaming it on lack of sleep. Though I definitely wasn't complaining, nearly every night Max and I would leave the club, drive to my place, and make love until sunrise. We'd catch a few hours of sleep, then wake and sate our hunger all over again. We'd fallen into a pattern of barely leaving the bedroom.

After his membership application had been approved, Max arrived early with me and helped me set up the bar. Occasionally we'd take a break from our bedroom Olympics—after all, you could only go for the gold so many times—and we'd share a picnic in the park, see a movie, or go shopping.

The bond between us was growing stronger every day. I was content and happy and, for the most part, able to ignore the two shadows looming over us—the worry of pregnancy and the direction I needed to pursue.

Early on, Max and I agreed to wait two weeks before breaking open any of the home pregnancy tests. I tabled deliberating Sammie and Samantha until we knew whether or not the rabbit had died.

As the two-week mark grew steadily near, my anxiety level skyrocketed.

Standing in my usual spot behind the bar, I tried to focus on the Doms and subs at play. But niggling in the back of my mind was the knowledge that when Max and I woke tomorrow afternoon, I'd break open one of the test sticks, and my future would be determined for me. Either I'd spend the next few years changing dirty diapers and saving for college tuition or dodge a life-altering bullet.

Lost in thought, I jumped when Max placed his hand over mine. "Stop torturing yourself, Sam. We'll be fine with whatever comes our way."

I nodded, not wanting to discuss our situation with so many ears around. Gossip had a way of sprouting wings and taking flight. As I skimmed a glance over the dungeon, my heart skipped a beat. Eli was cuffed to a cross. I watched as Mistress Monique, a young, raven-haired Domme, dragged her glossy red fingernails up and down the sub's back. A pang of guilt sliced me. Max glanced over his shoulder to see what had captured my attention.

"You didn't think the boy was going to wait forever, did you?" he softly asked.

"No," I replied in a quick, harsh tone.

Grabbing the bar rag, I polished the gleaming surface while inwardly cursing myself for neglecting Eli's needs. Purposely avoiding the urge to watch his scene, I focused on serving beverages instead. I was already juggling too many worries. I had no business tossing more into the mix. Eli's needs were being taken care of. That was all the mattered.

A few minutes later, I noticed Mika standing at the end of the bar. He was darting a glance between Max, Mistress Monique, and me. I tried to mask my shame for failing Eli, but I wasn't fooling anyone, not even myself. Mika had always been able to see right through me. The man didn't miss a thing when it came to his club, employees, or the members. Still, I worried my lack of desire to work the boy had irked Mika. Without a word, he turned and walked toward the hallway.

"Is there a problem with you not scening Eli?" Max arched his brows.

"I'm not sure." I shrugged.

Tony and Joshua stepped up, joining Max. The three began talking. Soon other Doms joined the men while their subs sat clustered at one of the tables across the room, visiting as well.

Behind me, the house phone buzzed. I answered, knowing Mika was on the other end.

"When things slack off down there, would you come to my office for a minute?"

"Sure thing, boss. Joe can take over for a few. I'll be right up."

"Thank you."

As I headed past Max, he shot me a curious look, but I continued my march toward the archway, feeling as if I were making a trek to the principal's office. Climbing the stairs, I broke out in a cold sweat as a wave of nausea hit me.

It's just nerves, I told myself. Shoving down my fears of what the pregnancy test would reveal, I sucked in a deep breath. When I reached the door to Mika's office, he opened it wearing a thin smile.

"What's wrong?" I asked as I entered.

He closed the door behind me and frowned. "I wanted to let you know that I asked Monique to work Eli *before* they'd decided to negotiate a session. It seems both were a bit too anxious to get some playtime in. I apologize, Sam. The look on your face…well, I know this was a surprise."

"It's all right. I'm well aware that I've been shirking my responsibility with the subs, especially Eli. I'm the one who owes you an apology."

"Accepted, but I'm curious. Why *have* you been avoiding the subs?"

"The bar's been busy. I've been a little tired lately, and I have a lot on my mind."

Even to my own ears, the excuses sounded lame.

"Do you need to take a few days off?"

"No. I'm fine."

His piercing amber eyes flickered slightly at my lie. "If you need to talk about anything, you know I'm here for you."

"I know that, and I treasure our friendship."

"I do too, so stop blowing smoke up my ass. You know how I hate that. Does your sudden departure from Dominance have anything to do with Samantha? Because I thought you worked that out weeks ago."

I closed my eyes and issued a heavy sigh. "I tried. But I discovered I haven't really come to terms with it like I thought I had."

"I see. And you didn't bother to come talk with me about that, because…?"

"Because I'm still working through it. I haven't reached any conclusions yet."

Mika frowned and stepped closer. He squeezed my shoulder. "You're a terrific asset to the club, Sam. You embody the code of the lifestyle and strive to ensure the subs' needs are achieved."

I could hear a big ol' *but* coming.

"But until you know where your heart truly lies, I have to ask you to refrain from working the subs. Not that you would ever lose your shit during a scene. I know better. But I can't have a Domme revert to sub mode in the middle of the dungeon. I'm doing this to protect you and them."

I felt as if he'd punched me in the stomach. I swallowed the bile rising in the back of my throat and nodded. I'd failed my boss…my friend…the one person who'd been a constant in my life over and over again. Inside I was howling in shame and regret.

It took me several long seconds to fight back my tears and find my voice. "I understand. I'm sorry that I've let you down, Mika."

"It's not that you've let me down, Sam. I'm worried about you. I see now that you've come to that familiar fork in the road…the one you didn't want to face again. I'm here for you, sweetheart. I'll do anything to help… and I *do* mean anything. If you need me to walk through fire for you, I'll do it."

I threw my arms around his chiseled body as a tear slid down my cheek. Though I didn't know why, I wanted to curl up in Mika's arms and sob like a child. But I knew that would worry him even more. Without a word, he held me as I struggled to glue myself back together.

"Twenty-four hours obviously wasn't long enough to make such a major decision. That's on me, sweetheart. I'm sorry."

"No," I said with a sniff. "I should have dealt with Samantha years ago instead of ignoring her. I've prolonged the process too long and shot myself in the foot."

"What's Max's take on all you're trying to deal with?"

All you're trying to deal with? Another sickening wave coiled in my belly. Had Mika somehow gotten wind that I was struggling with *more* than lifestyle issues? The room grew hot, like an oven, and started to spin. A veil of darkness clouded my vision, and then everything went black.

Somewhere in the distance, I heard Max calling my name. I opened my eyes to try and find him, but a harsh light had me slamming them shut again.

"Thank fuck, she's coming around," he cried. "Sam. Come on, baby. Open your eyes for us."

"Too bright," I grumbled.

"That was my fault, honey. I was checking your pupils."

The unmistakable voice of Master Sam had my eyelids flying open. I was lying on Mika's long leather couch. Max, Mika, Cindy, Liz, and the good doctor hovered over me wearing uneasy expressions. Well, all except Max, whose face was ghostly white and etched in terror. His confident veneer had shattered, sending adrenaline to ramp up inside me. I lifted my hand and cupped his cheek in hopes of wiping away his fear. His expression stayed the same as he pressed a beefy paw over my hand and continued to hold me with a desperate stare.

I was unsure how or why I'd ended up on Mika's couch, and a surge of embarrassment rolled through me. I tried to sit up, but Max dropped his hand to my shoulder, forcing me to remain flat on my back.

"Whoa. Don't try to move. Just lie here a little bit longer," he whispered. "You passed out, baby. Let Brooks take a look at you. All right?"

Dr. Samuel Brooks, ob-gyn surgeon by day, Master at Club Genesis by night, was the last person I wanted poking and prodding for answers as to my unexpected blackout. I knew the first question out of his mouth would be…

Oh, hell no!

While I desperately wanted to deny I was pregnant, I couldn't. I'd never passed out before in my life. My stomach pitched and rolled. The tiny salad I'd eaten for dinner was coming up. Panicked, I launched off the couch and pushed past my friends. Skidding to my knees next to Mika's desk, I grabbed the trash can and promptly tossed my cookies.

A split second later, Max was behind me. With one hand, he gathered up my hair and softly stroked my back with the other.

"I need a few minutes alone with Sammie," Brooks announced as he, too, knelt down beside me.

As the others paraded out of the room and the door snicked shut, I wiped my mouth on the back of my hand and collapsed against Max's chest.

"I'm staying," he informed Brooks.

"Sammie, are you okay with that?" I nodded. "All right. Have you ever fainted before?"

"No," I answered.

"Is there any chance you might be pregnant?" Brooks asked.

So it wasn't the first question, but close. I closed my eyes and inhaled a deep breath.

"We planned on taking a home test in the morning," Max answered.

"How many periods have you missed?"

"Who knows?" I shrugged, wanting to give a lackadaisical impression, but the strain in my voice gave away my fear. "I've been irregular for about a year."

"If you'd rather come by my office tomorrow, we can do a blood test," Brooks offered. "It's much more accurate."

"No offense, Doc, but this is something I'd rather find out in private."

Brooks nodded in understanding. "If it comes back positive, I need to see you. I'll want to keep a close eye on you."

"Why?" Max blurted out. Concern tightly wrapped around his one word.

"I don't like to use the term *high risk*, but the chance of complications rises with women over the age of thirty-five."

"Great," I mumbled. "Can I go back to work now?"

"No," Max barked. "I'm taking you home so you can rest."

"But I feel—"

"Max is right," Brooks interrupted. "You need to take it easy for a few days."

Oh, god. This cannot be happening!

"You're not going to say anything to Mika or the others, are you?"

"Of course not," Brooks assured.

"Thank you," I exhaled in relief. "For now, we'll just tell everyone I have the flu."

"You might have to come up with a different ailment in a few months," Brooks teased. "Maybe a hernia or a stomach goiter…hell, we'll think of something."

"You're not funny, Samuel," I groused with a scowl.

The two men bit back grins. I simply groaned.

"I'll grab your purse from behind the bar," Max announced and stood. "I'll be back to get you in a minute."

After he left, Brooks helped me over to the couch and sat down beside me.

"What kinds of things can go wrong with a high-risk pregnancy?"

"We'll cross that bridge if we need to later. Right now, all I want you to do is rest and take it easy. Are you having any morning sickness?"

"No, but food hasn't been my friend for a couple days. Nothing sounds good or tastes good. I do force myself to eat, though it's not very much."

"I can tell you're less than thrilled at the prospect of being pregnant."

"I'm too old."

"No. You're not yet. If the home test is positive, come by my office. We'll discuss everything then."

"All right," I mumbled.

Mika poked his head in. "Safe to come back yet?"

"Sure." I nodded. "Sorry about the trash can. I'll get it cleaned out and—"

"You will not. I'll take care of it in a minute. I want you home and in bed until this flu bug is out of your system. Got it?"

I whispered an inward thanks to Max for using a case of the flu as a smoke screen. I didn't want to have to lie to Mika; he'd see right through me.

"Just wait until you're sick," I drawled. "I'll bark out orders to you left and right."

"You'll have to get in line. Julianna's like Nurse Ratchet," Mika said with a snort.

"Somehow that doesn't surprise me. I'll go down and meet Max by the back door. Thank you both. I'll feel better soon."

"We're walking you down," Mika demanded.

"Fine, but if I give you cooties, don't be pissed at me."

"I could never be pissed at you, Sam." Mika sent me a tender smile.

As both doctor and club owner helped me down the stairs, Max appeared in the alcove with my purse.

"Why don't you bring the car up to the back door, Max? She won't have as far to walk."

"See how you are?" I shot Mika a mock glare. "You *ask* him to get the car, but you *order* me to go home."

"He won't argue with me, because he's worried about you. You, on the other hand...well, your claws are out and you're hissing and spitting."

"I'd say Mika's already got your number, baby," Max laughed as he rushed out the door.

"Rest well, Sammie." Brooks smiled before heading toward the dungeon.

As Mika led me outside, Max was jogging up the stairs. Concern ate up his eyes and lined his face.

"Thanks man, I've got her from here." He lifted me off the ground and carried me to the car.

"Call if you need anything...anything at all," Mika yelled.

"We will," Max assured.

Racing toward my house, he threaded his fingers through mine. "I think I lost ten years off my life when Brooks tugged me off the barstool and told me you were sick in Mika's office."

"I didn't mean to scare you. One minute I was fine. The next, I...I don't even remember hitting the carpet."

"You didn't. Mika caught you and laid you on the couch, then radioed the DMs to send Brooks upstairs, stat."

"It felt like the whole damn dungeon was in the room when I came to."

"Just the resident medical crew. They love and care about you, like I do, Sam."

"I care about you, too," I whispered.

"I know." He squeezed my hand. Long minutes passed before he darted a glance at me. "I don't think waiting another day is going to matter. Why don't we take the test when we get you home."

A knowing dread inched up my body. I'd been living with my head in the sand, dismissing my loss of appetite and queasy stomach for days. But after passing out, I couldn't avoid the obvious any longer.

"Okay," I murmured.

I pressed a palm to my stomach, and somehow I just knew…

The test would be positive.

Max and I had created a life.

I was terrified.

A rush of panic swelled and a tear slid down my cheek. As we entered my subdivision, I had to bite my tongue to keep from ordering Max to drive around the block for several hours. That would only prolong the inevitable.

Still, when he pulled into the drive, I couldn't move. Couldn't open the door. Couldn't speak. I was frozen in fear. I wasn't ready for my life to change so drastically.

Would I be a good mother?

Was Max going to stay true to his word and help me raise this child?

What if he skipped town or—god forbid—died, like Desmond?

The thought of being a single parent was daunting. I'd have to quit the club and find a nine-to-five job. The cost of daycare would no doubt be staggering, not to mention diapers and formula and clothes…good god, the price of raising a kid was astronomical.

My mind continued to reel when suddenly I discovered I was already inside the house and sitting on the edge of my bed. I didn't even remember Max leading me from the car. Yet there he stood, test stick in one hand and his open palm extended to me with the other.

"I know you're scared, Sam, but we need an answer."

Digging deep, I grabbed all the strength I could muster and took Max's hand.

He pulled me in a tight embrace and held me there for several long seconds. "No matter the results, I'm here and I'm not going anywhere. Got it?"

"Let's do this before I chicken out."

Together we entered the bathroom. After I situated myself on the toilet, I took the stick from Max and placed it between my legs. As I voided, I sent up a silent prayer.

Wrapped in each other's arms, we stood with our eyes glued to the plastic wand lying on the sink for what seemed an interminable amount of time.

Ever so slowly a second line appeared.

I was pregnant.

CHAPTER NINE

"I KNOW THIS isn't what you wanted, but I meant what I said, Sam. I'm beside you a hundred and ten percent."

I could barely hear what he said. The roar of hope collapsing within was deafening. Wiggling from his arms, I raced to the toilet and promptly threw up. Kneeling beside me, Max once again gathered up my hair and stroked my back.

"What have I done? How could I have screwed up my life like this?" Tears rolled down my cheeks as a feeling of desolation consumed me.

"Aw, Sam. It's going to be all right, baby," he soothed as he grabbed a glass of water and dampened a cool cloth. He bent and pressed the fabric to my forehead. "*You* didn't do anything. *We* created life. I won't lie...I'm overwhelmed as fuck right now, but at the same time, I'm excited as hell. We're going to be parents!"

The wonder in his tone raked my flesh like the biting tacks of a vampire glove.

"Please...just shut up," I sobbed.

Instead of heeding my command, Max softly chuckled. There was nothing remotely funny about any of this. I wanted to grab a flogger and beat the happiness out of him.

"What are you laughing at?" I spat. "You're not the one who's going to blimp out to the size of a hippo. It's not your body that will be covered in stretch marks like a damn road map or crave crazy shit like pineapple and peanut butter sundaes. You're not the one who'll be forced to wear *sensible shoes* because your feet swell like cinderblocks."

Scooting away from the toilet, I drew my knees to my chest, hung my head, and sobbed.

"You're worried about having to wear sensible shoes?"

"No," I groaned. "I'm worried about everything!"

"I know, baby, but don't be. Dammit, how many times do I have to tell you you're not alone? Yes, this is a lot to take in, but it'll all be fine. I promise," he softly cajoled.

I thought him delusional but let the opinion of his mental state simmer on my tongue. Lifting me off the floor, Max cradled me in his arms and carried me to the bed. I continued to cry as he undressed us both and then crawled in alongside me. He didn't say a word, simply threaded his fingers through my hair while holding me tight to his chest as I cried myself to sleep.

Sunlight seeped through a gap in the curtain and bathed the room in a golden hue. My eyes felt like I'd spent the night facedown in the sand…gritty and sore. Max lay softly snoring beside me as all that had happened last night rushed back in a foreboding flood.

I pressed my palm to my stomach as an ember of awe dimly pulsed within.

Bittersweet memories crowded my brain. Desmond and I had tried to conceive a child for a couple of years but to no avail. I'd always wanted children. Wanted to be the warm, loving, encouraging influence to my child, like my own mother had been. But over the years as my biological clock kept ticking on and on, I'd given up hope.

Stop thinking it's the end of the world. You have the chance you've always wanted, right now!

Strumming my stomach, I wondered if the growing cells inside me would be a girl or a boy. It didn't matter which, only that they be healthy. Would he or she be blonde like me or have chocolate-brown hair like on Max's arms?

The ember within flickered slightly higher.

Though the life inside me was only the size of a pea, or maybe a tiny tadpole, I felt an overwhelming desire to protect the growing cells. I needed to eat a better diet, get more exercise, and do everything within my power to help our child grow strong.

Peeking up at Max, I studied him as he slept. From head to toe, he was ruggedly defined and sensually masculine. I could easily imagine a son or a daughter having their daddy's bright smile, sparkling green eyes, and gentle, loving soul.

A lump of emotion clogged my throat and tears filled my eyes.

Fine. If I'm pregnant, I'll give you the kid to raise. How's that?

The cruel and heartless words I'd spewed that were fueled by fear whipped through me like an icy winter blast.

I'm sorry, I inwardly whispered. As I gently caressed my stomach, guilt and remorse made my heart bleed. *I didn't mean a single word...I swear. I love you, little one, and I'm going to spend the rest of my life proving that to you by showering you with unconditional love and happiness. You're going to have a beautiful life. I promise.*

A new sense of resolve rooted deep within. I would strive to be the best damn mother on the planet.

"Turn off your brain, baby. It's clanging louder than an alarm clock," Max teased in a groggy voice.

"Smartass," I chided. Lifting my head off his chest, I watched all traces of humor drain from his face.

"Are you all right?"

"Yes." I nodded.

"Talk to me, Sam."

"While I'm still trying to digest the fact that we're going to be parents in nine short months, I'm through freaking out."

All of a sudden, Max sat up. A look of shock blazed across his face. His mouth fell partially open as he stared at me, dumbfounded.

"What?" I asked.

"Who are you, and what have you done with my Sam? You look like her, talk like her, but you're not her."

"Ha, ha. Very funny," I drawled and slapped him on the chest. "Just because I'm rationally coming to terms with this doesn't give you permission to make fun of me."

I started to launch off the bed, but Max banded a thick arm around my waist and hauled me to the sheets.

"I'm proud of you, Sam." He gripped my nape and slammed his mouth against mine, plunging his tongue past my lips like a wild animal. The heat of his skin melded with mine, and the force of his kiss reduced me to liquid silver.

"But I'm still going to tease you," he murmured against my lips.

With a growl, I nipped his tongue.

"There she is... There's the wild tigress I know so well."

I bit his lip and gave it a feral tug. "Keep it up, mister. I know several deviant ways to make you cry."

Max inched back and flashed me a lazy smile. "The only crying I'm going to do is yelling your name when I come."

Sparks of want zinged through me. "Do you always think about sex?"

"Mostly. I think about food from time to time. Like now...I'm starving. Let's go out for breakfast. Afterward we can drop by Brooks' office..."

I don't like to use the term high risk, *but the chance of complications rise with women over the age of thirty-five.* The doctor's words slashed through my brain like lightning.

I gave Max a pensive nod. "We'll go talk to him after breakfast."

Max pressed a kiss to my forehead. "You're through freaking out, remember?"

"I thought I was."

"Sam." Max arched his brows in warning.

"No. I am. I won't fold beneath the questions and fears that are pressing in around me. We'll talk to Brooks and meet whatever challenges await us, one-by-one, head on."

"Yes. We will. We're a team now, Sam. You can lean on me when you need to. Got it?"

"You might be taking that offer back soon."

"Never."

After filling our stomachs at a popular chain restaurant, Max drove across town to the hospital. As we entered the medical building attached to the facility, butterflies dipped and swooped. The strength of Max's strong hand in mine fed my courage. But as he reached for the knob of Brooks' office, I tugged him to a stop.

"You *do* want this baby, right?"

Max stilled. A tender smile curled the corners of his mouth as he stroked the side of my cheek.

"The only thing I want more in this world besides a healthy, happy baby is *you*." He brushed his lips over mine. "Breathe, Sam. Everything's going to be fine."

The conviction in his voice reinforced my resolve. I lifted my chin and placed my hand over his. Together we opened the doctor's door. After waiting only a minute or two, a young blonde nurse ushered us back to an exam room. She had me leave a urine sample, then weighed me and took my blood pressure before leaving us alone.

Seconds later, Samuel Brooks entered, darting a dissecting gaze between Max and me. A broad smile tugged his lips as he shook both our hands.

"Congratulations, Mom and Dad. Based on the estimated date of conception, you two will be holding a little bundle in your arms the middle of next April."

The butterflies dancing in my belly dove like fighter pilots. Max let out a whoop, then kissed me hard. I laughed as excitement bubbled up from inside me, then quickly sobered.

"You mentioned last night that my age might be a risk to the baby. What kind of dangers are we talking about?"

"I'm going to send you down the hall so we can draw some blood, then we'll go into my office and discuss them," Brooks stated in a purely professional tone.

By the time we'd climbed back inside the car, my head was spinning.

Brooks told me to reduce stress. I nearly laughed in his face. How the fuck was I supposed to stay calm after he'd tossed out words like *increased fatigue, hormonal and emotional changes, morning sickness, Down syndrome, preeclampsia, gestational diabetes,* and had scheduled an amniocentesis—a genetic profile of the baby—in two months? Even Max had turned pale a time or two before Brooks was through.

Neither of us said a word as we sat in the hospital parking lot for several long minutes. Finally, Max shoved the key in the ignition, then paused and looked at me.

"I had no idea the potential harm that could come to you and the baby. I feel guilty now for getting you pregnant. What if—"

"Hey." I interrupted him by leaning over to cup his cheeks. "You're the one who sees the silver lining in everything. You can't crumble on me. I need your strength and that positive attitude of yours, or I'm going to come undone. Got it?"

My voice shook. I was raw with fear, but I asked for his strength instead of lashing out—a fact that spoke volumes about the level of trust I'd placed in him over the past few weeks.

He cupped his hands around mine and drew each of my palms to his lips. After kissing my flesh, he sent me a weak smile. "I'm not crumbling, Sam. This is only a slight aftershock born from an earthquake of understanding. Don't worry, baby, I'm always going to be your rock."

Tears of gratitude and hope stung the backs of my eyes. Max leaned in and kissed me, then started the car and pulled out of the lot. I'd assumed we were going back to my place, but Max drove east toward Lake Michigan. A smile tugged the corners of my mouth.

"A walk on the beach would be nice." I placed my hand on his leg. "Watching and listening to the water always calms me."

"Me, too. It's the only place, besides bed, that I wanted to be with you right now. We've got a lot to talk about, Sam."

"I know."

Strangely enough, the idea of discussing a future with Max and our child didn't fill me with an ounce of dread. While I wasn't looking forward to delving into a lifestyle conversation yet, I knew that time was drawing near. I'd have to make a decision. But today I wasn't ready to pull my head out of the sand…I needed it beneath my feet and between my toes and to ground myself with Max.

I drank in the warmth of the sun and the sound of the water gently rolling ashore as we walked. Max's strong hand was linked in mine.

"Do you want to tell anyone about the baby?"

"Not yet." I felt my brows tug together. "I'd like to keep this our secret for a few weeks."

"Not a problem. I'll be taking possession of my new house in six days."

"Wow. That was fast. I can't wait to see the inside."

A week ago, we'd taken a drive to North Shore. Max had pulled to the curb of his soon-to-be stately and beautiful, two-story Cape Cod. It was shaded by several hulking elm trees, and colorful flowers surrounded a white-framed, covered porch. He'd apologized for not being able to take me on a tour; the current owners were in the process of moving out. Still, Max beamed with pride as he described the layout of the four-bedroom; three-and-a-half-bath, with gleaming hardwoods throughout.

"I'm anxious for you to see it, too. What do you think about… Shit…" Max paused. A hint of annoyance flickered in his eyes. "I don't even know if you own or rent your place."

I chuckled at seeing him so flustered. "I rent. Why?"

"I want you to think about moving in with me."

"Do what?" I blanched.

"Move in with me," he repeated slowly.

"It's a bit soon for that, don't you think?"

"In terms of the amount of time we've known each other…probably. But I'm measuring my invitation on what's in here." He lifted my hand and pressed it against his heart. "You and our baby mean the world to me, Sam. I want us to be more than baby daddy and baby momma. I want us to be a family."

Family. I could barely remember what that felt like. Though Mom was still alive, she was close to a thousand miles away. I hadn't shared my space, twenty-four seven, with anyone since Desmond. I wasn't sure I could remember how…or if I even wanted to.

Sensing my uncertainty, Max squeezed my hand. "Don't give me an answer now, just think on it."

"I will, but you need to do the same. I've lived alone a long time. I'm not laid-back and even-tempered like you." Max started to laugh and I smacked him on the arm. "Don't you dare say it."

"Say what?" he asked still chuckling.

"*No shit.* Or *I hadn't noticed,*" I replied sarcastically, dipping my voice low like his.

"Would I ever say anything like that?" he asked in feigned innocence.

"In a heartbeat, and we both know it."

Grinning, Max wrapped me in his arms and kissed me.

His lips were like warm velvet.

His tongue was pure, liquid heat.

Though my head and heart locked horns more times than I wanted to count, there wasn't anyone or anyplace on earth I wanted to be…than here, with him. Our lips melded as one while our tongues dueled and danced. I'd found the serenity I so desperately sought right here in his arms.

Max reluctantly released my lips and eased back to study the contours of my face. He smiled and tucked me against his side before we started walking along the sand again.

"I don't get it."

"Get what?" he asked.

"You're so calm…and still here. Aren't men the ones who freak out and head to the hills when they knock up a girl?"

"Jaded much?" Max laughed. "First of all, I already told you…I'm not like most men. Secondly, I'm looking forward to both being with you and also becoming a daddy."

"So, you're saying that you're not the least bit nervous about being a father?"

"Of course I am, but not like you think. I'm worried about your health and the health of our baby." He paused before his expression turned grim. "I'm sorry that deep down you don't want this child, but I do, Sam."

I stopped dead in my tracks before pivoting to face him. "You're wrong, Max. I *do* want this baby. I know I said those horrible, unforgivable words at first. But I didn't *mean* any of them. I was scared...no, I was terrified and lashed out in mean and hurtful ways. I'm sorry. I'm so damn sorry." Tears spilled over my lashes but I continued. "When I woke up this morning and realized there was actually a baby growing inside me, I wanted to stand on the rooftops and scream it to the world."

"So, you're telling that you're not afraid anymore?"

"No. Of course I am, especially after all the things Brooks told us, but I'm not going to cow down to my fears. This isn't about me, or you...it's about him or her." I cupped my stomach as tears streamed down my cheeks. "I'm going to do my damndest to drown our baby in love. And I'm going to bust my ass to make sure he or she has a life filled with happiness. Trust me. I *want* this baby...want it with all my heart."

His eyes glistened in unshed tears. Max pulled me to his chest and buried his face in the crook of my neck. He dragged in several ragged breaths. I clung to his shoulders, sobbing as he stole yet another chunk of my heart. I had no idea what I'd done to deserve this intuitive, sensitive, and powerful man. But I was never more thankful that he'd stormed his way into my life than I was at that moment.

We stood on the beach meshed together for a long time. Finally, Sam lifted his head and flashed me that infamous crooked smile. My heart melted and I issued a watery smile of my own as I wiped my eyes.

His expression darkened. "From now on, there'll be no more lashing out when you're afraid. You'll open up and tell me your feelings. I don't care if they're good, bad, ugly, or unfounded...you *will* talk to me. Is that clear?"

Max had never used such a Dominant and commanding tone with me before. Instantly, the ache to submit, surrender my all to him, pulsed in time with my heart. Every cell in my body screamed and begged to glide to my knees and give myself over to him.

But Max would want more than a taste.

He'd want Samantha's heart and soul to shape and mold.

Would that be so bad? He's strong enough to peel back all those layers and expose what's in your heart. You know what's there…waiting for him. Stop ignoring what you truly desire. You'll forever deny your own happiness if you don't at least try.

I swallowed the lump lodged in my throat as I stared into his emerald eyes. I didn't know if I'd succeed or fail the man. I only knew that he'd protect the sub still haunting the depths inside me.

The time had come to let go of Desmond, break the chains that kept me bound to the past. Yes, he'd loved me…loved me with every breath in his body, but he was gone and never coming back.

Max had been right…it would kill Desmond all over again to see me struggling in this paradox of pain and confusion.

Change was inevitable. I'd survived the horrors of the past, and they'd brought me here, to this crossroads with Max. He was patient to a fault and accepted all the complex parts that didn't quite align inside me. But most of all, he was the father of my child. I owed him the same honesty and truth he'd always granted me.

I opened my mouth and drew in a quivering breath, then cast my eyes toward the sand.

"Yes, Sir," I softly whispered.

His entire body tensed. Doubts slowly crawled up my spine. After several interminable, silent seconds, a gust of air exploded from between his lips before Max gripped a strong fist in my hair. His heated breath spilled over my lips as he guided my head back.

"Look at me, Samantha," he instructed in a deep and raspy tone.

A shiver slid through me as I slowly raised my lids and locked eyes with his. The blazing fire of command and need that reflected back at me nearly stole my breath. His Dominant power all but crackled in the air. The submissive inside me rose like a phoenix and spread her wings once again.

"You have from now until we're inside your bedroom to decide if you wish to hand your power over to me. That includes asking any questions or giving me a list of your hard limits. Though you won't need to worry about those right now, I want you to feel free to tell me what feeds your submission. But once we step inside that room, your power is mine until you use the word…*mistress*. That is your safeword from now on. Is that understood?"

My whole body trembled. "Yes, Sir."

"Good girl. Let's go."

With his hand pressed to the small of my back, we hurried from the beach to the car.

The whole way home, my mind spun like a centrifuge. But there was an unmitigated peace that surrounded me. I was encased in a forgotten white light, poised on the gossamer wings of freedom.

"I used to like pain," I whispered. "I'm not sure if I do anymore or not."

Max simply nodded. "Are you afraid to surrender to me?"

"Yes, but I'm not afraid of *you*."

"Good. You'll never have reason to fear me, Samantha. I promise." Max darted a solemn expression my way before turning his attention back to the road. "Tell me what you're scared of."

"Of failing…and not failing."

"You can't fail me, Samantha. I already know that in my soul. What do you fear about not failing?"

"That all this time I've been simply playing the role of Domme. That my true nature is and has always been a submissive."

"Did you feel like you were pretending when you worked Eli?"

"No. I was in command and control of him…granting him the serenity he craved."

"Yes, you were. As I've said before, your Dominance is stunning. I know it nurtured a part of you, but it couldn't fully fill the needs you'd buried inside you…the ones that were starving for the chance to fall at the feet of a commanding Dominant like yourself, could it?"

"No," I murmured.

"No, Sir," Max gently reminded.

"No, Sir."

"I've seen the whole dog and pony show where Dominants take the stage for the whole world to *look at me* more times than I can count. You weren't pretending a thing, pet. You *were* in control and command of the sub. You simply found the way to satisfy an aching voice within you. And at the end of the day, isn't that really what we *all* do—Dom and sub alike—find a way to sate those cravings burning inside us?"

"Yes. It is, Sir."

"I suspect that in a twisted kind of way, you were able to give your inner sub a bit of sustenance."

"How so?"

"Well, you were providing the submissives what they needed. Isn't that a backhanded form of submission in itself?"

I couldn't help but laugh. "So, you're saying that you and the other Doms are submi—"

"Don't twist my words, girl," Max warned with a look so fierce I felt my panties grow wet. "I'm talking about what *you* gained, not me."

"So what is it that you gain…Sir?"

Max smiled when I added the late honorific. "The immensity of combining my power and a sub's is staggering. The sheer magnitude of trust a sub places in my hands humbles and inspires me. I wield my control by dissecting their psyche with such finite precision they sail off to a magical and peaceful subspace. As they float away, I'm riding my own different wave…Domspace. Have you experienced that, as well?"

"Somewhat. I've experienced a high, but I think it was mostly pride for helping the subs achieve what they needed."

"Yes, there's a bit of that mixed in, as well, but for me, it's the responsibility of holding all that precious power and control in my hands."

Comparing what we each derived as Dominants sent my submissive headspace askew. Like the scales of justice, control weighed far heavier within me now. I couldn't solve this dilemma riding a roller coaster. Closing my eyes, I shoved aside my Domme perspective and focused on unfurling my submissive wings once more.

When I opened my eyes, Max was pulling into the driveway. He turned off the engine and turned toward me. During the drive, there had been a palpable change in him, as well. I could feel the force of his Dominance as if it were a living, breathing thing, reaching out to me like a live wire. The air hummed with a familiar, ancient energy, and I welcomed the sensation…let the contentment spill over me like a waterfall.

As his gaze raked over my flesh, I dipped my chin and lowered my lashes.

Max stroked my cheek so fragile and tender I wanted to weep. "What do you want, Samantha?"

"To please you, Sir."

His fingers instantly stilled. "You already have, pet."

Hastily exiting the car, he jogged to the passenger side before opening my door. He didn't say a word, simply extended his hand. Not in chivalry but in a silent Dominant invitation. Once I laid my fingers in his palm, I would be placing my power and control into those masterful hands.

Lifting my arm, my fingers trembled. I sucked in a shallow breath and slid my flesh into his. Once more he pressed his palm to the small of my back as we entered the house. Without a word, he prodded me toward the bedroom and paused just outside the doorway.

"You're safe. I won't let you fall, Samantha," he whispered in a whiskey-smooth voice. A shiver slithered up my spine, and I gave him a resolute nod. "Good girl."

Mentally casting off my fears and insecurities, I could almost feel them fall to the ground before I stepped through the doorway and into my bedroom. Max followed and closed the door behind him. He stood drinking me in with a steady gaze, shoulders squared, legs parted, and hands behind his back.

Intimidating.

Regal.

Commanding.

He glowed with an imposing sense of strength and power.

My heart thundered in my chest. My body trembled in anticipation and fear.

"Strip off your clothes for me, Samantha."

His words were forceful. Direct. This was it, the answer to the final question that plagued me. I had to know where I belonged in the lifestyle. Backing down now wasn't an option.

With trembling fingers, I lifted the sundress over my head and let it flutter to the floor. Heat flared in his eyes as he watched me peel off my bra before I slid my thong down my legs. Max raked a stare up and down my naked body. Lust and approval flicked in his eyes, but it was the potent wave of his command that made my pussy weep and ache.

Long, anxious seconds passed before he lifted his feet from the floor and moved in close. His palpable command grew even more intense, and I ached to fall to my knees before him. Of course, I wouldn't...couldn't, not until he issued the command.

Max bent and pressed his tongue flat against the fluttering pulse point at the base of my throat. My nipples grew stiff and my pussy contracted. I wanted to toss my head back and moan, wrap my hands against his head, and pull his mouth to mine. Instead, I stood inwardly melting from the submissive flames that licked at my soul.

He lifted from my flesh and threaded his fingers through my hair. Tugging my head back, Max pinned me with a compelling gaze. "Tell me what you need, little one."

"To serve you, Sir."

"Are you ready to surrender your heart, mind, body, and soul to me, Samantha?"

"Yes, Sir," I whispered.

"Your safe word is mistress, don't forget."

"I won't," I promised.

He drew in a deep breath. His nostrils flared and his chest expanded before he slanted his mouth over mine. His kiss was hungry and feral but only lasted a second before Max pulled back and released my hair. "Hand yourself over to me, sweet girl. Kneel."

A burst of lightning exploded inside me…blinding and euphoric. A rush of tranquility, pure and sure, rippled outward and enveloped my limbs.

With my eyes locked to his, I slowly sank to my knees.

Floating in clouds of splendor, I was lost…lost in an emotional and spiritual reverie of long ago. While my heart still ached to bow before Desmond, I'd moved past pining for a ghost. Max was in control of me now, and I knew without a single reservation that I was safe, treasured, and protected once more.

My heart soared as I spread my thighs and rested my hands, palms up, upon them. Drinking in one last look at Max, I lowered my head in reverence and respect to the Dom before me. He began to slowly walk in a circle around me. I could feel his dissecting stare singe over every inch of my naked flesh as he appraised my submissive pose…judged the sincerity of my silent plea to serve him. Chills raced up and down my spine, sending goose bumps to pepper my flesh. It was as if his gaze were conjuring the submissive rebirth churning inside me. I felt raw yet painfully alive, like never before.

Max paused before squatting down beside me. He placed the tip of his finger between my breasts and slowly dragged his digit up my chest and stroked my throat. His movements hauntingly mimicked those of my dream, stilling the air in my lungs. Gently lifting my chin, Max tilted my head back before bringing the pad of his warm finger to rest on my lips. My back now arched and my breasts thrust toward the sky, I was stretched out in supplication to his every desire.

The reckoning within wasn't the cataclysmic pitch and yaw I had expected, but more a gentle shifting on the wind across an open field. Samantha sighed in satisfaction. Like the echoes of a heartbeat, Max's touch revived the submissive—so fragile and small—who lay curled in the safety and protection of her Master's palms.

"You're fucking beautiful in all your submissive splendor, Samantha." His praise swept over my soul with a passionate kiss. "Tell me what you're feeling, my slave."

"Free," I whispered. "Alive again."

"Thank fuck," Max murmured on a heavy sigh. "Drink it in, pet. Savor the peace…let it fill you up and wrap around you like a soft, warm blanket."

"Oh, I am. It's wonderful, Sir." The words rolled past my lips on a breathless, tranquil slide.

Max flicked the tip of his tongue over my earlobe. "Tell me more, pet," his whispered words spilled down my neck.

"I feel calm and small, and so ready to serve you, Sir."

"You are, sweet girl. You please me greatly following my instructions and telling me how you feel."

A contented smile tugged the corners of my mouth. "Thank you, Sir."

"You're welcome, my treasure. I can smell your cunt…you're aroused, aren't you?"

"Yes, Sir. I ache but it's a low throb…a needy reminder."

"Reminder of what?"

"That you'll give me what I earn and not what I want, Sir."

"That's true. I aim to make you earn all the pleasure you could want and more, gorgeous."

Demand hammered through me with a potent throb. Max gripped my hair once more and twisted my head back until our faces aligned. "You want me to fuck you hard, don't you, Samantha?"

"Yes," I answered on a mournful plea.

"Yes? Yes, who?"

"Yes, Sir."

"You want to suffer for me too, don't you, precious?"

Immersed in the placid peace of submission, I'd crawl through fire to please this amazingly powerful man. "Anything for you, Sir."

"Mmm," Max growled. "Yes...I like that. Rise and climb onto the bed. Lie on your back and spread your legs wide for me, Samantha."

Every time he whispered my name, a rush of ecstasy sang beneath my flesh. His command sank deeper and deeper into my bones. With his hand still cinched in my hair, I slowly rose to my feet and walked to the bed. Max released me as I climbed into position. I watched as he unbuckled his belt and slid it from the loops of his jeans.

"I'm going to bind your hands, pet. Remember your safe word."

"Yes, Sir."

I raised my arms above my head and watched as Max looped the leather around my wrists before securing the strap to the brass rungs of the headboard.

Bound.

Immobile.

Tears of absolution and happiness spilled freely. Max brushed them from my cheeks and eased down on the mattress beside me. An almost frantic expression lined his face as he searched my eyes, anxious to gain insight into my tears.

"Tell me, Samantha...tell me what it feels like, baby."

"It's been so long..." My voice quivered and cracked. "I'm at the mercy of your pleasure...your pain...your benevolence."

"Yes, you are. Does that frighten you?"

"No. I-I finally feel whole again."

CHAPTER TEN

"OH, MY PRECIOUS, precious, girl," Max murmured before claiming my lips with a soul-stealing kiss.

I gave back my heart, using my mouth to say all the things mere words could not convey...the depth of gratitude, joy, and the completeness he'd brought back to me. With his unyielding command, Max had swept the clouds from the sky and showed me the most brilliant sun. The rays saturated every cell, filling me with a blissful warmth and peace of mind I never expected to find again.

I didn't regret my decision to forge Sammie from the ashes of my past, but it was painfully obvious...I had to let her go. The cry to seize my submission was beyond a throbbing or visceral need...it was a merciless demand. There was only one man savage and commanding enough to set me free—Max.

He tore from my mouth. The ruthless gleam in his eyes set me on fire. Bending once more, he sank his teeth into my bottom lip and gave an animalistic tug.

"Whose mouth is this?"

I sucked in a quivering breath. "Yours, Sir."

Max smiled and inched down the mattress a bit farther before latching onto one of my pebbled nipples. He flattened the tissue against the roof of his mouth, then nipped and laved the hardened peak. Reaching across my body, he plucked and pinched, showering my other with the attention it needed. On a purring moan, I lifted my shoulders slightly off the bed, offering him all of me.

"Who do these pretty pert breasts belong to, Samantha?" he asked, twisting the now throbbing tips.

"You...only you, Sir," I gasped.

"So, you're really giving me your body to use as my own personal playground?"

"As long as I get to play on your jungle gym." I flashed him a sassy grin.

"It's about time." Max narrowed his eyes, but he gave himself away when the corners of his mouth twitched.

"About time for what?"

"For you to start getting mouthy. I knew you'd show your claws eventually, kitten."

"I can bring out a lot more than claws if you'd like me to…Sir."

"Sweet girl, you can try to unleash anything you want. Just remember, I'll be the one keeping you in line…and I, too, possess a few not-so-gentle means of persuasion skills."

"I can't wait, Sir."

Max softly chuckled. "Somehow that doesn't surprise me, pet. Now hush that sinful mouth of yours before I have to go digging around in your toy bag for a ball gag."

A sudden chill cascaded over my skin. Over the years, I'd amassed a lot of toys. Mostly CBT—cock and ball torture—devices that had given hours of painful pleasure to numerous subs. It was going to be a shame to have to give them—

"Samantha." His word, harsh and threatening, pulled me from my wayward thoughts. "I don't want you focused on anything but the sound of my voice. There'll be time to process the rest later."

I flashed him a tentative nod.

Max cupped my breasts and strummed my nipples as he leveled a commanding stare at me. "Follow your heart, Samantha. What do you desire deep down inside?"

"To please you, Sir."

As the words rolled off my tongue, the tension stringing inside melted away. I sank deeper into the mattress on a blissful sigh. He knew what phrases to say, what questions to ask. Coupled with his husky and compelling voice, Max guided me down that silky path of surrender.

Climbing between my legs, he spread my thighs wide. His gaze fixed on my weeping sex, and when he lowered his head and dragged his tongue up my wet folds and teased my sensitive clit, I gasped. As he lifted from my core, I bucked and arched. I fought to bite back the curse words blistering my tongue, the leather strap binding my wrists, and the overwhelming urge to take control. I was helpless, at Max's mercy, and no longer in charge of my destiny. Panic surged and swelled inside, but before I could voice my dread, he drove two fingers into my sweltering core. Homing in on the tingling bundle of nerves hidden deep inside me, Max studied me with a cutting stare.

"Tell me, Samantha," he demanded. "Does this belong to you?"

His husky words vibrated over my clit, and I clutched tightly around his fingers.

"No. My pussy belongs to you, Sir," I purred and slowly melted beneath his powerful voice.

"Anything else, pet?" he wheedled with a mischievous smirk.

His roguish expression pulled me slightly to the surface, at least enough for my brain to partially clear. "No kids, animals, asphyxiation, choking, scat, snuff, golden showers, humiliation, branding, broken bones, permanent marks, or impact play that could hurt the baby."

Max's expression softened. "Thank you for sharing your hard limits with me, Samantha. We can work around those, no problem."

He bent and circled his tongue around my tight bud. I knew then all conversation was over, or at least I hoped so. Each lap and lave sent me swirling deeper beneath his assertive spell. I lay before him, legs spread and heart open, offering every particle of my being for him to claim and own.

I suddenly realized I'd kept my submissive desires locked away, not for fear of losing Sammie or to malign the bond Desmond and I once shared. I'd stolen the chance of this blissful freedom by forcing myself to believe that no other man was powerful enough to tame me.

Max was more than formidable enough. I had no doubt the man would quench my submissive thirst and drown the abandoned woman I'd become with his spine-bending Dominance and affection.

As his fingers stroked the heightened nerve endings inside, his tongue lashed my swollen, tingling nub, and I felt myself sailing toward the stars. Stroke after luscious stroke, he nibbled and suckled my clit, turning my blood to liquid fire. I clutched the sheet. Writhing and whimpering, I feared he'd leave me suspended on the brink of blissful oblivion until I lost my mind.

"Please…" I mewled.

"Please what, my beautiful, needy slut?"

"Let me come."

"No," he growled. "You promised to suffer for me, and that's what you'll do, pet. Is that clear?"

I nodded, but inside I was screaming. There was no way I could hold back the brutal orgasm churning inside me for long, but at the same time, the thought of failing Max was crushing. Taking control of what I could, I set my mind toward a different path, far from the epicenter of the pleasure he bestowed. I'd no more begun to focus on what I needed from the grocery store when a sharp slap to my clit shot me straight back to his wicked tongue.

"Don't try to cunt-block me again, girl," Max warned with a feral roar. "You'll stay here in body and mind, focused on every drag of my fingers or cock and every lick or nibble of my tongue. Is that clear?"

"Yes, Sir…but I won't last," I wailed.

"I don't expect you to." A cunning expression lined his face. "I want to hear you beg for mercy, pet. Beg…loud, long, and hard."

Relief flooded my veins. He'd given me a lifeline—or the illusion of one—I could cling to without failing him and ultimately myself. Unfortunately, my reprieve didn't last long. Max draped my legs over his shoulders and hoisted my hips off the bed before his tongue laid siege to my tiny puckered rim. He alternated thrusting his fingers into the slick fire of my pussy with plunging his wicked tongue into my crinkled backside. Shards of lightning ignited my clit as I rocked against his face and hand.

Breathless and keening, I tugged at the leather restraints. My limbs tingled and the roar of release thundered in my ears. The lifeline Max had given me, along with my will, disintegrated.

"Please!" I screamed. "Oh, god. Please. Help me…I can't—Master!"

"Come, my sweet slut. Come hard," Max bellowed.

His fingers filled me as I clamped down hard around them. Guttural cries of rapture tore from my throat as convulsions racked my body. Before I stopped quaking, I heard the sound of a zipper, and half a heartbeat later, Max was driving his thick, delicious cock through my quivering tunnel. In and out with frenzied thrusts, I rode the waves cresting and ebbing within as I whimpered and mewled. He fucked me hard with exacting stabs of brutal force. My tunnel burned with friction even though I was still saturated with my own release.

Suddenly, Max pulled from inside me and rolled his shoulders, sending my legs back onto the bed. Grabbing his cock, he fisted himself with a ragged jerking motion. I watched as ruthless pleasure played fiercely across his face. He locked his eyes on me.

"Mine!" His thunderous decree rolled off his tongue as he showered my stomach and breasts with his hot, milky seed.

Streaming ropes of silky come continued to splatter my naked flesh. Tears poured from my eyes. I understood the significance of his release.

Max had claimed me.

Marked me as his own.

I was bound to him…his girl, his pet, his sweet slut…his *One*. He now controlled my submission, my world, my decisions, and my path…all the independence I once possessed now lay safely tucked in his masterful hands.

Slowly, his eyes refocused. A look of affirmation and satisfaction smoothed his striking features. Max reached down and gathered his spilled seed. Drawing his fingers to my mouth, he watched as I greedily slurped down his offering, gliding my tongue over his digits to clean off every drop.

He smiled at me.

It was the proud and fulfilled smile of a Master pleased with his sub.

"I will claim you fully, Samantha. But we'll need to work on a bit of anal training first. You're my pride and joy, my most treasured possession. I won't hurt you, sweet one."

Anticipation fluttered through me, and while I wondered how many years it would take before I could accommodate his massive cock in my ass, I simply sent him a timid nod.

As if reading my mind, Max laughed. "I'll make it feel good for you, pet. I promise."

"You always do, Sir."

"Master. You'll address me as Master, like you did when you begged to come."

I didn't remember using the term, but then the fear of failure had mixed with the conflagration of demand so violently I could have called him Santa Claus at the time. I found it ironic how easily it had been to slide back into a submissive mindset. Well, once I'd decided to at least give it a try.

A peaceful sense of balance and harmony, like a gentle flowing stream, settled deep inside me.

I felt as if I'd spent the last decade lost in a labyrinth and had finally discovered the calm center where I'd once belonged.

Max stood and tucked his cock into his jeans before striding to the bathroom. He returned with a warm washcloth and a towel. After he sat down on the edge of the bed beside me, he set the items on his lap. Releasing my wrists from the leather belt, he massaged my fingers and palms.

With a wary expression, he raised the washcloth and extended it toward me.

Warning bells and buzzers went off in my head. Max was testing me, or rather testing to see how much—if any—of Sammie remained inside me. I knew in my heart, she'd not been vanquished. I honestly didn't want her to disappear. There were times in my previous submissive life when I needed the kind of strength and perseverance she offered. In a way, I'd always had a bit of Sammie in me. It was only after Desmond died that I needed her to step up and lead me down the road of recovery.

I stared at the washcloth, then lifted my eyes to Max's. Without a word, I simply spread my legs and sent him a gentle smile. He sucked in a deep breath. His chest expanded. Max dropped the cloth and sank a hand in my hair. Tiny sparks of painful pleasure skittered over my scalp as he pulled me to his lips.

"You amaze me, Samantha," he murmured before claiming my mouth in a brutal, dizzying kiss.

After cleaning my folds and back passage, he patted me dry and returned to the bathroom. On his way back to the bed, he plucked my robe from the overstuffed chair by the window and held it out for me. I rolled out of bed and slid my arms through the silky fabric. Max tied the sash, then pressed his palm to the small of my back once again and led me to the kitchen.

"I want you to make yourself a cup of tea, then grab me a beer and meet me on the couch."

"Yes, Master."

I knew he wanted to dissect what had transpired, and while it was best to lay a foundation of communication from the start, I wanted a few minutes to gather my thoughts and feelings first.

That's why you're in here making tea…duh.

There were times I really wanted to slap the lips off my subconscious. Now was one of them. As I heated water in the microwave, and while letting the tea steep, I began aligning the sensations still thrumming within me. Though they had shifted a bit, I still felt my submissive glowing presence.

I joined Max in the living room to find him sitting at one end of the couch. His legs were crossed at the ankle and resting on the coffee table. He smiled and opened his arms, inviting me to curl up beside him—which I did of course, after handing him the beer.

We talked for hours, pausing to inhale the pizza Max had phoned in to be delivered. I confessed that surrendering to him was easier than I'd expected. He wasn't surprised at how seamlessly I'd transitioned into that mindset, but then again, he'd been the one to see the submissive inside me all along.

"How far do you want to take this…exchange?" A hint of uneasiness snaked through his voice.

In other words, was I willing to come out of the closet among the members of the club? The thought filled me with angst.

"I'd like to keep this between us, here in the safety of this house, for a while."

"Fair enough, but you *will* kneel for me at Genesis, Samantha. You know that, right?"

I bit the inside of my lower lip and gave a not-so-encouraging nod.

Max strummed his thumb along the inside of my wrist. "Your friends will be happy for you. The rest…" He shrugged dismissively. "They don't matter. Haters are always going to hate, and dipshits…well, they'll keep stirring the pot with or without a spoon. You can't let them bother you, pet."

"I know, it's just…I haven't had time to totally wrap my head around all this yet."

"I know. I'll give you time, but there will be a limit. When we do finally scene together, if anyone has anything negative to say to you, I damn well want to know about it. That's my hard rule, Samantha."

"I understand."

A smile spread over his lips. I shot him a quizzical look.

"What do you think about Julius Maximus Gunn if it's a boy?" He grinned.

I felt my face fall and my mouth gape open. "What? You're not serious…are you?"

"Why not?

"Julius Maximus? No! He'd have to go through life dressed like a damn gladiator."

"My Dad's name is Julius."

I wanted to sink into the couch cushions. Instead, I smirked. "Did he grow up wearing gladiator outfits?"

"No. Overalls," Max laughed.

As the night progressed, the conversation moved from lifestyle topics to more general, vanilla ones. Though I truly didn't suffer from multiple personality disorder, I was acutely aware when Samantha decided to sink into the shadows and allow Sam to rise to the surface.

Max obviously noticed the change in me, as well. "I don't want a TPE—total power exchange, where one gives their submission, tangible property, and income to the Master—I simply want us to find a happy medium between Dom and sub, and man and woman. After all, someone will have to cook, take out the trash, empty the dishwasher, do the laundry...and eventually change our baby's diapers. I want to share those responsibilities with you."

"When you put it that way, the prospect of keeping Samantha around isn't nearly as daunting." I brought our clasped hands to my lips and kissed his knuckles. "Thank you."

Max smiled. "I intend to make sure you're happy, Sam. That's why I want you to move in with me."

My stomach knotted and my heart rate doubled. I didn't know if I was ready to give up the roof over my head and my independence to a man I'd known less than a month.

"Don't go pressing your luck, mister. I've already accepted two major changes in my life—a baby in the spring and rediscovering my submission. I think that's enough for one day," I quipped with a crooked smile.

Laughter twinkled in his eyes. "True. Okay, we'll tackle the topic of moving in together tomorrow."

I feigned a gasp and rolled my eyes.

"And I thought subs were the only ones who were supposed to be brats," I mockingly scolded, which only made him laugh.

FOUR DAYS LATER, I squeezed into a corset, a pair of black leather pants, and my signature stilettos as Max sat on the bed watching me.

My bedroom, like the rest of my house, was in shambles. Boxes, packed to the gills, lined one wall. Others sat empty, scattered haphazardly across the floor, waiting to be filled. Three days ago, I'd made the decision to move in with Max. I wasn't altogether thrilled about giving up the security my rental home afforded. My emotions were mixed, but Max had vowed long ago that he was in for the duration. The least I could do was promise the same.

"You don't have to go back to work so soon, baby."

"I know. But I feel fine. Besides, Mika needs me. I know he's had to persuade the members to fill in for me. I'm sure they'll be happier scening than working the bar and picking up the slack for me."

"I doubt they've minded."

I shrugged. "It's still my responsibility, not theirs." I turned and looked at myself in the mirror. My heart sank. My skin crawled. A frown wrinkled my brow. "Dressing like this makes me feel like a fraud."

"Then wear something else."

I spun on my spiked heel and shot him a scowl. "You know I can't."

With a sympathetic nod, Max stood and wrapped me in a tight embrace. "You can do anything you want to, Sam. No one…not even me, has the right to act as judge, jury, or executioner when it comes to your happiness. Remember that."

"I know," I mumbled. "But I haven't even talked to Mika about everything. I respect him too much not to tell him face-to-face."

"Are you going to mention the baby, as well?"

"I have to, but only him…for now."

Max nodded. "We can tell him together if you'd like."

"No. I'd rather talk to him alone if you don't mind."

"Not at all. Do what you need to. I've got your back"—a flicker of something wicked danced in his eyes—"and your front."

"You have all of me." Lifting to my toes, I kissed his luscious lips.

He gripped the cheeks of my ass with his wide hands and pressed my pussy against his growing erection. I wanted to strip out of my *costume* and drag him to bed. Unfortunately, it was time to face the music, starting with Mika.

Max dropped me off at the club before grabbing takeout from

Maurizio's for us to eat before Genesis opened. As I took the stairs up to Mika's office, butterflies were having a field day in my stomach. At least I'd eaten a protein-packed lunch and wouldn't pass out on the man again...or I hoped not.

Lifting my hand, I rapped on his door.

"Come in," he called from the other side.

I peeked in to find him sitting behind at his desk, which was scattered with papers. He lifted his head and sent me a broad smile.

"Sammie! What the hell are you doing here? You're supposed to be resting," he chided as he rose and gave me a hug.

"I feel fine."

"Good."

He led me over to the couch and we both sat down. I was unsure which topic to broach first, the baby or rediscovering my submission.

"I haven't seen Max around lately. Has he been taking care of you?"

In ways you can't imagine.

"Yes. He's been amazing." I smiled nervously.

"Spit it out, Sam," Mika softly coaxed.

"I'm pregnant."

As the words rolled off my tongue, he reared back. His eyes widened in shock, then ever so slowly, an annoyed expression lined his lips. "Son of a bitch! She was right...again!"

"Huh? Who was right about what?"

"Julianna. I told her you'd passed out the other night and the first thing out of her mouth was, 'Sammie's pregnant.' I told her she was crazy...but she nailed it." Mika shook his head. "She's never going to let me hear the end of this. Fuck!"

I couldn't help but laugh. Mika pressed a palm to my stomach and grinned.

"When are you due?"

"Around the middle of next April."

"And Max? Is he good with this?"

"He's over the moon." I beamed.

"So, is there a wedding date...or are you two going to live in sin, like Julianna and me?"

"Live in sin, I guess. We haven't talked about tying the knot, which is good. I'm still trying to wrap my head around being a mom and..."

"And what?"

"I'm moving in with him. Max picks up the keys to his house in a couple days...Friday to be exact. We've hired some guys and a van to come haul my stuff over on Saturday morning."

Of course, moving in with Max wasn't what I'd intended to tell Mika, but I wasn't altogether sure how to introduce the topic of becoming Max's slave, either. I nervously licked my lips and lowered my lashes.

"Sammie?" Mika's voice was soft. "Or should I call you Samantha now?"

He'd always been an observant S.O.B., I thought with an inward scoff.

I raised my eyes. A weak smile formed on my lips and I nodded. "Samantha."

Mika sat back as he continued to stare at me. A lazy grin followed. "I knew it. If anyone was ever going to lead you back into the light, it'd be Max."

"Why did you think he'd be able to?"

Mika laughed. "Because there's never been another Dom who got under your skin the way he does. He's compelling enough to keep you in line and, at the same time pamper you the way you deserve."

"How do you know?"

"Remember that night you kicked us out of your private room?" I nodded. "Max and I spent the rest of the night in my office talking about the lifestyle. I'd pretty much connected the dots a few days before, but I wanted to see if he had enough mettle to tackle you."

"What's that supposed to mean?" I scowled.

"Come on, Sam. Don't get your feathers ruffled. You know what I mean. You've been a Domme for years. You're not the kind of woman to let a man run roughshod over you, and you'd sure as hell never willingly submit to anyone who wasn't one fucking powerhouse of a Dominant. I'm confident that Max can handle your inner Domme while letting your submission shine."

I couldn't help but grin. "I do, too, but...what about the club members?"

"What about them? Sure, most everyone will be surprised that you've decided to take a walk on the submissive side, but that's only because they don't know about your past."

A spark of hope ignited in my brain. "I think I have an idea. I need to run it by Max first, but if he agrees, I'm going to need your help."

"Anything for you, sweetheart." Mika's expression shifted to concern. "Are you sure you're ready to come back to work tonight?"

"Totally sure. Oh, but aside from Julianna, I'd like to keep this all between the four of us...for the time being."

"You don't even have to ask, Sam. It goes without saying."

"Thank you." I kissed his cheek before hurrying down to the bar.

Max was waiting for me, opening up the Styrofoam boxes and setting out the plastic ware and napkins. As I sat down beside him, he arched his brows waiting for me to fill him in on my meeting with Mika.

"It's all good." I kissed him, long, slow, and passionately.

As we ate, I talked to him about my idea, then filled him in on my conversation with Mika. Just as we finished eating, the man himself came storming into the dungeon. Mika's milk-chocolate complexion was dark red. His nostrils flared like a bull.

"That cocksucking, motherfucking son of a bitch!" he bellowed.

"Who? Jesus, Mika, what the hell is wrong?" I cried in alarm.

In tandem, Max and I both leapt from the bar and headed Mika's way.

"Kerr! That wimp-assed player opened a BDSM club, a block and a half down the street, two weeks ago. I just found out. Justice called to tell me that Kerr's soliciting all the members of Genesis. He's trying to entice them to leave this club and join his. He's calling it Club Control. That motherfucker doesn't know the goddamn meaning of control."

"Oh, my god!" I gasped. "Surely no one is going to drop their memberships with Genesis and follow that miserable prick, are they?"

"I'll be more than happy to pay him a visit," Max volunteered with a chilling smile.

"Don't tempt me," Mika fumed. "I'm not worried about competition. I'm concerned about the newbies...the subs who don't know the difference between abuse and the beauty of the lifestyle. Dammit! I fucking hate players!"

"I say we infiltrate...try to warn as many subs as we can," Max offered.

"How? He knows all the members here." I nibbled the inside of my lip.

"He doesn't know *I'm* a member. He thinks I was here visiting. I could go in undercover…start talking trash about Genesis…Mika in particular." He shot a look of apology toward the owner. "No offense, man, but it might keep Kerr from getting suspicious."

Though visibly livid, Mika cracked a half smile and nodded. "I think that's a fantastic idea. But how are you going to approach the collared subs? Either Kerr or their Masters will kick you out in seconds. The man didn't honor the boundaries of the unowned subs, but he never spoke to the collared ones. He knew he'd have his ass handed to him."

"I could go with Max and—"

"No. There's no way Kerr would let you step foot inside his club, Sam. There's too much animosity between you two," Max pointedly explained.

The three of us stood silently pondering the situation. Suddenly, Max's eyes lit up.

"I've got it. I'll need to talk to Dylan, Nick, and Savannah first, but I know they'd be willing to help."

"Talk to me, man," Mika urged. "What's cooking in that devious brain of yours?"

A cunning grin lit Max's face. "If I can get Dylan and his entourage on board, I say the four of us go to Kerr's club. We'll all but beg to join since I had a one-night stand with Sammie, and Mika found out I'd only used her to get a piece of ass and banned me from Genesis. Of course, Dylan, Nick, and Sanna couldn't stand to see me kicked out for such a ridiculous reason and got so pissed that they tore up their contracts and left, as well. We'll tell Kerr we're looking for a new club to call home."

I'd happily let the prick think me a helpless bimbo if it meant saving subs from his cruel abuse. I darted a glance at Mika and could practically see the wheels turning in his head.

"I think it's brilliant. Give them a call. Ask if they'll come in early so we can sit down and make this happen," Mika eagerly urged.

Max grinned and plucked out his cell phone. While we waited for the trio to arrive, I began setting up the bar.

Drake dropped by to check in on his way home, but when Mika explained the situation with Kerr, Drake pulled out his phone and told Trevor he'd be a little late. Justice arrived next, clearly ticked off about being invited to join Control. Soon, several more trusted friends arrived, grumbling about Kerr's solicitation, but began buzzing with delight after hearing Max's plan.

"What I don't understand," Justice began, "is how did Kerr get all our phone numbers?"

Everyone turned to Mika. His face grew redder by the second, and I could have sworn steam was rising off his bald head.

"That's a damn good question. I'll be right back." The owner turned and raced toward his office.

With a frown, Drake followed. Even more friends soon arrived, including lead DMs: Ink and Bent-Lee. Many offered their assistance, even concocting more horrendous stories about Genesis and Mika in hopes of joining Max's subterfuge. I just stood behind the bar, grinning at my usually loving family who had suddenly turned bloodthirsty and vengeful.

"It's time to teach that little weasel a lesson. When you mess with one of us...you mess with *all* of us," Master Quinn declared. His Scottish brogue was thick and rich, and I could almost picture the man as a highlander in a past life.

"Kerr is a troll," Ava, Quinn's submissive/wife, stated flatly, wrinkling her nose in revulsion.

"He's a jobby," Quinn spat.

"A what?" she chuckled.

"A pile of shit...a worthless pile at that."

A collective murmur of agreement and a few laughs rippled through those gathered at the bar. The telephone behind me buzzed. I picked it up, but before I could answer, Mika barked that I send Ink and Bent-Lee to meet him at the back door. As I passed along the message, the rest of us followed to see what was up.

We quickly discovered the keypad lock had been tampered with. The club had been open and unguarded for three days, or so Mika and Drake could tell based on the time-stamp of the security footage they'd been poring over upstairs.

They had proof that Kerr had broken into the club, not only stealing several toys from the wall—that had gone unnoticed—but he'd also picked the lock on the door to Mika's private office. The ballsy bastard had even sat at the man's desk while he copied phone numbers off the members' applications.

Mika and Drake looked as if they were ready to kill. The privacy of our kinky family had been invaded. Kerr's head was going to roll...maybe not today but soon. I could feel it in my bones.

"I'll get a couple trustworthy friends in law enforcement to come over and take a look at that footage. See if we can get Kerr on a B and E," Justice announced before lifting his cell phone to his ear and heading toward the dungeon.

The back door opened. Ian, James, and Liz blinked in surprise at the welcome party that greeted them.

"We've got trouble. I need your help," Mika addressed the two men who'd arrived.

James had been a former officer with Chicago P.D. but was now partnered with Ian, who owned a small security company. Liz watched with her mouth agape as her two Masters followed Mika up the stairs to his office. Slowly she turned toward me.

"Mistress Sammie? What's going on?"

I nearly cringed at the word, mistress. Instead, I wrapped my arm around her waist and smiled. "Why don't we go sit at the bar? I'll get you something cold to drink."

Liz darted a worried glance at the others huddled near the back door, then nodded and went with me. Across the room, Justice paced, gesturing with his hand as he talked on his cell phone. I poured Liz a cola, then filled her in on the current events.

"I hope they nail his ass to the wall. I wish Master Sam, Cindy, and I hadn't taken that Hippocratic oath. We should have let Kerr bleed out that night on the floor," Liz huffed.

"No, honey. None of you would have been able to live with yourselves. You all did the right thing," I assured.

"I know, but still...Kerr's done nothing but cause trouble. Why do people have to act like that?"

"Because they're ego driven...and probably have tiny little dicks." I grinned.

Liz burst out laughing. "Oh, my god. You are too funny, Sammie." She quickly slapped a hand over her mouth. "I'm sorry. Forgive me, Mistress. I didn't mean any disrespect to you. Oh, god. My Masters will tan my hide if they knew I was being so—"

"Comfortable with me?" Oh, how I wanted to spill my guts if only to ease Liz's embarrassment.

"Yes, Ma'am," she mumbled.

"Well, I'm certainly not going to tell them. You won't, either." I reached out and patted the back of her hand. "It'll be our little secret, all right? Besides, I'm sure they have enough on their minds right now. Mika will probably want the whole club's security system revamped."

"Thank you, Ma'am, but I *have* to tell them." Liz hung her head in shame.

"No worries, girl. We'll tell them together. I'll assure them you were a shimmering example that they should be proud of."

Liz sent me a grateful smile. "God, I love you, Mistress."

The others wandered into the dungeon. Dylan, Nick, and Savannah followed Max toward the bar. Justice ended his call and jogged down the hall. It was a bevy of commotion, and we hadn't even unlocked the front doors. I quickly glanced at the clock and cursed under my breath.

"It's show time," I announced to the group. "Any volunteers to check in members?"

"Ava and I will be happy to do it," Quinn called out.

"Thank you." I smiled.

After grabbing the keys, I hurried to the foyer and disengaged the lock. Several people filed in. Their anticipation and happy energy hummed in the air. This was why I'd chosen to remain in the lifestyle. I couldn't give up the camaraderie of this like-minded family.

"Welcome, all." I grinned. "Master Quinn and his beautiful girl, Ava, will have you passing through the velvet curtain just as quickly as they can."

As I turned and walked away, Eli stepped out from behind Peanut and flashed me a nervous smile.

"Mistress, I-I wanted to make sure you weren't angry for me scening with Mistress Monique the other night."

I sent him a gentle smile and cupped his chin before he could drop his gaze to the floor. "No, sweet boy. I'm happy she's helping you find subspace. I'm sorry if you feel I've failed you. That was never my intent."

"Oh, no, Mistress. I didn't think that. I know how hard you work, and the times you've been able to scene with me have been an honor. Is everything all right? You've been gone for days…I was worried that…well, that I'd upset you."

"No, pet. I was sick. But I'm much better now," I assured. "Go back and get in line. I'll have a cherry cola waiting at the bar for you."

He flashed me a smile filled with relief. "Thank you, Mistress."

As I walked away, a lump of emotion clogged my throat. My eyes burned and I quickly blinked back my tears. Of all the members I hoped would embrace my new role as a submissive, Eli's acceptance was important to me. I owed it to him to sit the boy down and explain everything one-on-one.

Suddenly, I was a knot of nerves.

Was I doing the right thing? A wave of panic threatened to take me over. Then I looked toward the bar. Max's gaze was locked on me. Worry reflected in his eyes as he stood and barreled my way.

"What's wrong?" He clutched my elbow and pressed me up against the wall, shielding me from the other members.

"Nothing. I'm fine."

"Samantha."

My eyes flashed wide as I darted them first to the left, then the right. We'd agreed that Max would call me Sam until… "Not here," I whispered tersely.

"Then stop telling me nothing's upset you, girl," he growled lowly. "What the fuck is wrong?"

"I-I just had a little freak out. I'm fine."

"What caused you to freak out?"

"Eli. I had a bout of guilt, is all. I feel like I'm tossing him aside."

"You're not. You're fulfilling your own desires, just as he is. Monique is stepping in to give him what he needs. He's not your worry anymore."

"Maybe not by club standards, but in my heart, he is." A tear slid down my cheek, but I hastily brushed it away.

"We have time to settle you into your new role, baby. Just breathe. All right?"

"I don't want to wait. I want to do what we talked about this Saturday."

"All right. Saturday it is."

Easing in alongside Max, Brooks cast a quizzical glance between us. "Are you feeling dizzy or sick again, Sammie?"

"No. I'm fine." I forced a smile. "We were just having a little discussion."

"Sorry, didn't mean to interrupt, but you look a little pale." The doctor nodded. "I'll leave you two to finish your talk."

I sucked in a ragged breath. "I need to get to work and we're making a scene here."

"We can give them a scene, Samantha, right fucking now," Max murmured between clenched teeth.

"No, Master. I'm sorry. It's…god, this is hard."

"I'm not trying to be unreasonable; I'm simply making sure you're not putting too much stress on yourself or…"

I followed his gaze as he palmed my belly gently. Another tear escaped as I felt his benevolent command seep into my pores.

"I'm fine, Master. I don't know why I'm always crying, but it's pissing me off."

"Hormones, pet." Max grinned before leaning in close. "Pregnant women cry all the time."

"Lovely," I drawled derisively.

"We'll talk later. Just relax."

He walked me back to the bar before disappearing through the archway with Dylan, Nick, and Savannah. It didn't take long for me to find my rhythm once more as the sights, sounds, and scents of the dungeon enveloped me.

When Max and his friends failed to return, I assumed his plan was in motion. I hoped Kerr would buy their deception, and between the four of them, they'd be able to reach out to as many subs as they could and lead them to Genesis. If things went well, the Saturday morning sub sessions would grow in size.

Mistress Monique had Eli on the cross again. A sliver of regret burned deep, but I lifted my chin and reminded myself change was inevitable. I'd survived releasing Dark Desire; I'd survive both Eli's transition and my own, as well.

Tony had Leagh tied to a spanking bench, and when she sent him a naughty grin over her shoulder, he landed the leather strap to her pink cheeks with a mighty backhand. She yelped and buried her face in the padded leather. I bit back a chuckle and filled more drinks.

Suddenly I saw Ink sprint across the dungeon and disappear down the hall. Master Sam and Cindy were quickly making their way in that direction again.

"Good lord, now what?" I murmured.

No sooner had the words left my lips than Max hurried toward me.

"I need the key to your room."

"What's happened?" I asked as I pulled it from my pocket and placed it in his palm.

"I blew our cover at Kerr's, but I've got eight subs out of there. One girl's ass is opened up pretty badly. Brooks and Cindy are going to fix her up."

Those pesky tears threatened again. "How bad was it there?"

"It wasn't even a real club…just a loft with a crude slapped-together cross and a scuffed-up picnic table. I wanted to smash that prick's face in."

"You didn't pulverize him, did you?"

"No, but I sure as fuck wanted to." Max's lips thinned. "The only thing that stopped me was the worry of being hauled away to jail. I'm not leaving your side. I gave you a promise. Remember?"

I blew him a kiss before he rushed away.

CHAPTER ELEVEN

"JOE," I CALLED over my shoulder as I stared at Max's retreating back.

"I know. Watch the bar," he replied. The sub's face was pale and lined with anguish.

"I'll be back as soon—"

"Just make sure that fucking monster didn't hurt her so badly she'll give up on submission."

"I will."

As I raced toward my private room, I wondered how we were going to protect others who might find Kerr first instead of Genesis. My stomach rolled at the thought of the harm he could do to the whole community. A group of subs—two male and five female—stood near the end of the hall. They looked scared and confused as they huddled together.

"The package is safe. You've got a green light. Go," Justice barked into his cell phone.

I was stunned, not that he was likely talking to the cops but that he'd raised his voice. I sent the Dom a sideways glance. Ending the call, Justice turned and stormed out the back door, leaving me with the group of anxious subs. I sent them the most reassuring smile I could before introducing myself and promising they weren't in danger now.

"Symoné used her safe word and that prick, Kerr, just ignored it," a tall middle-aged man spat. "He wouldn't stop. If that big, bald wall of a dude hadn't stepped up and gotten in Kerr's face, the bastard would probably still be beating the poor thing."

I knew instantly the big wall of a dude who'd gotten in Kerr's face had been Max. Part of me wished that my secret Master had beaten the shit out of the slimy prick.

"We have a member who's a doctor, along with a couple of ER nurses. Symoné is getting professional medical attention right now," I assured. "Don't worry, we'll take care of her and of you all. You have my word."

Visible relief rippled over their features.

"Thank you, Mistress," the angry male sub stated. "I'm Woody."

After he introduced the other subs, I sent them a soft smile. "Try to relax. I'm going to check on Symoné. I'll be back in a minute and let you know how she's doing."

"Thank you, Mistress Sammie," a young, doe-eyed sub named Maple said with a respectful smile.

When I tapped on the door of my room, Max answered. He led me inside, where I found Savannah hugging Symoné—a pretty auburn-haired girl. Brooks and Cindy were applying a large gauze bandage to the upper part of Symoné's thigh.

"Keep the wound clean and bandaged, sweetheart," Brooks advised before lifting the sheet to cover her backside. "Take some over-the-counter ibuprofen or acetaminophen to help with any discomfort. All right?"

Symoné turned and brushed back the curls from her face. When she looked up at the doctor, her striking aqua-colored eyes were rimmed red. "Thank you, for both rescuing me and mending me up." Her voice was soft, almost sultry, but held an undertone of self-assurance. She might have endured a submissive's worst nightmare, but this girl had spunk. She wouldn't let this deter her from achieving her submissive goals.

She hugged Savannah and smiled. "Thank you so much for keeping me calm. You all have helped me in ways I can't put into words. Masters Dylan, Nick, and Max, thank you for un-cuffing me from that nasty cross, but mostly for taking my friends and me out of that disgusting place." Gratitude shimmered in her unique-colored eyes, conveying her depth of appreciation.

"You're welcome, pet. Kerr's a pig," Nick grumbled.

"That's an insult to pigs." Symoné smirked shyly.

"How did you get mixed up with him?" Dylan asked.

"I met him and the other subs that were in his *club*"—Symoné rolled her eyes—"online, a couple years ago. We'd meet up at Maple's apartment and he'd scene with us…well, until he got shot. We thought our submitting days were over. But then Kerr messaged us and said he was opening up his own dungeon and invited us to come by…so we did."

"And he'd never gone off the deep end before?" Dylan asked in disbelief.

"No. Not until tonight." She shook her head, sending her chestnut-colored curls to bounce. "I should never have let him cuff me to the cross. I sensed something was off. He seemed different…angry. Once he had me bound, he turned into a monster."

"Filthy prick," Max mumbled under his breath as another knock came from the door.

Justice, Mika, and a uniformed officer stood at the portal.

"This is Officer Lennox. He needs to get a statement from the victim," Mika announced.

"Are you up for answering some questions, Symoné?" I asked.

"Yes," she answered forcefully. "I'll do anything to get that animal behind bars."

"He already is," Mika replied as the three men entered the room. "Kerr's been arrested not only for assault, but for breaking and entering my club."

Justice moved in beside me. The second he laid eyes on Symoné, his whole body tensed as he stared at her, seemingly awestruck.

As Mika introduced Lennox to the group, I watched Justice continue to gape at the girl, but yet another knock on the door stole my attention. When James and Ian entered, floor space inside my small room became a premium.

"Lennox? Damn good to see you, man," James greeted with a huge grin.

"I hoped you'd be here, Bartlett." Lennox grinned as the two shared a manly hug and clapped one another on the back. "We sure miss your crazy ass at the station, bro."

Grateful that the cop who'd arrived to take Symoné's statement turned out to be a former co-worker of James', I smiled and inched toward the bed.

"I'm Mistress Sammie. Your friends outside are anxiously waiting to see you. Is there anything you'd like me to tell them?"

"Yes. Please tell them I'm fine and I'll be out to join them as soon as I can."

"Will do. Sir Max and I will get them situated at the bar. It's just down the hall past the archway. We'll be waiting for you." I smiled as I looped my arm through Max's and started dragging him toward the door.

He arched his brows and flashed me a wicked grin. "Are you asking or ordering, *Mistress*?"

Leaning in close to his ear, so only Max could hear, I whispered, "I can't very well beg, now can I?"

"You will later," he mumbled as we left the room.

After I relayed the injured sub's message, the visitors followed us down the hall. As I poured their drinks, all but Symoné, Mika, James, and the cop filtered into the dungeon.

Max flashed me a wink. "I'll be right back." He slid off the barstool and met up with Dylan, Nick, and Justice.

"This place is nice. And it's clean," Woody stated as he watched the various scenes being played out. "This is a *real* club. We should have hooked up here club instead of with Kerr."

Joe introduced himself, and as the subs talked, I pretended to look busy while I listened in on their conversation. As Symoné had stated earlier, the group relayed how they'd met Kerr and the chain of events that led to the girl's injuries.

"When Kerr told us he was opening a dungeon," Maple chimed in, "we all jumped at the chance to help him. We should have told him to kiss off."

"Were there any other Doms there?" Joe asked.

"Just one," Woody replied with a roll of his eyes. "But he got scared when Symoné started screaming. When your friends quickly stepped in, the dude left."

"What a douche," Joe drawled as I bit back a curse. "If he was any kind of Dom at all, he'd have stopped Kerr and helped your friend."

"Oh, my god, Woody. You know that idiot wasn't a Dom," Maple scoffed. "Every time he spanked me, he looked like he was going to cry. He told me to tell him to stop if he hit me too hard. I *ordered* him to shut up and keep spanking."

"Oh, good grief," Joe chortled. "You all need to join Genesis, but for shit's sake, don't ever try to order the Doms here around. Of course, you wouldn't have to."

When Mika and James led Symoné into the dungeon, her friends let out a cheer. I couldn't help but grin as I watched their happy reunion. As the young girl introduced Mika to her friends, they respectfully thanked the owner before inundating him with questions about the club.

Symoné quickly darted a glance toward the front of the club as a slight blush colored her cheeks. I turned to see Justice standing in the shadows, intently watching her, too. When he caught me looking at him, he scowled and exited through the velvet curtain. I couldn't decipher his behavior, but before I had time to analyze it further, Peanut requested a bottle of water.

At the end of the evening, Max and a group of Doms walked the visiting subs back to retrieve their cars while Joe and I closed down the bar for the night. I was exhausted and couldn't wait to get home, take a hot shower, and climb into bed.

As I sat beside Max in the car, he gave me a play-by-play of what had happened at Control. He was as disgusted by Kerr's disregard for the sub as I was. Thankfully, he and the others had been there to help Symoné and rescue her and the others.

As we left the city, I closed my eyes and drifted off to sleep. When I opened them again, Max was unlacing my corset. He peeled the fabric aside and leaned in, sucking an already erect nipple into his warm, silky mouth. I sent him a sleepy moan.

"I know you're tired, baby. I was just going to tuck you into bed, but then this"—he nipped my pebbled tip between his teeth—"and this"—then the other—"well they were just begging for attention."

"They were, huh?" I replied with a lazy grin.

"Uh-huh. And if you weren't totally exhausted, I'd start at the bow of your ripe, lush lips and kiss my way down your sinful body…latch my mouth onto your hot little cunt, and make you scream my name."

"Sounds like one hell of a plan. Don't let my snoring stop you."

Max clasped each nipple between his fingers and thumbs and pinched until I blinked wide and let out a cry of pain.

"Thank you for giving *me* permission, Samantha."

I sucked in a deep breath between clenched teeth as the burn lingered, spreading out to warm my limbs.

"Until you're ready to reveal to the world that you're my submissive, you will leave your Dominant mindset at the club each night. Is that clear?"

As if Max had flipped an internal switch, the submissive in me ached for his forgiveness. I instantly wanted to please the man in any and every way I could.

"Yes, Master. I'm sorry. I wasn't thinking about—"

"You should never have to *think* about it, girl. Yielding to me should be an automatic reflex and always in the forefront of your mind." He laved his tongue over each throbbing tip. I exhaled on a blissful sigh and he stood. Max didn't say another word as he removed my shoes and tugged off my leather pants, then drew the covers around me.

"Go to sleep, precious," he instructed before kissing my forehead.

When he turned and left the room, I felt alone…orphaned.

Was he punishing me for not tossing my crop aside and peeling off the skin of my alter ego before leaving Genesis? Dammit, I'd tried to do my best. With the exception of a few awkward moments early on, I'd worn my Dominant veneer at the club seamlessly…the way I was supposed to.

No, you're supposed to stay true to your heart.

Feelings of being a fraud stabbed deep once more. An oily film slid over my skin. My stomach coiled. I bolted upright. Tossing the covers aside, I gulped for air. I didn't want to be branded a player like Kerr. Acid, caustic and hot, swirled in my belly. Launching from the bed, I raced to the bathroom and slid to my knees in front of the toilet.

Max gently gathered my hair back as I wretched and spit. I hadn't even heard him enter.

"I'm sorry, Master," I choked, swiping the tears dribbling down my cheeks.

"You've no need to be sorry, baby. They call it morning sickness for a reason."

"No. Not for this…for failing you."

Max didn't reply, simply drenched a washcloth in cold water and dragged it over my face. "Are you finished now?"

I nodded.

Picking me up in his arms, he carried me back to bed. This time, he kicked off his shoes and crawled in beside me.

"You haven't failed me, Samantha," he softly whispered as he threaded his fingers through my hair. "It's going to take time to figure out how to navigate the waters. The tides around you are rising and ebbing at the same time."

"So why did you punish me by leaving?"

"That wasn't punishment," he bit out incredulously. "You were tired, girl. When, or if, you earn a punishment, you'll damn well know it. I'll tell you my displeasure in no uncertain terms. I was simply giving you parameters to help you transition from Domme to sub at the end of your workday. That's all."

"I should have stopped you before you left the room."

"Yes, you should have. Communication is a must. You know that." He kissed the top of my head as I lay against his chest.

I did. And I needed to keep that in the forefront of my mind if our relationship had a chance in hell of working.

"I'd like to discuss Saturday night with you, Master."

"I think we should."

Easing off his chest, I made my way off the bed and knelt on the carpet. Max sat up and smiled as he swung his legs off the edge of the mattress. He bent and traced his knuckles down my cheek.

"You may begin, gorgeous."

AS I TAPED up the last box in the bathroom, I dragged my arm across my forehead to wipe the sweat from my brow. The movers were scheduled to arrive at eight in the morning. Max had left over three hours ago to pick up the keys and oversee the cleaning crew he'd hired so we'd have a spotless house to move into. I wandered into the living room and stared at the stacks of boxes that held the contents of my life. Before I had time to second-guess my decision, the rumble of Max's new half-ton pickup roared into the driveway.

Tearing open the door, I stood on the porch expectantly. He rushed from the truck. Wearing a triumphant smile I thought might split his face, Max raised the key in the air. I let out an excited squeal and ran across the lawn before leaping into his arms.

"Would you like to hop in and go see our new home, Miss Radcliffe?"

"You bet your sexy balls, Mr. Gunn."

"Sexy balls, huh?" he laughed.

"The sexiest. Let me put some shoes on and grab my purse. I'll be right back."

Max cinched his arms around me tightly. "Are you asking or

instructing, pet?"

I rolled my eyes and flashed him a saucy grin. "Oh, great Master of my heart, mind, body, and soul, may I please beg your permission to put on some shoes and fetch my purse so we can see our *new house?*" I was so excited my voice rose to a near scream by the time I finished my over-dramatic plea.

"Oh, I'm going to have fun taming your smartass tomorrow night, pet." Max swatted me on the butt. "Get in there and get your things before I take you over my knee on the front porch and embarrass you in front of your soon-to-be ex-neighbors."

With a laugh, I hurried into the house. After gathering my things, I ran to the truck and jumped inside.

"Let's go. Let's go!" I giggled like an impatient child.

"Still trying to push limits, huh? Fine. It's your ass," Max warned with a wicked grin.

"It'll be my lucky day. A new house *and* a red ass? What more could a girl want?"

Max's eyes twinkled as he shook his head. "I didn't say anything about a *red* ass, pet."

"But you said…" My eyes grew wide and I found it hard to breathe. "But we haven't done much in the way of anal training yet, Master."

"We've done enough. You can handle my fat cock in your ass, Samantha."

"But…but…"

"I can't think of a better way to christen the house, can you?"

"Sure I can. How about a blow job on the kitchen table?" I offered as a slow-roiling wave of fear careened through me.

"I can't think of a better house-warming gift than a blow job *before* I flip you over the kitchen table and claim that perfect puckered hole of *mine!*"

Once he'd discovered that anal play turned me inside out, he pushed that sizzling hot button as often as he could. But images of Max trying to shove his fat cock in my tiny opening filled me with fear. There was a huge difference between his thick fingers and his massive cock invading my crinkled passage. He'd likely split me in two.

The air froze in my lungs as a shudder quaked through me.

"Relax, pet. I'm not going to claim your ass yet."

"Then why did you—"

"I was teasing and we were having fun, but then you stopped bantering. Why?"

"Are you giving me some kind of test again?"

"Maybe." He shrugged. "Answer my question."

"I didn't know if you knew something I didn't. I mean, I can't tell how wide you stretch me with your fingers. It feels like you working open the Grand Canyon, but then I *know* perfectly well how big you are and…well."

"So you were willing to trust me but still had reservations, is that it?"

"Exactly."

"Next time, you'll voice your worries to me. Understand?"

"Yes, Master."

Max sent me a brilliant smile. "Good girl."

I never understood why two simple words, *good* and *girl,* filled me with pride or calmed and centered me the way they did. Maybe there didn't need to be a reason. Perhaps it was simply because being in a submissive headspace was an amazing and glorious place to be.

Instead of pulling to the curb of his new house, Max whipped the truck into the driveway this time. My stomach tumbled and he took my hand.

"I hope you like it, Sam."

"I know I will."

He leaned over and kissed me, then vaulted from the truck and raced to my door. He took my hand and led me up the curved walkway to the porch. The white door framed with rainwater glass panels looked both homey and inviting, but when Max shoved the key in the lock and opened the door, I couldn't keep from gasping. Glossy hardwoods beckoned me inside. Sunlight streamed through huge picture windows throughout, and when Max led me into the kitchen, I instantly fell in love. Rich marble countertops lent an airy vibe. Double doors led to the backyard with its inlaid slate patio and hot tub near the house. Huge fir trees surrounded the property line, and I grinned knowing we'd be cloistered in privacy for a little hot tub fun.

After we checked out the finished basement, Max led me upstairs. Of the three empty rooms on the second floor, I chose the one directly across from the massive Master bedroom as the nursery. It still seemed surreal that I was actually moving in with the man. That we were going to have a baby soon was even more mind-boggling. When I checked out the master bath with its Jacuzzi tub and glass and travertine shower, big enough to hold a football team, I was ready to toss my pillow on the glossy marble floor and sleep right there.

"It's simply breathtaking…like you." I threw my arms around his neck and kissed him.

Bright and early the next morning, the movers loaded up the truck. I said good-bye to my house and my independence. As Max and I drove away, a pang of fear and regret sliced deep. I inhaled a deep breath and searched for my Zen.

Max reached down and squeezed my hand. "No regrets, pet. You, me, and our baby are going to be happy."

The conviction in his voice chased the bulk of my insecurities away.

Dylan, Nick, and Savannah met us at the new place with bundles of groceries and a case of beer. The day was a whirlwind as we directed movers hauling boxes to the correct rooms. Midmorning a delivery truck arrived, chock full of furniture Max had ordered. A whole new wave of chaos ensued.

As if sensing my dismay, Sanna pulled me aside. "Why don't we let the guys deal with the new furniture and you and I go pick up some pizzas so we can feed these beasts?"

"I say yes. We both could use a break from the pandemonium."

After we offered to get lunch, Nick thanked Sanna and kissed her hard before handing her the keys to his truck. Dylan and Max were in a hot debate regarding which direction the kitchen table should face.

"I bet you money neither one of those two have ever watched HGTV before," I said with a laugh once Sanna and I were outside.

"And you didn't really think that Sir Max picked out all that gorgeous furniture himself, did you?"

I hadn't given much thought when the delivery truck arrived. I'd assumed Max was the one responsible for the seemingly never-ending lugging parade ensuing as Sanna and I had left.

"He didn't?"

"Nope." Sanna smirked as she shook her head.

"Did you help him?"

"Me?" She blanched. "No way. Master Dylan hooked him up with an interior designer friend. Next week she'll have her whole crew crawling through every room of your new house, hanging drapes, pictures, and adding special touches everywhere."

"Oh, Max...you sneaky little rat," I drawled with a laugh.

Changing topics as she drove, Sanna happily informed me that the subs from Control had reached out to Mika. He'd invited them to attend the weekly sub meetings, which, ironically, were being held that very minute.

"That's wonderful. I can't wait to start hitting the meetings so I can get to know them better."

Sanna shot me a look of confusion. "You're joining the sub meetings? Why?"

Shit! Shit! Shit! I'd shoved not one but both feet in my mouth.

"Sorry, Mistress. It's not my place to ask."

"Please, don't apologize, Sanna. Though I can't explain right now, things will make sense tonight at the club. *If* I survive this move, that is." I laughed softly.

"Oh, a surprise. I can't wait." She grinned. "We're all so thrilled that you and Sir Max are moving in together. I have to confess, when I first met the man, he intimidated the socks off me. But after he stayed with us a couple days, all that changed. From the outside, he might look like a scary badass, but underneath those tattoos and all those muscles is a kind and generous man. Still, he has that strict Dom vibe like a couple other Masters I know and love."

"That he does." I nodded, anxious to feel Max's strict Dominance again.

You'll be basking in his power forever.

After returning with the pizzas, we ate and went back to work unpacking boxes. The afternoon whizzed by, and soon we waved goodbye to the helpful trio before preparing for our special night at Genesis.

Butterflies tore through me in a mass migration.

"Everything ready for tonight, Samantha?" Max's eyes twinkled.

"Yes, Sir. I'm nervous though."

"I expect you would be, but do try to relax. I'll always be right by your side, pet."

When I stepped into the enormous shower, I closed my eyes and let the hot water melt my anxiety. Max joined me. We not only christened the spacious stall properly but he effectively wiped all worries from my brain, too.

Though he'd sated me—and then some—I grew impossibly wet as he watched me primp and dress with a heated stare.

"The scent of your cunt is intoxicating, pet," he growled.

My knees nearly buckled as he helped me climb into his truck. While Max drove toward the club, I sat quietly pondering the evening ahead.

"Mika phoned while you and Sanna were picking up the pizza. Everything is ready to go. The caterer should already be there setting up the dinner buffet. Oh, and he spoke to Eli. The boy will meet you in your private room in thirty minutes. While you're talking with him, I'll fill Dylan in on what's happening tonight."

The reality of what I was about to do slapped me across the face. A part of me wanted to tell Max to turn around and take me home, but that would be caving in to my insecurities.

My heart knew what it desired; I simply had to direct my head to get on the same page.

I placed a palm to my stomach.

So many changes were taking place in my life, and at such breakneck speed, I simply wanted things to slow down so I could take a deep breath.

Of course, Max read me like he always did and placed his hand over mine before gently squeezing both mother and child.

I'll always be right by your side, pet.

Yes. He would.

CHAPTER TWELVE

ELI TOOK THE news better than I'd expected. There were tears, which I'd anticipated, but in the end, he was happy to gain a submissive sister. Still, he was understandably sad to lose me as a Domme.

A few minutes after he left my room, Max entered wearing a smile so bright it nearly blinded me.

"Are you doing all right, pet?"

"Yes, Master, just a bit...I really am trying to calm down. I'm scared and excited."

"Scared of what the members are going to think of you?"

"No. I mean, yes. There's that, but I just don't want to stand up there and start bawling. I cry at the drop of a hat these days. I hate it."

"I've noticed, so I tucked some tissues in my vest, just in case." Max pulled me to his chest and enveloped me in a warm, reassuring embrace. "You're stronger than you think you are, baby. You'll do just fine. If the tears come, I'll sip them from your cheeks."

His promise sent goose bumps to pepper my arms. Drinking in the tears—the tangible sacrifice of a sub—was heady and potent for a Dominant. Knowing that I would be feeding his command filled me with purpose...gave me an even stronger conviction than standing before the members to strip off my Domme cloak and unveil my inner sub.

Max slightly pulled away. He brought his fingertips to my chin and tilted my face back. "You look gorgeous, my sweet slut. There's not a happier or more honored Master on the planet tonight."

My heart soared and flew even higher when he slanted his lips over mine and claimed me with a passionate, hungry kiss. I clutched his wide shoulders as that familiar arc of electricity surged between us. The current didn't only sizzle, but grew hotter...more exacting. I felt Max fortifying me with his strength, meshing his control to mine so I could face the members with dignity and poise.

Savannah's words rolled through my head: *underneath those tattoos and all those muscles is a kind and generous man.* She'd been spot on about that.

Max ended the kiss when a knock sounded at the door. The knob turned and Mika poked his head in. "Everyone is here and seated. Are you ready?"

I nodded and swallowed tightly and smoothed my hands over the ivory silk gown.

"Make your Master proud, Samantha," Max whispered as he squeezed me tight, then released me.

With his wide, warm hand splayed at the small of my back, he led me down the hall. Before we breached the archway, I could hear murmurs coming from the dungeon. Mika had personally invited everyone to join him for a buffet dinner and surprise.

I assumed the food would be spectacular but hoped the surprise would be well received. When I entered the dungeon, I nearly swallowed my tongue. My knees began to shake and my palms grew sweaty. It would be a small miracle if I could keep from puking into one of the trash cans situated by the various stations.

"Easy, Samantha," Max murmured. "Take a deep breath, pet. You're going to do fine."

Breathe? Really? I could barely walk, let alone breathe. But the minute I spied Eli—his dark eyes glassy with tears—wearing a huge smile of encouragement, the icy fingers of fear clawing at me melted. I wrapped Max's compelling strength around me and inhaled a calming breath.

"That's my girl," he whispered in a tone teeming with pride.

I was so preoccupied with bolstering myself inwardly that I totally missed Mika's introduction. It wasn't until he turned to me with a smile and moved alongside Max that I realized it was time for me to address the crowd.

Renouncing my Dominance was a small price for the chance to bask in the joy and honor of being Max's girl…his pet…his slut…his *slave*. I lifted my chin.

There was no longer any shadow of doubt.

I was on the path of my heart's desire once again.

Courage bloomed as I scanned the smiling faces of longtime friends like Julianna, Drake, Trevor, Ivory, Dark Desire, and so many others, to newbies like Woody, Maple, and Symoné. I returned their caring smiles and cleared my throat.

"Thank you all for coming this evening. I mean…who'd turn down a free dinner, right?" I joked as the members nodded and laughed.

"You all know me as Sammie, or Mistress Sammie. Anonymity is a fundamental must in this lifestyle, but the time has come for me to reveal the woman behind the curtain, so to speak."

All eyes were riveted on me, even Master Justice, standing at the back of the room, partially concealed in the shadows.

"Before moving to Chicago and having the honor of becoming friends with Mika…who isn't only a mentor, but a cherished friend, I lived in New Jersey. I was a different woman then. I was eighteen when I married a man named Desmond. He was my childhood sweetheart. Together we discovered the lifestyle. Through a bit of trial and error, our Master/slave relationship eventually began to flourish. It was…amazing." My throat tightened and I paused, biting back my emotions. "On September eleventh, two thousand and one, my whole world crumbled. Desmond was aboard United Airlines flight one seventy-five…the second plane that crashed into the World Trade Center. I not only lost my husband, that day, but my *Master* as well."

Several members gasped and murmured in shock. Trevor covered his face in his hands and wept while Drake brushed a tear from his rugged face. I wanted to join them…break down and curl into a ball on the floor and sob like a baby. But I'd already done that…already purged the pain I'd carried for so many years.

Today was a chance at rebirth. I paused as I sensed Max moving in close behind me. When he gently slid his fingers up my spine, I greedily absorbed his strength. Gathering the fortitude he offered, I continued.

"Desmond's death annihilated me. I was lost and aimlessly drifting out to sea. I knew in order to stay sane, I had to leave New Jersey. His ghost was everywhere. Every time I stepped out of our brownstone, I saw survivors mourning…wearing empty, vacant expressions like my own. I began to liken us to nine-eleven zombies. So I packed my things and started driving. The void of losing my husband was all consuming, but the loss of my Master was black and ugly. I had no direction, no purpose. I knew that if I didn't find new meaning in life, I'd simply blow away.

"Luckily, a lifestyle friend back in New Jersey had me get in touch with Mika, and he introduced me to Club Genesis. When I confessed this story to him and explained I couldn't kneel to another Master again, Mika took me under his wing. He taught me how to find a different kind of fulfillment within the lifestyle. He gave me a second chance on life with a new and wonderful kinky family."

I darted a glance over my shoulder. Through my blurry vision, I saw Mika crying...proudly displaying the tears that trickled down his cheeks. I sucked in a shaky breath and quickly wiped my eyes. I didn't dare look at Max. I'd break down and never finish what I needed to say.

"My years as Mistress Sammie have been more rewarding than I can express in words. I've found tremendous joy scening and working you amazing subs. The trust you granted me to send you off into that lullaby of subspace has been a humbling honor. Thank you for allowing me to aid in your journey, as you've helped me grow in mine."

"Oh, god," Trevor wailed. "You're not leaving us, are you, Mistress?"

"Hush, boy!" Drake barked.

"I'm sorry, Master, but"—Trevor issued a mournful howl—"she can't leave..."

The utter pain in his voice was my undoing. A strangled sob slid from the back of my throat. I shook my head but couldn't push any words past my lips. I turned toward Max as another sob shook me to my toes.

"No, Trevor. She's not going anywhere," Max assured in a tone thick with emotion. He reached into his vest pocket and handed me a tissue. Accepting it with a watery smile, I knew these tears weren't the ones Max intended to sip from my flesh. I blotted my cheeks and sucked in a ragged breath.

"*I'm* not going anywhere, but Mistress Sammie is. She's leaving...me, and in her place will be the submissive I locked away sixteen years ago."

Mika stepped up and wrapped his arm around my waist. "Ladies and Gentlemen of Club Genesis, it's my pleasure and my heartfelt honor to introduce you all to slave Samantha."

After a split second of stunned silence, the members launched to their feet. Deafening applause, cheers, and whistles filled the dungeon. I was stunned. Overwhelmed. Speechless. My heart swelled. I was shaking with shock and joy at their unequivocal acceptance.

Max moved in alongside me and banded his arm around my waist as Mika stepped forward and raised his hands in the air.

"Settle down...settle down," he instructed. "We're not quite finished yet."

"There's more?" Ian barked out. "Mad Max, you're not going to the other side, too, are you, man?"

Max laughed. "Not in a million. Someone has to keep Samantha on the straight and narrow."

"Oh, holy shit! Are you fucking serious?" Trevor squealed as he jumped up and down.

"You'll be paying for that filthy mouth of yours for weeks, my incorrigible slut," Drake bellowed.

"Beat me, gag me, shove your cock in my mouth for a month, Daddy... I'll gladly take any punishment you give me, but I've got a new *sub sister*!"

Trevor bounced into the narrow aisle between the rows of chairs and started dancing. I couldn't help but laugh. With a scowl, Daddy Drake stood and wrapped a beefy fist in his lover's long blond hair. He then yanked him back to his chair and narrowed his eyes. Trevor cupped Drake's face and kissed him, hard.

"All right. All right. If you'll all settle down, I'm going to pass things over to Master Max."

Mika smiled and kissed me on the cheek. "I told you all this would turn out fine, sweetheart."

"Yes, you did. Thank you. Thank you for...everything." My voice cracked. Mika wiped a tear from my cheek, then turned and sat beside a weeping Julianna before wrapping an arm around his slave.

"Many of us, in and out of the lifestyle, spend years searching for that special someone who completes us. Many have been blessed and have found that missing puzzle piece of their soul. Others continue to search. To those of you who've not yet found them, don't give up. When you least expect it, your One might do something as ordinary as opening a door...and your whole world will change." Max sent me a knowing smile I could barely see through the tears pouring from my eyes.

"Oh, but don't get bent out of shape when, after you introduce yourself, she asks if that's your porn or stripper name."

My cheeks caught fire as the whole room roared with laughter.

"That just means she's really into you but doesn't want to admit it," Max added, cupping his hand to his mouth in a conspiratorial gesture. He flashed me a wicked smile as he waited for the laughter in the room to die down.

"I've spent weeks in a battle of wills with this tenacious woman, trying to crash through her walls and lay a foundation of trust, communication, and honesty...the cornerstones necessary for all of us to grow and thrive. We've laid open our souls, and though neither of us has spoken the words until now, I want the whole world to know"— Max turned with a blinding smile—"from the moment I first saw her, I fell in love with Sammie, fell in love with Sam, and fell in love with Samantha, who I will treasure and hold with the greatest care of a man and a Master forever."

The damn inside me burst. Sobs tore from my throat and tears spilled from my eyes. This time, Max didn't bother with a tissue; he simply pressed his lips to my cheeks and drank in the love spilling from inside me.

"I love you, Maximus...I love you, Master...I love you...love you with all m-my heart," I sputtered between sobs.

He growled and kissed me like he'd never kissed me before. The whole world spun and dropped out from beneath my feet. The room erupted in cheers and applause once again.

Max begrudgingly pulled away and smiled. "About fucking time we got that out in the open."

I laughed and sniffed.

I felt like a waterfall as more tears cascaded down my face. Max glanced toward Dylan with a barely perceptible nod. He was on his feet and standing beside Max in front of the crowd. The members grew quiet and anticipation lined their faces.

"A Master is never complete without a slave. *You* complete me, Samantha." I opened my mouth to reply, but Max pressed a finger to my lips. "After Master Desmond passed away, you honored his memory by vowing to never kneel before another, but in the process, you locked your own heart away. I know he's watched down on you with pride, admiration, and joy, but also sorrow because you've forsaken the peace and serenity you deserve. It's time for you rise from the ashes, pet, and kneel once again to another Master who loves you."

He turned toward Dylan, who placed a shiny silver necklace in Max's hand. Facing me once more, Max lifted the dainty silver chain with a cluster of three diamonds dangling from the center.

"I'd be remiss not to thank Master Desmond for igniting the spark of submission that burns so brightly inside you. No matter how much you wanted to deny that burning ember, I saw the glow inside you from day one. While I'd never be so bold to think of replacing him, Samantha, I simply ask for the honor to be your Master today, tomorrow, and till the end of time.

"The circle of love never ends, pet." Max placed the necklace in my hand and pointed to the diamonds. "See? Desmond. Max. Samantha. The decision is yours, my sweet slut...if you wish for me to guide, protect, and lead you along your submissive path, then kneel and allow me to claim you."

Max took a step back. He squared his shoulders, parted his brawny legs, and tucked his hands behind his back. Forceful. Commanding. He called to me as a woman and a submissive in a primal and passionate way.

I stood before him, trembling, sobbing, and tracing my fingertip over the circle of diamonds. I was astonished that Max had paid such homage to Desmond and the impact he'd had on my life, not only as his wife but his slave. Adding a separate stone in acknowledgment completely decimated my heart.

Yes, I wanted to kneel before Max, but most of all, I ached for him to claim me.

I lowered myself to the floor and felt as if I were surrendering to him for the first time. Blissful love burst through my whole being and my heart soared as if it would explode. Resting my butt cheeks against my heels, I spread my thighs and lowered my head as Max draped the delicate chain across my palms. I inhaled a deep breath as the chain sent a warmth and calmness to radiate through me, then raised my arms, offering Max the necklace to bind to my neck.

The collar was unconventional, but then so were we.

"Look at me, Samantha."

Heeding his command, I raised my head and lifted my lashes. Max seized me with a look of love so raw and sharp it stole the air from my lungs. How on earth could I find the right words to convey the depth of feeling that thrummed inside me? My heart ached with the love that burned inside me. I suddenly realized that if I accidently tangled up my words, it wouldn't matter. Max had always possessed that mystifying and innate ability to know what I was feeling...thinking, even when I didn't say a thing.

He needed to hear the songs my heart had never sung to him before.

"It no longer matters if Maximus Gunn is your stripper or porn name." I grinned when he tossed back his head and laughed along with the rest of the crowd.

"God, I'm going to love taming your sassy tongue, wench," he barked.

"So am I." I exhaled on a sigh before turning sober. "You uncovered the submissive buried inside me, but you did more. You saved her...saved me. You forced me to face my fears with compassion and love. Even when I drew the blade of my wicked tongue, you simply tossed up a shield. With the patience of a saint and the determination of a warrior...you never backed down."

"Retreat was never an option, gorgeous," he softly whispered.

"Thank god," I murmured before continuing. "Your eyes show me a future I once refused to even dream about again. Your arms shelter and protect me when I need refuge from insecurities. Your voice, whether silky with praise or harsh with command, fills me with the unequivocal demand to surrender. Here, at your feet, I am whole...I'm complete."

Tears streaked from my face and dripped to the floor between my thighs. I stretched my arms as high as they could go...beseeching him to lift the collar from my palms.

"I kneel before you begging that you will bestow the honor and privilege of claiming me as your slave. I ache to serve and please you, and willingly offer you my heart, mind, body, and soul. You are my world, Master...my whole world is *you*."

I dropped my chin to my chest. As I bit back sobs, I waited one...two...three thundering heartbeats before I felt his fingers brush my palm. I choked back a strangled cry of joy as I lowered my arms and rested the backs of my hands on my thighs.

Max knelt in front of me and cupped my chin. Lifting my head back, I gazed up at him. Tears glistened in his eyes and his chin quivered once before he clenched his jaw. Dylan moved in behind me and gently lifted my hair as Max worked the clasp of the necklace open.

Bending, he draped the chain around my throat and pressed his mouth to my ear, and as the latch snicked shut, he whispered, "It's my privilege and honor to own *you*, my beautiful Samantha."

Max sipped my free-flowing tears before he claimed me with a silken, fiery kiss. I melted against his chest as my whole being blazed in completeness, and the club erupted in applause and cheers. Sliding his arm around my waist, Max hauled me to my feet. We faced our friends, now on their feet, still clapping. I wiped my cheeks and choked out a watery laugh. Gliding my fingertips over the three diamonds, I looked over at Max. He was beaming with pride and joy.

"I love you, Master."

"I love you, too, sweet slave," he growled, then kissed me again, long and hard.

"All right. All right," Mika barked above the cacophony. "Usually we put the guests of honor at the front of the food line, but these two love-birds might stay up here all night sucking tongues while we starve to death."

I grinned against Master's lips as Mika chuckled.

Suddenly, Max tore from my mouth.

"We'll finish that, later," he said with a wink before giving Mika a mock scowl. "God knows I don't want anyone starving to death. Let's eat!"

More cheers went up as Max pressed a strong hand to the small of my back and led me to the tables lined with silver chafing dishes. As I reached for a plate to hand to my new Master, Trevor nearly tackle-hugged me with a squeal.

"Samantha, Samantha, Samantha. Lordy, girl, it's going to take some time for me to get used to calling you that…but, oh, my god! You're a sub!" Trevor screamed. He was more excited than I'd seen him in years.

Drake shot me a look of apology, yet there was a tremendous look of relief flickering in the man's gray eyes. I flashed the burly tattooed Dom a look of warning followed by a barely perceptible shake of my head for leniency on Trevor's behalf. Drake's lips slowly kicked up with an incredulous grin as he opened his arms for a hug.

I giggled and wrapped my arms around his robust and hairy chest.

As he squeezed me tightly, Drake settled his mouth next to my ear. "Remember your place, girl. I decide if my sub needs a punishment, just as your *Master* will decide your fate."

I tensed and swallowed tightly.

"Easy, Sam," Drake murmured. "We're still friends, honey. I'm simply trying to help keep your head where it needs to be. This is going to be a big transition for all of us, but I'm so fucking happy for you, baby."

He released me and planted a big kiss on my forehead.

"Thank you, Daddy Drake...Sir." My voice trembled. I hadn't thought about the affect my submission would have in regard to my longtime Dom friends.

"Don't worry, honey. In private, I'm still Drake, and you're still Sam."

"Are you hitting on my slave, Drake?" Max chuckled.

"Please," the Leather Daddy drawled.

"Samantha's safe, Sir Max." Julianna grinned. "Daddy Drake hates vaginas."

"Which is a damn good thing for me." Trevor grinned.

I suddenly realized both maternal figures were there without their children. "Where are the babies tonight?"

"Tristan and Hope are at our place." Julianna sent Mika a pleading expression. He didn't say a word, simply nodded. "We...um, we hired a nanny since another Baby LaBrache will join our family the first part of March."

"Oh, sister!" Trevor squealed and hugged her tight. "Another baby! I hope it's a girl; then Hope will have a brother and a sister."

"I hope so, too." Julianna wiped a tear away. I knew then it wasn't just me. Pregnant hormones were hell on all women.

"And you swore you'd never go through labor and delivery again during Hope's birth," Trevor teased with a laugh.

"It was the pain talking, not me." Julianna laughed. "I honestly can't wait."

"You're due in March?" Savannah asked breathlessly. Nick flashed his girl a wink. "February twenty-fourth, here," she announced, softly rubbing her belly.

Leagh pinned Mellie—whose mouth hung agape—with a knowing grin.

Joshua cleared his throat and placed his masterfully artistic fingers over his girl's belly and smiled proudly. "February twenty-second, here."

"What?" Sanna screamed. "Some sister you are! Why didn't you tell me?"

"Ditto, wench! Why didn't you tell *me?*" Mellie countered. The two pregnant sisters started to laugh and cry and hug each other as *I* teared up.

More waterworks...great!

Tony held up his hands. "Okay, nobody drink the fucking water around here unless you want to be knocked up."

"I've never heard of getting pregnant by drinking water, Sir. However, I've heard of it happening after too much tequila," Symoné laughed.

Tony blinked at the new sub in stunned silence for several seconds before a grin crested on his mouth.

"You'll do just fine at this club, girl," he chortled. Raising a hand in the air, he pointed at Symoné. "Looks like we have another feisty sub to keep you Doms on your toes. Step up...the line forms here!"

Symoné's face turned bright crimson with embarrassment. She flashed a nervous glance at Justice before dropping her eyes toward the floor.

"Pick one line or the other, man, and make it snappy. We're hungry," Justice called out as his features quickly morphed from a scowl to a manufactured smile.

The others bought the man's ruse and started harping at Tony to fill his plate and move on. I, however, wasn't fooled. Justice clearly had his balls in a twist. I suspected it had to do with a certain auburn-haired, aqua-eyed submissive named Symoné. With the focus on Tony now, Justice stood with his jaw clenched, looking awkwardly uncomfortable as he darted covert glances the sub's way. And even more so when Symoné lifted her lashes in his direction.

I couldn't wait to see how this prickly waltz played out in the coming weeks.

When Max and I finished filling our plates, we walked back toward the center of the dungeon. Thanks to some fast-working subs, the chairs used during our ceremony were now repositioned around the tables. He held out a chair, and once I was seated, he eased in beside me.

"Since the others have announced their due dates, did you want to do the same, pet?"

I shook my head. "I'd rather wait until we get the results from the amniocentesis, in case something—"

"Our baby is going to be healthy and happy. I know it in my heart."

I wanted to share his conviction, but I was barely pregnant, and I was thirty-eight years old.

"Clear your mind, Samantha, or I'll tie you to that spanking bench and clear it for you," Max said with a sensual growl.

My heart skittered and my blood warmed as a mischievous grin played at my lips. "You know that storage space, next to the workout room?"

"Yes," Max replied before taking a bite of his dinner roll.

"Wouldn't that space make a wonderful dungeon?"

"Christ, I love your kinky mind, slave."

"I'm glad you didn't mention that kind of furniture to your interior decorators."

Max quirked a brow at Sanna as she, Dylan, and Nick sat down at our table. "You've been telling tales about me, little one."

Sanna's eyes grew wide as a blush rushed up her cheeks. "I-I have?"

"I was teasing him about the interior designers."

"Oh, I didn't realize that was a secret." She blanched.

"It's not. I'm only teasing you, Sanna." Max grinned.

"Don't be giving her a hard time. She's pregnant," I chided. Even before Max turned to slam me with an angry, badassed Dom glare—that made my pussy clutch—I knew I'd fucked up. I'd have to backpedal, and fast. "Um…I mean, err, please, Sir. Don't be mad at Sanna…or me…especially now that I've royally screwed up…my sweet, loving, oh, so kind and *forgiving*, Master."

Nick and Dylan roared as I tried to dig myself out of trouble. Sanna quickly covered her mouth, but her whole body shook in silent laughter.

Max simply smirked at me and nodded. "You realize I *am* keeping track of your Dominant outbursts, don't you, pet?"

"Oh, god," I whimpered. "You can't possibly—I mean, no Sir, I didn't."

The men across from us only laughed harder.

"I am. So keep that in the forefront of your mind, Samantha."

"I will, Master." I swallowed tightly as I anxiously glanced at several of the play stations across the room.

We ate our meal surrounded by friends, talking and laughing. The evening had been nothing short of magical. Altering my status from Domme to sub was met with joyful acceptance. A steady stream of members congratulated Max and me, driving home the fact that all the hours I'd spent fretting over their rejection had been a waste of time. But even more mind-boggling was the number of deliveries the stork would be making come spring.

Still warring with my waning appetite, I nibbled at the food on my plate but mostly just pushed it around with my fork.

"Try to eat a few more bites, love," Max murmured.

With a nod, I smiled. I thought it ironic that a month ago I would have snapped at the man and told him to mind his own business. Mika had been right; no other Dom before Max had ever crawled so deeply under my skin. I was damn glad he had.

When dinner was done, Quinn, Ava, and Joe hurried behind the bar as the play stations quickly filled. It was strange to watch others do my job but blissfully relaxing to spend unhurried hours with my Master and our friends engulfed in the sights and sounds of the dungeon.

Max draped his arm across the back of my chair and pulled me close to his side. "I'd love to cuff you to the cross and redden your ivory ass, but I'm exhausted. Besides, I think we've given the members enough to process for one night."

The mere mention of being tired had me yawning. "I couldn't agree more, Master."

"Come on, pet. Let's thank Mika and say good night to our friends so I can take you back to our new home and tuck you into our new bed."

An hour later, Max led me into the bedroom, but we didn't crawl between the sheets. Instead, he filled the massive Jacuzzi tub in the bathroom as he slowly peeled the clothes off my body.

Earlier in the day, I'd unpacked a box with my collection of candles and had placed them around the edge of the tub. Max lit them all before he turned off the lights and stepped into the churning hot water to join me. Nestled between his long, muscular thighs, I leaned my back against his chest. With his strong, ink-colored arms banded around my waist, I closed my eyes and issued a sigh of pure contentment.

"Thank you for the fairy-tale evening, Master."

"You're welcome, precious." Max kissed the top of my head. "I was proud of your courage. You did fantastic, Samantha."

His praise warmed me and a lazy smile tugged my lips. As I toyed with the diamonds on my collar, Max's fingers joined mine.

"Including Desmond in our union melted my heart, but I don't ever want you thinking or feeling that you're competing with a ghost."

"I don't, baby. But he's the primary reason you are who you are. Adding his symbol to your collar is a reminder of where your journey started. The third diamond is me...that's where your journey will end, when we're both old and gray."

"So, you're planning to stick with me all that time?" I teased.

"Baby, I'm sticking with you till the *end* of time."

He sank his fist into my hair and tugged my head back before he claimed me in a kiss so filled with passion it stole my breath. We made love in the tub. His every touch was tender and reverent, as if I were made of glass. Any sliver of my heart that wasn't already lost to Max, he claimed then and there.

CHAPTER THIRTEEN

THE DAYS SLID into weeks, and before I knew it, almost two months had trekked by. Yet every morning, like clockwork, Max sat beside me, holding my hair as I heaved into the toilet. He'd carry me back to bed before bringing me hot tea and crackers. The morning sickness left me feeling as if I'd been hit by a train. Thankfully, the nausea would pass quickly and not interfere with the rest of my day. It was a small price to pay and would be nothing but a faded memory by the time our little bundle of joy made its way into the world.

"Did you want to go to the submissive meeting at the club this morning?" Max asked as he stepped from the bathroom wiping shaving cream off his face.

"I'd like to." I gazed at his naked body. The desire to drag my tongue over every inviting inch climbed inside me. "But I'll pass if you have something else in mind…"

I set my teacup down and climbed out of bed, smiling as Max raked a heated stare over my bare flesh.

"I've got nothing on my calendar except making you beg and plead until Monday afternoon."

"What happens Monday afternoon?" I purred as I raked my nails down his chest and slowly stroked his awakening cock.

Max sucked in a ragged breath and cupped my already wet mound. "I've got a job interview with Dylan and Nick."

"What?" I blinked in surprise.

"I can't spend my nights being a club bum now that we've got a baby on the way. I need a *respectable* job. It was either work for Nick and Dylan or take a lion tamer job," he replied with a taunting grin.

I stuck my bottom lip out in an overdramatic pout. "But I like spending my nights with you at the club and sleeping…or rather playing half the day away."

"I do, too. Though I've got plenty of money in the bank, we need to start saving for our little one's college education now."

"I can give my notice at the club and find a respectable job, too."

"No. I want you to keep doing what you love, surrounded by people who love you." He slapped me on the ass as a hungry fire leapt in his eyes. "Get in the bathroom and get ready for the sub meeting before I change my mind and tie you to the bed, slave."

"Do I get to vote on which *I'd* rather do?"

"No, you don't, my sweet slut. Now, get moving." He grinned.

An hour later, I sat with the other subs of the club while Max and the Doms gathered at the bar.

"Today's topic is sub-drop. Has anyone here ever experienced it?" Julianna asked. Several raised their hands, including me. "Wow, that's a lot. Okay, does anyone want to share what that was like for you?"

"I will," I volunteered. "It happened with my former Master. We'd gone to a new club and played hard. I was still sailing on endorphins when we went to bed, but the next morning, I woke up and started crying. I cried…for hours. I couldn't figure out what was wrong. I'd been given tons of aftercare, so I knew that wasn't the issue. So Desmond sat me down and we started dissecting my bizarre emotions."

"It happened that way with me, too," Woody stated.

"Not me. I turned into a defensive asshole." Peanut cringed.

"Did you ever discover what triggered your drop, Samantha?" Julianna asked.

"Sort of, but we didn't recreate the situation again to know for sure. We'd gone to a new club in New York. The place was small and packed with people. They were literally standing in line to use the stations. When it was our turn, Desmond didn't warm me up the way he usually did. Though I sailed off into subspace fast, he pulled me out quickly. I'd been fine during the endorphin rush, but when it wore off, I crashed. Hard. He held me as I cried and apologized and promised we'd never visit that club again. And we didn't."

"Ah, that makes sense," Julianna stated. "I can imagine it freaked you both out."

I nodded, noticing that the room had grown incredibly hot. As some of the other subs began telling their experience with sub-drop, a dull, aching pain began throbbing low in my stomach. I thought I might have to throw up again.

"Excuse me," I interrupted. "I'll be right back. I need to hit the ladies' room."

When I stood, Liz's eyes grew wide. She jumped from her seat and grabbed me by the arm. Cindy vaulted up next as several subs gasped.

"Sam. Max!" Cindy cried.

They were visibly shaken, and their worried expressions sent a wave of panic blasting through me.

"What's wrong?" I asked. Looking down, I saw the stain of red blood on my white yoga pants.

"Oh, god!" I cried. "My baby! My baby! Master!"

"Baby? You're pregnant, too? Oh, shit," Julianna's voice trembled with fear.

"Oh, god. No!" Max wailed in terror as he stared at the blood between my legs.

"I need you to lie still on the floor for me," Brooks calmly explained.

Before I could even bend my knees, Max lifted me into his arms and gently placed me on the ground. I began to shiver, partly because of the cold tile beneath me but mostly from the horror consuming me.

"Please, don't let me lose this baby," I begged, staring into the doctor's eyes.

"I need you to relax, Samantha. Take some deep breaths for me." Brooks turned toward the crowd now gathered around me. "I need some clean sheets, towels, surgical gloves, lube, and several blankets."

Like a bullet, Julianna and Mika both took off running.

"I'm scared," I whispered to Max. He'd gone pale and tears welled in his eyes.

"I know. I am, too love. But try to calm down and breathe. Okay?" I nodded and tried to drink in his soothing words. "Close your eyes and relax. I'm right here by your side."

"You're doing well," Brooks murmured. "Are you experiencing any pain?"

"No. Not now. Earlier I felt a little, but it's gone." My eyes flew open wide as a new wave of dread pulled me under. "I didn't lose the baby already, did I?"

"I don't know yet, sweetheart. Just calm down," Brooks gently urged.

Mika and Julianna returned with their arms filled. Brooks eased me onto my side and placed a couple sheets beneath me. He tucked several of the blankets around my trembling body.

"I'm going to take your pants off and check you, Samantha."

"Okay." I nodded, staring into Max's shimmering eyes. I was trying to draw strength from him, but he looked as scared and worried as I felt.

"Everyone move to the bar. Let's give them some privacy here," Mika instructed as the Doms and subs moved away. Only Cindy, Liz, Brooks, Max, and I remained.

"Bend your knees for me and spread your legs, Sam," Brooks instructed.

The cold lube on his invading fingers made me gasp.

"Sorry, sweetheart. I know this isn't the least bit comfortable for you." The doctor's voice was low and calm as he drove his fingers in deeper and pressed on the outside of my stomach. "Ah," he smiled. "There you are."

"What? Do you feel the baby?"

"Yes. He's still in there. I think you're merely spotting," Brooks explained. A wave of relief sang through me as Max released a mighty exhale.

"He's still in there." He smiled.

"She," I corrected in a trembling voice.

"We're going to get you to the hospital so I can do an ultrasound…check things out a bit further. Just to be on the safe side."

"I'll call an ambulance," Liz announced before racing toward the bar.

"Wait," I called out, but she was already gone. "Can't Master drive me instead?"

Brooks shook his head, pulled off his glove, and tucked the covers around my legs.

I knew then, either I wasn't out of the woods and could still lose the baby or the doctor was simply being overly cautious. Either way, I wasn't going to argue.

"I'm riding with you," Max assured. "and holding your hand the whole way."

"I love you."

"I love you, too." He brushed a gentle kiss over my lips.

James and Ian trailed behind Liz as she hurried back toward us.

"If you want to give me the keys to your truck, Max, Ian and I will follow the ambulance and leave it at the hospital for you," James offered.

"Thanks, man. I appreciate it." Max dug his keys out of the pocket of his jeans and tossed them to the Dom.

The seconds dragged on like hours before I heard a siren in the distance. Of course, it could have been a cop, but I knew in my gut it was my ride coming. As the EMTs loaded me up, Brooks squeezed my hand.

"I'm taking off now so I can get scrubbed up before you arrive. I'll see you soon. Just stay calm for me. All right?"

"I'll do my best. Thank you, Sam."

Staying true to his word, Max held my hand and tried his best to keep me calm as the ambulance, with sirens wailing, sped toward the hospital. One of the EMTs checked everything from my blood pressure to my heart rate, lobbing questions about pain and checking beneath the blanket to see if I was still bleeding. All the while terror thrummed through me.

"Looking good. Hang tight." The young man smiled. "We're only a minute or two away."

I was aware the ambulance was flying, yet everything around me appeared to move in slow motion. Locked in his own fear, Max was too quiet. But the feel of his sturdy fingers threaded through mine felt like an anchor. I clung to him, drinking in his strength and safety.

Brooks and Cindy were both waiting for me when they wheeled me into the ER. When one of the nurses on duty tried to escort Max to the waiting room, I thought his head was going to explode.

"You're wasting your breath," he told the nurse. "I'm not leaving her side."

"I need him to stay with me." I played on the woman's sympathy, knowing I'd likely fall apart without him there.

Cindy assured her co-worker that Max could say. With a nod, the nurse left.

Brooks spread a dollop of lube on my abdomen before holding up a plastic square. "This is a fetal Doppler device. We'll be able to hear the baby's heartbeat."

Though his bedside manner was cool and collected, I didn't miss the split-second glance between the doctor and his sub nurse, Cindy.

The moment of truth was here.

As he glided the monitor over my stomach, I held my breath. Then I heard a soft swishing noise. Both he and Cindy broke out with wide smiles as Brooks turned up the volume on the device. The echo of the baby's heartbeat was music to my ears. Max squeezed my hand and wiped a tear from his cheek with the other as I lay sobbing in relief.

"That's the best sound I've heard all day," Brooks chuckled.

"Me, too," Cindy sniffed before hugging me tightly.

"I still want the sonogram," Brooks began. "In light of your spotting, we're going to hold off on the amniocentesis for a few more months. I don't want to do anything invasive to this little guy for a while."

"Little girl," I corrected once more with a watery laugh.

"Well, if it is a girl, I guess we *could* name her Julius Maximus, and call her Julie for short," Max teased.

"No way. Our daughter is going to dress in pink and purple ribbons and lace, not gladiator wear," I scoffed.

"Baby, I don't care if it's a girl or a boy," Max murmured against my lips. "I just want momma and baby to be healthy."

"That's all I want, besides you, too." I kissed him with all the love in my heart.

We both breathed out a sigh of relief when the results of the sonogram came back perfectly fine. But Brooks put me on bed rest for a week, which was not fine at all.

By day four, I was so bored out of my head that I was nearly climbing the walls. Though I'd all but demanded he go, Max postponed his job interview to wait on me hand and foot. While the former Domme in me would have basked in the attention, I felt as if Max had collared an invalid. I sorely lacked in providing him an ounce of submission.

It was vital that I rest so our baby could grow healthy and strong, but the need to give myself over to Max, to surrender to his command, rode me hard.

It was a void I couldn't fill.

Blaming my funk on fluctuating hormones—the ones Brooks had warned me about—I decided to give myself five minutes to grieve the fulfillment I couldn't give Max. After the time limit was up, I was going to hike up my big-girl panties and toss away my futile feelings of ineptness.

As Murphy's Law would have it, Max entered the bedroom carrying my lunch on a tray three and a half minutes into my sob-fest. Fear filled his eyes as he lowered the salver to the dresser and rushed to the bed.

"What's wrong? Are you spotting again?"

"No," I wailed.

"Then what is it? What's wrong, Sam?" He all but barked the questions.

"I-I'm sorry."

"Sorry for what?" His forehead wrinkled as his brows slashed in confusion.

"For being such a shitty slave," I blubbered.

He looked at me like I'd completely gone off the deep end for three solid seconds before his expression softened and he dragged me into his arms.

"Baby, you are not a shitty slave. You're doing exactly what I ordered you to do the day we came home from the hospital. Stay in bed and rest."

"I know, but I'm bored and…aw, shit. I sound like a spoiled brat 'cause I can't have my way. I'm sorry."

I felt his body shake in silent laughter. It only made me cry harder.

"You need a hard hand across your ass, girl," Max growled.

"I do, but…you won't give it to me, because I have to lie in this stupid bed." I angrily wiped the tears from my cheeks and huffed. "I loathe these out-of-control hormones. How do pregnant women keep from going stark raving mad?"

Suddenly, Max stood and shucked off his pants. His eyes blazed with heat and that luscious command I'd so desperately missed.

"What are you doing? You know we can't make love for another three days."

"I'm not interested in filling your cunt, girl," Max snapped. "Your mouth will do nicely for now."

A rolling ripple of heat careened through me. My tears evaporated as Max fisted his cock and strode toward the bed.

"On your back, slave," he commanded in a low, raspy voice.

I complied as a blanket of peace slowly settled over me. Max climbed onto the mattress and straddled my chest. I stared up into his emerald eyes and sent him a weak smile.

"Thank you, Master. Thank you for always knowing what I need."

"Raise your arms above your head, gorgeous." His soft smile faded as a wicked grin replaced it. "Now open your mouth and suck your Master's cock so my seed can scald your throat and warm your belly long after I wear out your soft, pretty tongue."

Staring at his bulbous crest, dripping in need, I opened wide and moaned as Max fed inch after delicious, hot inch past my lips. Each swirl of my tongue and guttural groan that rumbled from his chest sent the tension of longing inside me to uncoil and fall silently away. Surrendering to this amazing man filled me with peace of mind, peace of heart, and an unequivocal peace of soul.

I'd foolishly tried to deny myself this unparalleled fulfillment. If not for the persistence of my strong, intuitive, and glorious Master, I'd still be trapped inside a cage and resisting my submission.

ABOUT THE AUTHOR

USA Today Bestselling author **Jenna Jacob** paints a canvas of passion, romance, and humor as her alpha men and the feisty women who love them unravel their souls, heal their scars, and find a happy-ever-after kind of love. Heart-tugging, captivating, and steamy, Jenna's books will surely leave you breathless and craving more.

A mom of four grown children, Jenna and her alpha-hunk husband live in Kansas. She loves reading, getting away from the city on the back of a Harley, music, camping, and cooking.

Meet her wild and wicked fictional family in Jenna's sultry series: ***The Doms of Genesis.*** Become spellbound by searing triple love connections in her continuing saga: ***The Doms of Her Life*** (co-written with the amazing Shayla Black and Isabella La Pearl). Journey with couples struggling to resolve their pasts and heal their scars to discover unbridled love and devotion in her contemporary series: ***Passionate Hearts***. Or laugh along as Jenna lets her zany sense of humor and lack of filter run free in the romantic comedy series: ***Hotties of Haven***.

Connect with Jenna Online
Website: www.jennajacob.com
Email: jenna@jennajacob.com
Facebook Fan Page: facebook.com/authorjennajacob
Twitter: @jennajacob3
Instagram: instagram.com/jenna_jacob_author
Amazon Author Page: http://amzn.to/1GvwNnn
Newsletter: http://bit.ly/1Cj4ZyY

OTHER TITLES BY JENNA JACOB

The Doms of Genesis Series
Embracing My Submission
Masters of My Desire
Master of My Mind
Saving My Submission
Seduced By My Doms
Lured By My Master
Sin City Submission
Bound To Surrender
Resisting My Submission (March 21, 2017)
Craving His Command (May 23, 2017)

The Doms of Her Life – Raine Falling Series
(Co-authored with Shayla Black and Isabella LaPearl)
One Dom To Love
The Young and The Submissive
The Bold and The Dominant
The Edge Of Dominance

The Passionate Hearts Series
Sky Of Dreams
Winds Of Desire (Coming Soon)

Hotties Of Haven Series
Sin On A Stick
Wet Dream

Made in the USA
San Bernardino, CA
12 January 2018